PRAISE FOR *CALDER'S ROSE*!

"A sheer delight! Brilliant and fast-paced . . . sizzling with sensuality, seasoned with humor, and peopled with vibrant characters, this fun story is a pure joy to read."
—Sue-Ellen Welfonder, author of *Devil in a Kilt*

"Delightful and witty battle of the sexes. *Calder's Rose* is a light, fast, funny read!"
—*Sensual Romance Reviews*

"If you want to read something fresh and sexy, funny and heart-warming, don't miss *Calder's Rose*!"
—*Escape to Romance*

"*Calder's Rose* is a stellar reading experience complete with quirky characters and a plot that demands to be read in one sitting! Five stars."
—*Affaire de Coeur*

"Ms. Angell has written a delightful story. If you like intrigue, magic, and passion, you're going to love *Calder's Rose*."
—RomanceJunkies.com

"A humorous read with great characters."
—Marlene Breakfield, Book Isle Paperbacks

STEAM AND BODY HEAT

"You thought to sneak in and sneak out before I finished showering?"

She nodded. "I thought to be quick."

"Not quick enough, sweet cheeks." Leaning forward, he rested his hands on the sink on either side of her hips. She had no wiggle room. "There's a penalty for getting caught."

A penalty? "A shove out the door?" she asked hopefully.

He held her gaze in the mirror, bold and decisive, and slowly shook his head. "Towel me off," he breathed near her ear.

Dry him off? The man was delusional.

On impulse, TZ turned slowly. "Head to toe?" she asked.

"A full-body rub down."

With cool porcelain at her back, she faced his hot body. She couldn't let Cade intimidate her. Couldn't let him know how one look at his broad chest made her fingers itch.

Instead, she teased him. She was living dangerously, and she knew it. But she couldn't resist.

Other *Love Spell* books by Kate Angell:

CALDER'S ROSE

DRIVE ME CRAZY

KATE ANGELL

LOVE SPELL   NEW YORK CITY

LOVE SPELL®

March 2004

Published by

Dorchester Publishing Co., Inc.
200 Madison Avenue
New York, NY 10016

ISBN 0-505-52559-3

The name "Love Spell" and its logo are trademarks of Dorchester Publishing Co., Inc.

Printed in the United States of America.

Visit us on the web at www.dorchesterpub.com.

Drive Me Crazy

For my mother, Marion Brown, with love.

Debbie and Ted Roome
for supportive, close, and lasting friendships.

Cindy Smith, who always has my back.
You have a little TZ Blake in your soul.

Jean Lorenz, who has the patience of a saint.

Sue-Ellen Welfonder,
marvelous author and good friend.

Many thanks, once again,
to Alicia Condon, Editorial Director.

Four-footed, furry friends:
Griffin, Sara, Shine and Cosmos.

Author's note: SunCoast Run is purely fictitious,
as are many of the cities in Florida.

Chapter One

"*Male drivers!*"

"*Female drivers!*"

The man in the black Sting Ray exited the vehicle, madder than hell. Hands on his hips, he waited, ready to kill, as TZ Blake stepped from her candy-apple-red Mustang.

Ignoring him, she immediately checked the damage to her car. There was a significant dent in the door just below the window. Her heart sank. The '67 Mustang had been a gift from her aunt Elise, and TZ treated the classic car as if it were her child. A child now with a nasty scrape.

"You took two inches of paint off my car door," the man said to her back as he huffed down her neck.

TZ turned and came close enough to Cade Nyland to breathe the same air. She'd seen Cade from a distance, but never up close, and never so angry. The orange-tinted lenses of her pink Retro shades cast him in a hellish glow. His look condemned her. She slid her sunglasses down her nose with one finger and looked at him over the rim. In the late afternoon light, he stood tall and solid, his nostrils flared, and his muscles flexed. He was an imposing male animal. She knew him by reputation alone: a bad-boy ladies' man known as much for his bar brawls as for his sinfully good looks.

Pitch-dark hair brushed the collar of his gray polo; his shirt was tucked into snug black jeans. Beneath dark brows, his eyes were the deep color of twilight. His mouth was sexy, even with his nose out of joint. His jaw was set, strong and stubbled.

The man was carnal.

TZ pushed her shades to the bridge of her nose. "You should be more careful."

"*Me*, careful?" He looked incredulous. "You swung your door wide, as if there wasn't another car in sight."

The handle had slipped from her fingers, TZ silently admitted. The door usually creaked open, but today, it flew from her grasp. She was always so cautious and careful, and she hated the fact this might be her fault.

"You shouldn't be backing into parking spaces at the speed of light." She jabbed a finger at the diagonal stretch of his Sting Ray. "No parking lot etiquette. You've taken up two spots."

"I'd have taken up three if I'd known some college kid in a rush to party would park next to me." He waved his hand, encompassing the lot. "Look around, I'm not the only driver who's taken up two spaces."

College kid? TZ blinked. The man was no judge of age. She was pushing thirty, not twenty. He must have been misled by her ponytail, freckles and bare feet. That was his problem, not hers.

Glancing over her shoulder, she checked out the lot. Two lanes over, a '65 Cobra and a '66 Maserati were also parked diagonally. The drivers of the classic cars entered in the SunCoast Run had parked to protect their vehicles.

While TZ couldn't blame the other drivers, she could point a finger at Cade. "We pulled in at the same time," she reminded him. "You, ass backward and me—"

"There's nothing backward about my driving," he said heatedly. "I saw you. You, however, didn't notice me before you flung open your car door in an all-fire rush—"

"I am in a hurry," TZ cut him off.

Cade blocked her path. "We're not done yet."

"Life moves on," TZ informed him. "Move with it or step aside."

Grabbing her straw bag from the front seat of the Mustang, she undid the clasp and pulled out a business card. "All Tune and Lube, ask for TZ Blake. Best repair job in town. On me, I have a running account."

He took the card, studied it. "You carry Blake's business card?" He shook his head. "You're an accident waiting to happen. The way you drive, I'm sure you keep the man in business."

The man? Nyland thought her male. TZ contained her smile. "I make him rich."

She spun on her heel and strode across the parking lot toward Chugger Charlie's, a local beachside bar favored by the townies. Within a very short time, the crowd would raise the roof as rallyists and groupies kicked off rally week with the tight butt contest.

Squinting against the sun, Cade Nyland watched the young woman with more attitude than driving sense weave around the parked cars and enter the bar. He fin-

3

gered the business card. Who was this female with a running account at All Tune and Lube? Hell, he hadn't even gotten her name.

His anger had nearly gotten the better of him when he'd heard the smack of her car door hitting his. Then he'd seen the culprit: a coed with an auburn ponytail, three diamond studs in each ear, and a stubborn chin. She wore shorts and a top that were two sizes too large for her slender frame. A two-inch scar ran just below her left kneecap. She stood barefoot, her toenails painted a bright pink. Several toe rings banded her toes, and a gold-link bracelet encircled her right ankle.

Cade had an eye for detail and the memory to shame an elephant. Something about the coed bothered him. He just couldn't put his finger on it. Not yet anyway.

To her credit, she'd shown concern over the dent in the Mustang. Undoubtedly she was more worried about the possibility her father would ground her over Spring Break than she was over the fact she'd damaged her old man's car. She had no business cruising in the Mustang, ready to party.

Chugger Charlie's was the place to party. The bar hosted the wet T-shirt and tight butt contests the weekend prior to the SunCoast Run, the father of all road races.

The coed had entered Chugger Charlie's as if she owned the place. She didn't, however, look old enough to drink. If she was in the bar, he'd find her before the evening ended. He'd get her name and the name of her insurance company.

Cade pushed off his Vette, and took one final look at the dent in the Mustang. He rubbed his hand over the gash. The car felt warm, pulsing warm, though it was parked in the shade. He glanced inside and caught his reflection in the rearview mirror. It was set at an odd angle, tilted right instead of left. He had the strangest sensation the mirror was staring back at him. He almost expected to see eyes . . .

He rubbed one hand over his own eyes and exhaled sharply. Man alive, he'd just imagined the Mustang checking him out. Perhaps he was more tired than he'd realized. The trip from Los Angeles to northern Florida had definitely taken its toll. He'd lived on little sleep, pumped on caffeine for the past three months. It was all part of corporate raiding, staying awake and one step ahead of the competition. He worked behind the scenes of Action Auto Parts, only called into play when buyouts slowed and the seller needed a nudge. Cade did the convincing, sealed the deals, while his two younger pencil-pushing brothers crunched numbers, built profits and kept their white collars clean.

His most recent buyout would claim a West Coast auto parts franchise. The takeover would soon double his family's fortune. Action Auto Parts would stretch coast to coast. Though his father wanted him to take his rightful place as CEO of the company, Cade felt as confined in suits and ties as he did in a boardroom. He found freedom on the open road. Just as his grandfather, Rayburn Nyland, once had. To this day, Rayburn understood Cade's restless spirit and never called him on the carpet for missing a meeting.

The moment he'd returned to Gulf Cove, he'd received a phone call from the rally committee, notifying him that Jay Wright, his partner in the race, had broken his leg waterskiing. Jay's hip-to-heel cast wouldn't fit in Cade's

Sting Ray. He needed to hire a new mechanic or his Corvette would turn into a damn pumpkin by midnight.

He'd been told local mechanic TZ Blake frequented Chugger Charlie's. It was further rumored two other drivers were in need of the mechanic's services. Cade hoped to connect with TZ after the tight butt contest. He would pay big bucks for the man's time and expertise.

He wanted this win, the final trophy in his grandfather's dreams. Rayburn had been an adventurer who rallied the stateside circuit in a '33 Duesenberg SJ Speedster. The rally gene had skipped a generation, but appeared stronger than ever in Cade. In the history of the rally, no other driver had won all twelve competitions. Rayburn had won ten races before a car accident had taken him off the circuit and confined him to a wheelchair. Cade wanted to finish what his grandfather had started. It had been a year of performance and handling and champagne in the winner's circle. He had one race to go. . . .

Turning on his heel, he headed for Chugger Charlie's. Once inside, sunshine slashed the archways of the open-air bar. Tracked-in sand scuffed wooden planks while overhead, paddle ceiling fans cooled the overheated crowd. The scents of salt air, coconut suntan oil and two-for-one banana daiquiris mixed with activated hormones.

A restless undercurrent quickened the pulse of the crowd. The wild pulse of anticipation.

From the doorway, Cade scanned the crowd for the coed with the auburn ponytail. The bar was packed, and he didn't have time to move about the room to look for her.

Easing forward, he elbowed his way through the thickening crowd toward the improvised stage. Chugger Charlie's was not his usual haunt. He preferred atmosphere that edged the darker side of midnight. Though he'd begged off the wet T-shirt contest, he'd been strong-armed by the rally committee into judging the tight butt competition. He couldn't believe he'd agreed to such lunacy. He had more important things to accomplish than casting a vote for sweetest cheeks.

The announcer and owner of the bar, Charlie Owens, soon spotted him. "Over here, Nyland. Judges' table sits front and center."

And so it did. Cade dropped onto the end chair, nodded to the other four judges, two women and two men, all of whom he knew from past road rallies.

To his left, Cade's chief competitor, Rhett Evans, nudged his shoulder. "Can you believe our luck? Scoring tight butts!"

Cade felt anything but lucky. "It can't get any better than this." His sarcasm was lost on Rhett. Leaning forward, Cade picked up his scorecard and scanned the necessary qualifications: firmness, roundness, no tan lines.

No tan lines? He dropped the card and blew out a breath. "Sun buns."

Directly in front of the table, Charlie Owens stood center stage. A burly man wearing white athletic socks and jockey shorts. He looked downright ridiculous.

"Bare fannies and granny panties, boxers and briefs, five grand for the sweetest cheeks," the announcer's voice boomed through the bar. "Clap and cheer for the tightest rear."

Catcalls and wolf whistles rose with the music as the contestants hit the stage and brought down the house. Cade watched as eleven women and four men in various stages of undress bounded onto the platform. Strip clubs had nothing on these dancers. Rump shakin' rocked the stage as the contestants played to the crowd.

The audience responded wildly, jostling for a clearer view of the stage. Contestants' names rose on an exuberant chant.

"Sweet cheeks" became the call of the wild.

Cade shook his head. The foot stomping and heavy breathing of the onlookers built like an orgasm. He wished the contest over. He was in need of fresh air.

A man bumped Cade from behind. "Tight ass, TZ!" he hollered near Cade's ear. "Tease me, baby."

TZ? Cade shifted on his chair and craned his neck. Which male dancer was TZ Blake? Not the pretty boy in the shamrock briefs he hoped. The man looked more vanity mirror than grease monkey.

"Give us all you've got," the announcer rallied the participants. "The judges are about to narrow the stage to five finalists."

"Damn, only five?" The man next to Cade sounded panicky.

Five . . . pressed for time, Cade tried to concentrate. He evaluated the buff behinds. While he liked the tanned, toned thighs on a leggy blond, her thonged derriere lacked the roundness of a perfect ten.

In a bid for finalist status, one redhead bared her breasts in an attempt to draw the judges' eyes from her cellulite to her magnificent chest. Cade mentally gave her points for distraction. The redhead should have won the wet T-shirt contest.

The male competitors, while all hard-bodied, didn't

hold the appeal of feminine fannies. Cade left the male scoring to the female judges.

Toward the back of the gyrating melee, a flash of hot-pink boxers caught his eye. The erotic sway of the dancer's hips held his glance until he was forced to blink. Contestant number nine held a subtle sex appeal the other dancers lacked. The sheer silken fabric of her boxers couldn't hide her flawless curves—flat stomach and tight ass.

She danced barefoot, her toenails painted a bright pink. A strobe light caught the glint of her toe rings and ankle bracelet.

Cade straightened on his chair as he skimmed her white crop top and his gaze claimed her face. With each shake of her head, wild auburn curls brushed the natural hollow of her cheeks and the flirty fullness of her mouth.

The coed from the parking lot! Scantily clad, she had a knockout body, a solid nine, pushing toward a ten. For a full thirty seconds he allowed her appeal to stroke him physically. He then swallowed hard and schooled his body against the attraction. While she was hot, she was also young. Too young for him. At thirty-six, he liked his women seasoned, older and wiser and aware of their actions.

The coed had also hit his car door and conveniently forgotten to give him her name. At least he knew where to find her. He couldn't miss her on the stage.

As the temperature in the bar rose, sweat beaded his forehead. Cade slipped a strip of leather from the pocket of his black jeans and tied back his unconventionally long hair. He further searched his pocket for a pack of Doublemint, removed a stick and popped it in his mouth. He

9

chewed slowly, thoughtfully, attempting to keep his cool in the overheated room.

"Tan lines, TZ!" Someone deep in the crowd shouted. "Bare it all, baby!"

Cade cringed. He wasn't interested in seeing another man's butt. Not now, not ever. Slouching slightly, he stretched out his long legs and yawned.

Bored, was he? TZ Blake caught Cade Nyland's yawn before he covered his mouth. A very sexy mouth if he'd relax and smile. He looked anything but happy. He appeared downright put out.

Prior to the contest, while waiting off stage, she'd seen Cade enter the bar and traverse the crowd. He'd walked with purpose, ignoring female double-takes and bold winks. The man had a healthy following of rally groupies.

While judging the contest he'd looked far too serious, except for the moment he'd recognized her. She caught a flash of surprise, then pure lack of interest. That pricked her vanity. Didn't he know how to have fun? He shouldn't be judging a contest that got his briefs in a bunch—if he even wore underwear. The man looked uncivilized.

He also looked bored. Something inside her clicked. She wanted him awake and watching and as wild as the crowd. It was time to shake the party animal's cage.

Moving to the front of the stage, she slowly pivoted, showing her backside. Curving her body into a sinuous S, she slinked to the floor and back, then rotated her hips. Her hot-pink boxers slipped down her buttocks with each rotation.

She whipped the audience into a frenzy. They wanted skin. "Moon! Moon!" The men hit their knees and prayed out loud to see her bare backside.

They didn't get their wish, however. Keeping a firm hand on the front elastic at her waist, she teased and tempted, but never fully revealed. When the song ended, she had Cade Nyland's full attention.

"Score, score, score!" The announcer was pressing the judges for their cards.

TZ held her breath as Cade crossed his arms over his chest and tucked his hands beneath his armpits. He sat low in the chair and chewed his gum, the slow roll of his jaw contemplative.

"Pass up your scorecards," Charlie directed.

The other four judges handed over their scores.

"Mr. Nyland?" the announcer prodded.

Cade scanned the contestants, his gaze eventually returning to TZ. He pursed his lips, picked up a pencil and tapped the eraser end on the scorecard. He was slow to rank his choice for tightest butt. Once completing the task, he stood and handed his card to the announcer.

The crowd shifted restlessly, awaiting the results.

"What are our chances?" Kimmie Thorn, TZ's closest friend since elementary school, came to stand beside her. Wearing a flesh-colored St. Tropez V-string and a tiny tube top, she left little to the imagination.

"One in fifteen," TZ counted for her friend.

Kimmie was all smiles. "Your sexy swivel brought the judges to their feet."

Every judge but Cade. "What do you know about Nyland?" she asked.

"That he's a loner and a known heartbreaker," Kimmie replied. "What about Rhett Evans?"

"Stockbroker and sharp dresser."

"I want him to father my children."

11

TZ started. "You don't even know the man."

"Just one look," Kimmie said simply.

And TZ understood. From the moment Kimmie first became interested in boys, she'd sworn she'd know her husband at first glance.

"Rhett's my ride to Key West," Kimmie announced with complete certainty. "I plan to make his Dow Jones rise."

TZ was not as optimistic as Kimmie. "Flag me down if the stock market falls and you need a ride home."

"What are you driving?" Kimmie asked.

"The Mustang."

"I'd rather walk."

"The car runs just fine."

"When it wants to. It's left you stranded so often, Checker Cab is on your speed dial," Kimmie reminded her.

"The 'Stang needs a lot of work."

Kimmie grinned. "How's the vibration? Still orgasmic?"

"It still vibrates, even after a change of tires and front-end alignment." TZ brushed her hair off her forehead. It had grown warm on the stage. "I wish I had time for all the repairs it needs."

"My wish is to win this tight butt contest," Kimmie said. "Where's the announcer?"

TZ glanced at the beer-stein–shaped clock that hung over the bar. Fifteen minutes had passed. Two minutes later, the announcer waved a piece of paper at the contestants. "All tallied."

Charlie's ear-splitting whistle gained the crowd's attention. "Bring your hands together for the winners of the preliminary round. First of the five, in no particular order, number two, Kelly Knight."

Kelly bounced forward, a brunette in a raspberry thong

and matching halter top. The crowd applauded its approval.

"A big rear cheer for number six, Kimmie Thorn," the announcer continued.

Kimmie hugged herself. "I made it!" Pleased to be a finalist, she blew a kiss to the judges. Judge Rhett Evans pretended to catch her kiss.

"Luck of the Irish, number thirteen, Chad O'Brien, step forward." The announcer motioned the man in the shamrock briefs to join Kelly and Kimmie.

Chad actually blushed at the female squeals.

The announcer grinned broadly. "Fourth of the five, number one, Shell Litton, come on down."

Pretty and petite, Shell backed toward the front of the stage. She was topless with adhesive breast petals covering her nipples. Only a whisper of pink nylon covered her fanny.

Charlie grinned. "I could bounce a quarter off her butt."

TZ licked her lips. One contestant to go. She desperately needed the tight butt win. The prize money would go toward the back taxes on All Tune and Lube, her aunt's three-bay garage. Six months before, Elise Blake had passed away in her sleep. She had been a free-spirited lady who had lived in a man's world and made it her own. When TZ had shown an interest in mechanics, Elise had taken her under her wing and taught her the business.

Amelia, TZ's mother, had been horrified. Amelia, acclaimed artist and gallery owner, had wanted TZ to refine her artistic talent and follow in her own footsteps. But TZ had set aside her pastels and acrylics for oil and grease.

Not until Elise's will had been read did TZ discover she'd inherited the garage. A garage deeply in debt. Her aunt could lube an engine, but hadn't kept up the books. Customer accounts were long past due, and the collection process was slow and tedious at best. The bank had threatened foreclosure. TZ had stalled the creditors for another month.

She had sworn on Elise's grave she'd bring the business into the black. A tight butt contest might be an unconventional method to raise the cash, but if she won, she'd be that much closer to clearing the debt.

Her breath caught in her lungs as the announcer paused for effect. "Last but not least . . . come forward, number nine, TZ Blake."

The breath she'd been holding whooshed out. TZ had made it to the final five! She took her place center stage.

The announcer swatted her on the butt. "Toned, tanned and very tight."

TZ smiled at his compliment, only to have her smile fade when she again met Cade Nyland's stare. His look had turned fierce. His nostrils flared as he chomped down on his gum. When TZ's name had been announced, his hands had stilled, then fisted. While the other judges smiled and applauded, Nyland looked ready to kill.

TZ had no idea why, but it was obvious the man had it in for her. The corners of his eyes and mouth were pinched. He looked as if he'd demand a recount.

The announcer saved her from Nyland's stare. He cleared the stage of all but the five finalists, then pushed the contest to the climax. "Walk the walk! Front, back, side to side, strut your tight butts."

The contestants split in five directions. TZ walked to the back of the stage, turned on her heel, then headed right. She clapped her hands to the roof-raising music, her steps light. Kelly Knight, whose focus was on the judges and not on the other contestants, bumped her shoulder in passing. At the front of the platform, Kimmie wiggled and giggled and flirted with the judges. It appeared she had Judge Rhett Evans wrapped around her little finger.

Chad O'Brien and Shell Litton's attention had strayed from the judges and onto each other. Over the past forty minutes, Chad had become as fascinated with the dimples on Shell's butt as she was in his shamrock briefs.

"Two minutes!" the announcer informed everyone.

TZ needed the judges' attention and approval. A table dance might gain their votes. She calculated the distance from the stage to where the judges now sat, then took a wild leap. She missed her mark by two feet. Instead of landing at the middle of the table, she hit the far end. It was Cade Nyland's face who stared up at her, his gaze as hard as the set of his jaw.

"Table dance, TZ!" the crowd cheered.

She picked up the beat of the music. She shimmied, then swayed to the left, intent on working her way down the table, away from Nyland. A hand around her right ankle stopped her progress as Cade clamped her to one spot.

His touch was strong and purposeful. He wasn't letting her go. TZ shivered and stepped back on her left foot. Her heel touched the edge of the table, and she nearly lost her balance. In one liquid move, Cade rose from his chair and grabbed the back of her thigh. His fingertips brushed her bottom as he pulled her toward him. He was soon face to satin fly with her hot-pink boxers. Although she was fully dressed, his look stripped her naked.

The crowd went crazy. "Nice save, Nyland. Reward him, TZ."

TZ had lost control of the dance. The music had long since ended, and she glanced to the announcer for assistance. Charlie Owens merely shrugged.

On impulse, she swiveled her hips low, until she was eye to eye with Cade. His hand fully cupped her left buttock. Her heart beat wildly as she stroked his stubbled jaw, then kissed him full on the mouth. It was a quick, light kiss meant to tease the crowd as much as Cade.

Cade did not take to her teasing. In a motion that left her breathless, he spun her around, lifted her off the table and set her back on the stage. Her feet hit hard, jarring her spine.

"I'm not part of the show," he said on a low growl. "I don't do public affection."

TZ retreated one step, then a second and backed into Kimmie Thorn.

Kimmie squeezed her elbow. "Great leap!"

TZ exhaled sharply. "I missed my mark."

"Doesn't matter. You're sure to win."

At the moment, TZ didn't feel like a winner.

The announcer signaled the contestants to center stage. "Who has the sweetest cheeks?" he asked the judges. "Make that tough, buff decision."

TZ waited impatiently for the judges to cast their ballots. She studied their bent heads, tried to make out the numbers they jotted on their scorecards. Once again, Cade was last to cast his vote. One by one he analyzed the contestants. No one but TZ seemed to mind his scrutiny. He unnerved her. However brief the kiss, she could still feel his mouth: warm, hard and unresponsive. He hadn't wanted her to kiss him. She'd bite her nails if she hadn't just gotten the best French manicure of her life. Pressing her hand over her nervous stomach, she met Cade's gaze boldly, refusing to step into the shadows of the stage.

After what seemed like a lifetime, Cade turned in his scorecard. The announcer disappeared for several minutes, then returned with the tally. "Well, well, well," was all he'd say as he stood to the left of the contestants and smiled broadly. "The judges' votes split two-two-one. We have a tie for tightest butt."

A tie? Disappointment settled heavily over TZ. Two winners meant a split in the prize money. TZ's hopes and prayers of settling her debt died a slow death.

"Your attention, please," the announcer shouted. "Put your hands together for . . . Kimmie Thorn!"

The crowd's enthusiasm hit a fevered pitch. The applause was deafening. TZ was truly happy for her friend. Kimmie needed the money for the rally as much as TZ did for All Tune and Lube. She watched as Judge Rhett Evans pushed back his chair and stood, clapping like a madman. Kimmie bounced to the front of the stage and accepted her half of the check with a grin.

"It takes two to tie," the announcer shouted. "Let's hear it for . . . TZ Blake!"

TZ summoned a smile she didn't quite feel. She met every judge's eye but Cade Nyland's as she smiled her appreciation. She clutched the check in her hand, wishing it were the full five grand.

It wasn't, however. Life would go on. Even before the applause died down, she hopped off the stage and headed toward the storeroom/dressing room at the back of the bar.

She planned to change her clothes before she mixed and mingled with the rowdy crowd.

A sharp knock on the dressing room door brought her up short. Imagining it was Kimmie, she called, "It's open."

Chapter Two

TZ Blake stood with her back to the door. She wasn't completely dressed, Cade Nyland was quick to note. A black demi-bra and satin string bikini covered very little of her slender frame. She had the sweetest cheeks he'd ever seen. Her head and arms were stuck in an animal-print top.

"Little help here, Kimmie," came her muffled request. "I'm hot and sticky and about to strangle myself."

The air left Cade's lungs in a low whoosh. "No problem," he muttered as he approached.

Her skin was warm—very, very warm—he noted as he helped her tug the material across her shoulders and down over full breasts barely contained by her bra. One final pull brought the fabric to her waist. The top hung loosely, concealing her figure. She looked as flat chested as a boy. He rested his hand a moment too long on the curve of her hip. He just couldn't resist one touch.

"You're not Kimmie!" TZ jerked back when she caught sight of him.

Cade swept one hand down his body. "No tube top, no V-string."

"Not funny." She tried to retreat farther, but the room was so tiny she couldn't move far.

Broken barstools and boxes of liquor were stacked against walls scored by grafitti. Only a hairbreadth separated TZ and Cade. Her scent was pure female: vanilla and spice. She'd removed her sunglasses and her light blue gaze now darkened with unease. "What are you doing here?"

He studied her closely. "I came to talk. Why did you play me for a fool in the parking lot?"

She shrugged. "You'd have to already be a fool for me to play you."

Smart-mouthed female. "Why didn't you tell me your name?"

"I don't usually talk to strangers."

He cocked a brow. "You don't look shy to me."

"I avoid controversy."

He shifted his weight onto his left hip. "You're standing knee-deep in scratched car doors."

"I'll fix the damage, no charge." She made a grab for a pair of khaki shorts. "Are we even?"

He nodded. "As far as the cars are concerned."

She stepped one foot in her shorts, then the other. She pulled the khaki up her long legs. He watched her zip the zipper and snap the snap. The shorts hung on her slim hips, baggy in the butt. An odd contrast to her tight butt attire.

She turned toward the cracked mirror, pulled her hair

into a ponytail and secured it with a beige Scrunchie. She stared at his reflection in the mirror. "You still here?"

"We need to talk," he said.

"Talk, now, in this tiny room?"

"Size doesn't matter—"

A touch of a smile flitted at the corner of her mouth.

"—it's what I have to say that counts."

She eased around to face him. "This conversation couldn't wait?"

"Once you hit the bar, you'll be lost to the crowd. I might not have another private moment with you."

She glanced toward the door. "I don't do private with someone I barely know."

"Cade Nyland." He held out his hand.

She was slow to take it. "TZ Blake."

Their hands brushed. The contact sparked with the intensity of a buzzer in his palm. Cade released her. He then dipped his head and confessed. "I thought you were a man."

Her light blue gaze narrowed. "A-ah, that explains the look."

"What look?"

"Your stunned expression when you discovered I had breasts."

She had incredible breasts, full and firm and well hidden beneath her top. He'd felt as if he'd slipped on an oil slick and couldn't regain his balance when he realized the mechanic he sought was a woman. A sexy exhibitionist in hot-pink boxers.

He jammed his hands in the back pockets of his jeans and continued, "I travel the rally circuit."

"So I've heard. Nice work if you can get it."

Her sarcasm punched him low. She believed rallying a road game, not a sport of strategy and skill. Most people knew of his life as rallyist and hell-raiser; few knew of his corporate and family ties. He kept that side of himself out of the public eye. He protected what he held most sacred.

Shaking his head, he wondered what had possessed him to follow TZ to the dressing room. Perhaps the flash of disappointment that tightened her mouth when she'd been told there had been a tie for tightest butt. Perhaps the slight slump of her shoulders when she'd hopped off stage. He'd been prodded by gut instinct to talk to her. He never argued with his intuition.

He stood stiffly. "Congratulations on your win, by the way."

"Don't you mean my tie?"

"A win's a win. Besides, Kimmie Thorn's a judge's dream. She's cute and cuddly with centerfold curves." He pursed his lips. "She's also calculating and looking for a husband."

She blinked. "You got all that from a nude V-string?"

"Call it sex sense."

"Did you vote for her?"

"I never vote and tell."

She smoothed her hands over her hips. "A-ah, a man of discretion."

"Impulse isn't my style."

TZ grinned. "My table dance?"

Cade frowned. "Your leap from the stage to the table could have landed you in the hospital."

"I've done wilder and crazier things."

He shook his head. "You're in need of a keeper, sweet cheeks."

"Interested in the position, rally man?"

Taking on TZ Blake would be a full-time job. She could drive a man crazy in a very short time. He didn't need her kind of insanity. He wondered if she could be serious during the four-day road trip from Gulf Cove to Key West.

"Why did you enter the tight butt contest?" he asked suddenly.

She bent over and straightened the gold link bracelet around her right ankle. "To show off my perfect ass."

Her ass *was* darn near perfect. It could bring a man to his knees. "The real reason, TZ."

"I entered for the money."

She gave him pause. "Are you broke?"

"Not broke, merely ambitious."

Ambitious . . . "What else do you do for money?"

Her lips curved. "What did you have in mind?"

She was playing him again, of that Cade was certain. He needed her serious, not turning his questions back at him.

He switched tactics. "Rumor has it you're a mechanic."

"I've been known to service an engine or two."

"Hopefully you give good service. I'm in need—"

"TZ, open the door!" The riotous pounding turned Cade around.

"Damn," he cursed. One step and he'd reached the door. He twisted the handle and pulled. Kimmie Thorn and Rhett Evans stood just outside.

Rhett waggled his brows. "Like minds," he greeted Cade, his gaze straying from Kimmie to TZ Blake. "Undressing in the dressing room?"

"More on the order of straight conversation," Cade replied evenly.

"Are you blind?" Rhett blurted. "How could you look and not touch?"

Cade shrugged. "My interests run elsewhere."

"Can you continue your conversation in the hallway?" Rhett asked. "That is, if talk is truly what you're after."

"It was all I was after." He turned slightly and nodded toward the door. "TZ?"

She stuffed her sunglasses, hot-pink boxers and white crop top into her straw shoulder bag. Still barefoot, she followed him out the door.

The hallway was jammed with two-legged wolves. Their congratulations and cheers stole Cade's private moment with TZ. He tried to snag her hand, but another man beat him to it.

She disappeared before his eyes.

He stood alone in the hallway. He leaned back against the cracked plaster wall, wanting to head out, but knowing he was stuck at Chugger Charlie's until he and TZ again crossed paths. He'd never had to depend on anyone for anything. He hated the fact he needed TZ Blake.

He pushed off the wall, deciding to hit the bar and nurse a drink. One beer, no more. A hangover could be as deadly to the driver as misfiring pistons to an engine. Cade wanted the SunCoast win. The rally lasted four days, weaving through both residential and commercial neighborhoods, along narrow beach roads and four-lane highways.

Cade prayed his mechanic could also navigate. Driver and navigator had to work as a team. Decisions were made on a dime, corners often taken on two wheels. Start, stop, pedal to the metal. He wondered how well TZ could read a road map.

He found an empty barstool between a redhead and a bleached blonde. The redhead smiled. "Been saving this seat for you, handsome."

Cade had never met the woman. He damn sure wasn't in the mood for intimate conversation.

The man dancing with TZ Blake was far too handsy, far too familiar. Introduced as a friend of a friend, Mick Wilcox was monopolizing her company. The dance floor was small and Mick was an extra-large man. He chose to dance slowly even to the fast songs.

Suffocated by his barrel chest, TZ sought a new partner. She scanned the crowd, only to find her male friends involved in pool or darts. She needed a savior. . . .

Her gaze found Cade Nyland. He'd turned his barstool toward the dance floor, and from there he returned her stare. Her heart quickened as his eyes narrowed, and he set down his beer. Sliding off the stool, he headed her way.

She tripped over Mick's feet. She wasn't ready to face Cade. Not now, maybe not ever. Taking over the lead, TZ danced Mick across the floor, distancing herself from the rally man.

Cade, however, tracked her. By the look in his eye, he wasn't amused that she'd danced beyond his reach.

"Can I cut in?" Rhett Evans's question took her by surprise. "Rally driver privilege." The lean, sandy-haired judge from the tight butt contest nudged an annoyed Mick Wilcox aside. Dressed in tailored gray slacks and a silver silk shirt, he looked as misplaced at the beachside bar as a surfer in the big city.

The music turned island, switching to reggae. While the

tempo allowed the dancers to remain close, there was no need to press flesh. TZ breathed more easily.

"Where's Kimmie?" she asked Rhett, keeping one eye on Cade as he zigzagged between the dancers. A brunette in a floral string bikini caught his arm. He dipped his head and spoke to her. Pouting prettily, she released him.

Several other dancers stopped Cade, slowing his progress as he made his way toward TZ.

"Kimmie's powdering her nose," Rhett told her. "Her trip to the little girl's room gave me the opportunity to thank you for the great tune-up you did on my Jag."

"So that was your XKE," she said admiringly. "The car was already on the rack when I came in. Scott, my vocational technician, must have taken your information. Nice wheels, by the way."

"My regular mechanic was on vacation," he admitted. "My father swears by All Tune and Lube."

"I've known Daniel for years." She liked his father. He'd been a good customer.

Rhett danced a little closer. He took her hands in his and swung her in a circle. "Ever consider rallying?" he asked when she passed beneath his arm.

"Driving with a madman for four days?" She laughed out loud. "Not on your life."

"Not all competitors are hell-bent," he assured her.

She pulled free of his hold. "Are you the exception?"

"I'm pretty even-tempered." He danced forward, nearly stepping on her bare toes. "I'm also in need of a mechanic."

TZ sidestepped, dancing around him. "I'm a mechanic with little sense of direction."

"Can you read a road map?"

"Couldn't tell an interstate from a side street."

Rhett moaned, disappointed. "I had such high hopes—you, me, the open road."

TZ swayed to the island beat. "Sorry, just can't—"

Her hip hit something solid. She blinked, turned and elbowed Cade Nyland in the gut. He didn't even flinch. He stood to her left, six solid feet of purpose and persistence. Her heart suddenly beat louder than the music. Every pulse point throbbed. She didn't like his effect on her.

"Kimmie's looking for you, Evans," Cade informed Rhett. "She's over by the bar surrounded by surfers. They're scoping her out like she's the next big wave."

"Later, TZ." Rhett departed with the speed of a superhero to the rescue.

TZ fanned her face. "Whew, it's hot. I'm in need of something cold."

Cade blocked her path. "Give me five minutes of your time, and I'll buy you that drink."

Five whole minutes. She'd sooner dance with the devil. She cupped her ear and raised her voice, far louder than was necessary. "What? I can hardly hear you. The music's loud—"

A switch in tunes shot her excuse all to hell. The classic oldie "Stand By Me" brought the dancers close. Everyone except TZ and Cade. He held her loosely and at arm's length. A third person could have danced between them.

In his arms TZ returned to Miss Farley's Ballroom Dance Lessons, where, at the age of twelve, her mother had insisted she learn the box step and social graces. She could still fox-trot and cha-cha, but seldom observed propriety. She was given to impulse.

She wanted Cade Nyland as off-balance as she. On a whim, she stepped on top of his booted feet, dancing with him as a child would with her father. He had big feet, long and wide enough for her to keep her balance. The extra height brought her barely to his chin. A whiskered chin in need of a shave.

"What the hell?" Cade cut her a sharp look. "The song's 'Stand By Me,' not 'Stand On Me.'"

"You wanted to dance." She breathed against his neck. "So dance."

Embraced by the scent of Polo and his immense irritation, she bonded like a skin graft. On a low growl he danced her over to the side archway, then shook her off his feet. His gaze burned darkly, and his expression turned as hard as the rest of his body.

Without warning, he snagged her hand, then led her outside and onto the beach, into the setting sun and rising tide. Every time she held back, dug her heels in the sand, he merely pulled her along. The tracks of her resistance were soon lost to the high tide.

"Where are we going?" she demanded as they climbed a sand dune.

"Not much farther." He stopped abruptly and pointed to an enormous piece of driftwood. "Have a seat."

"I'd rather stand."

"Then stand."

She sat down hard. "You always so bossy?"

He jerked the leather tie from his hair, then raked his hand through it. "You always so crazy?"

"Crazy? In relation to what?"

"Tight butt contests. Leaping from a stage to a table in

a single bound. Kissing me. Dancing on my feet. Life in general."

She shrugged. "I live for the moment."

"I'm looking for a four-day commitment."

"A commitment? From *me?*" A woman who stood in the aisles at the grocery store and couldn't commit to plain or crunchy peanut butter. Wheat or rye bread. Orange or grapefruit juice. She swallowed her laughter. Cade might not appreciate her laughing in his face.

"A commitment for cash," he added.

Cash? How much cash? Her amusement faded.

She waited impatiently as he shoved the leather tie into the pocket of his jeans, then removed a pack of Doublemint. He pulled out a stick and offered her a piece.

She shook her head. "No thanks."

While she watched, he unwrapped the gum, popped it into his mouth, then returned the pack to his pocket. The slight twist of his shirt sleeve gave TZ a glimpse of his tattoo. On his upper right arm barbed wire stretched over a red heart.

Guarded emotion. Limited entanglements. No complications.

He looked the loner, but required a four-day commitment.

She pressed him to continue. "Money talks."

"So it does," he agreed. "I'm in town for the SunCoast Run."

"So are a lot of drivers."

"One hundred, to be exact. Not all the drivers are in my predicament. I'm in need of a mechanic."

"So is Rhett Evans."

A muscle ticked along his jawline. "Did he make you an offer?"

"He asked if I was available to navigate."

"Are you?"

"Depends . . ."

"On the highest bidder?" He didn't look happy. "What's your price?"

Her price? TZ was stunned. "What's the going rate?"

"Depends on the level of desperation."

She studied him closely, caught the narrowing of his eyes, the flare of his nostrils, the widening of his stance. The flex of his tattoo. "I think you're pretty desperate, rally man."

"My mechanic was injured in a waterskiing accident," he admitted. "Without a navigator, I'm out of the race."

She couldn't read a road map.

He wouldn't appreciate driving in circles for four days. She turned to leave. "Sorry, no can do."

"Ten grand," he shot at her back.

TZ stopped, curled her toes in the sand. A flicker of hope swept away her disappointment over the tie in the tight butt contest. The ten thousand would help settle her aunt's debt and keep the bank at bay.

"Make it fifteen," he said.

She couldn't believe her ears. With the extra money she could hire Scott when he graduated from vocational school next month. "Will you be driving the Sting Ray?"

"It's a '63 convertible roadster."

"The plastic fantastic." A damn fine vehicle. She knew the engine well.

"The car's in mint condition."

The service she could handle. Direction would be her downfall. She dipped her head. "I honestly can't help you."

"Twenty thousand, and ten percent of my winnings."

A small fortune should he win. TZ threw back her head and stared into the twilight. Deep blues faded into the dark of night. The exact color of his eyes. "Trust me, I'm not who you need."

"Let me be the judge of that." He came up behind her. "Emergency service is my primary concern."

Her concern lay in charting the course. "Do you know the route?"

"We run from Gulf Cove to Key West. The rally master keeps the course secret until race time. SunCoast is as recreational as it is tricky and fast-paced. It's packed with rally code, checkpoints, brainteasers and nightly parties."

The parties she could handle. Codes and checkpoints would make her crazy. Under her direction they'd end up in Georgia instead of southeast Florida. "You intend to take first?"

"With the right navigator."

The road map dilemma. Again she debated, "I can keep your engine running, change a tire, but—"

He put one hand on her shoulder and turned her around, never letting her finish. He looked hopeful. "No more buts. Take the job."

He would pay her well. Her aunt's garage would be in the black within a week. She prayed the southern route of the rally would run west to east, diagonally across the state. If not, there was no telling where they would end up.

"Do we have a deal?" Cade pressed.

The man could bargain. "If you're absolutely certain."

"Damn sure, sweet cheeks." He actually smiled, the slow

satisfied smile of a man who had gotten what he'd gone after.

TZ knew she'd soon wipe the smile off his face. One wrong turn and he'd leave her on the side of the road. She wiggled her thumb. She could always hitchhike home. "I'll need some front money," she informed him.

He shrugged. "No problem. I'll write out a check in the morning."

She would deposit it before they hit the open road. If worse came to worse, maybe Cade would consider it a loan. She could dissolve the debts and pay him back in installments.

"Where can we connect tomorrow?" he asked.

"At All Tune and Lube on Gulfbreeze Boulevard."

"I'll pick you up at nine sharp. Pack light."

"One overnight bag and two toolboxes."

"Good ratio."

There was more to say, a whole lot more to admit, but he had cut off her confession. He would, no doubt, do so again.

He was a desperate man.

And she'd gone to desperate measures.

With a soft sigh TZ and her guilty conscience left Cade standing in the twilight that matched his eyes.

Chapter Three

"I plan to marry you, Rhett."

Rhett Evans nearly choked on his Caesar salad. Seated across from Kimmie Thorn at Calypso's Café, he rubbed his throat. The romaine went down as sharply as if he'd swallowed a bite of plastic fruit from the decorative bowl in the center of the table.

Kimmie, however, hadn't noticed his discomfort. She continued to eat with precise little bites. She'd finished her salad and had started on her tomato bisque. Calypso music played in the background of their secluded booth while waitresses dressed as Carmen Miranda delivered trays of food, their hips swaying to the West Indies beat.

Unnerved by Kimmie's directness, Rhett grabbed his water glass and took a long, cool sip. This wasn't the light, sexy banter he'd planned to enjoy when he'd invited her to dinner. The second they'd ordered, centerfold Kimmie had sent a verbal punch to his gut.

"You're rushing things a little," Rhett finally managed.

"We've known each other less than an hour."

"In that time I've come to know you quite well."

He picked up a spoon and tapped it lightly on the glass tabletop. "What do you know about me, Kimmie?" he finally asked.

She studied him so closely, he shifted on the banquette. "I *believe* you like fresh-squeezed orange juice and multi-grain bagels for breakfast, you usually skip lunch and eat a big dinner. You like big cities, baseball and imported beer."

Las Vegas, Florida Marlins, Heineken. He continued to tap the spoon, harder and little faster.

She gnawed her bottom lip, then continued, "You've grown up around women, but you're not a mama's boy."

Two older sisters and he adored his mother.

She gave him the once-over. "You always dress GQ and wear boxer briefs."

Propelled by nerves, the spoon flew out of his fingers and landed in her soup bowl. "How did you know?"

"It's in a man's walk," she said with a knowing smile. "A woman can tell." She scooped his spoon from her soup bowl with her own spoon. "Care for a sip of tomato bisque?"

He shook his head. He was slowly losing his appetite. He picked up his knife and rapped it on the table. Kimmie moved a little to the left. "I'm not a knife thrower," he assured her, then couldn't resist asking, "Why do you think we're compatible?"

"Just one look." She reached out and touched his arm, lightly, yet intimately. "Some things a woman just knows."

Some things a man just didn't. However adorable, Kimmie confused the hell out of him. Five foot three, eyes as green and sparkling as the slice of fresh lime in her glass of Perrier, she now sat Indian-style on the bamboo bench, all sweet and serene, and believing she'd found her soul mate.

While he believed in the heat of attraction and lust at first erection, love at first sight was a female myth. There was no room in his life for marriage.

He set the knife aside. Then, clearing his throat, he decided to live dangerously. "Just one look . . . what did you see, Kimmie?"

Her breasts rose on a sigh beneath her peach tank top, and her three belly rings sparkled at her navel. Low-rise white jeans snugged her hips and thighs in a way Rhett hoped to imitate with his own body before the end of the evening.

She set down her spoon and licked her lips. Candlelight cast a halo about her pale blond hair, and for a moment, she looked like an angel. An angel with double-D breasts. "We're both from Florida."

The foremost reason to propose.

"We're sparks off the same flame."

Wedding invitations would need to be printed. He couldn't comprehend how a woman who belonged in pink satin bunny ears and a white tail could compete with the tall, slim women of fashion he'd always dated. But somehow she did.

"We're both winners," she continued. "You in the rallies and me in the tight butt contest."

She'd tied for first. There was a big difference between her wiggling her firm ass and him driving a finely tuned engine. He just didn't have the heart to disillusion her.

He went back to his salad, silent and assessing, as Kimmie hit number four. "We both like classic cars."

An inducement to book a church. It had taken his promise that she could ride in his Jag to separate her from the surfers at Chugger Charlie's. "So much in common," he muttered around a bite of anchovy and cheese.

She pursed her lips, looking thoughtful as she uncrossed her legs and shifted on the bench. Rhett followed her movements beneath the glass table as she wiggled her bottom deeper into the bamboo seat, then rolled onto her left hip. She spread her legs, just a little. Just enough to make him groan as the jeans creased her inner thighs.

"I've another reason we should be together!" Kimmie snapped her fingers as she leaned forward. Her breasts squeezed together. Her scent teased him across the table, an exotic musk filled with silent promises. "You're a stockbroker, and I own some stock."

A definite reason to face a priest. Sadly, she hadn't a clue as to his true identity. He was a stockbroker by day, and a gambler by night. His life was a vicious cycle of highs and lows. He'd made a million, then lost it the same year. Easy come, easy go. He had a habit of betting on the ponies, professional sports and hitting more than twenty-one in blackjack. Only his shrink knew how deeply he was in debt.

After paying the entry fee for the SunCoast Run and placing a substantial side bet on its outcome, he had eighty-five dollars to his name. The way Kimmie had devoured the menu, he'd soon be down to change in his pocket. "What's your investment?" he asked.

She wiped her mouth, hesitated. "Burger Joe's."

He knew the stock. "The old-fashioned drive-in with 1950's music, waitresses on roller skates, delivery trays hooked to car windows. The franchise that's spreading as fast as the cook can flip the burgers."

Kimmie's family owned such a franchise, but she wasn't about to admit that her life revolved around burgers, fries and root beer floats. By the end of May, she would have enough saved from working at her parents' diner to open one of her own. Before she tackled sixteen-hour days, she wanted a little fun. That fun included Rhett Evans and the SunCoast Run. "Have you ever eaten at a Burger Joe's?" she asked.

"Only once. I ordered, then ate on the road during a rally. The food was great. Best onion rings I've ever eaten."

Kimmie sighed with relief. Unless he'd looked closely, Rhett would never have recognized her picture on the franchise logo. At seventeen, the founder of Burger Joe's had selected her from more than a thousand girls to model a tight pink angora sweater and swirling gray poodle skirt. She'd posed atop the hood of a 1950 hot rod, her legs crossed, flashing her bobby socks and saddle shoes. Over the years, restaurant owners across the country had blown up the logo and hung her picture over the cash register.

She'd become an advertisement for a half-pounder with the works.

"Buy low, sell high." She smiled, and touched his arm once again. She liked the feel of his shirt, all silver and silky.

"It's a solid investment," he approved.

"As solid as you and me."

"I know nothing about you," he reminded her.

Her gaze was as soft as her voice. "I'm your best wet dream and your sexiest daydream."

"My walking, breathing fantasy," he muttered as he ran

one finger beneath the collar of his shirt. "Can I interest you in something other than a walk down the aisle?"

She spooned tomato bisque into her mouth, swallowed. "I'd like to rally."

"Wedding or rally?" He blew out a breath. "Why not the moon, Kimmie?"

His sarcasm was lost on her. She went after what she wanted—and she wanted Rhett Evans. She'd flirted through life, wide-eyed and playful while waiting for this man. While she might not be the smartest V-string walking, now that she'd found Rhett, she'd grown determined and serious. He was her home, sweet home.

He'd lowered his gaze, his dark lashes veiling the heat in his eyes. She took an unguarded moment to study his face. Clean-shaven and chiseled. Beautiful for a man. The slight cleft in his chin split its symmetrical sharpness, giving him character.

He looked up, regretful. "Sorry, sweetheart. There's only room for two in the Jag. Driver and mechanic."

She thought fast. "Perhaps I could navigate."

He lifted one brow, asked, "Have you ever kept a mileage log? Ever charted starts and stops or timed travel between checkpoints?"

"No, but I could learn. You could teach me, Rhett," she insisted.

Reaching across the table, he ran one finger along the curve of her full bottom lip. Ripe for the Pickin' glossed her mouth a ripe peach. He'd watched her put on the flavored lipstick. By the look in his eye, he wanted to taste her peaches.

"There's not enough time for you to memorize the scoring penalties, track the color-coded checkpoints and speed changes. Throughout the rally a yellow legal pad fills with as much detail and data as a corporate tax return," he explained.

"Who will you find on such short notice?" The tip of her tongue flicked the tip of his finger, which still played at the corner of her mouth.

"I'll make some calls when I return to the hotel."

Hidden from other customers in the secluded booth, she stroked his wrist, then sucked his finger into her mouth, taking him to the knuckle.

She moved her mouth up and down on his finger, all swirling tongue and scraping teeth. His palm began to sweat. Beneath the narrow glass table, she noticed his erection tented his slacks. Kissing his finger one last time, she released him. His hand shook as he ran it down his thigh. The sweat from his palm flattened the knife-sharp crease in his pants.

"Where are you staying?" she asked.

"The Beachcomber." Rhett pushed his salad plate aside. "I want you, Kimmie."

"I want to rally."

"I'll give it some thought." His voice sounded as raw as the rare filet the waitress set before him.

"Think hard, Rhett Evans," Kimmie said as she accepted her surf and turf. "I'll expect an answer by dessert."

Dessert arrived, and Rhett poked at the pineapple upside-down cake with his fork. The cake soon became a pile of crumbs. His mind raced. He wanted Kimmie, wanted her bad, in his bed for the long night ahead. She, however, wanted to rally. He almost wished he could take her with him. He shifted on the seat, about to combust from her body heat.

"I have a final reason we should be together." She set down her dessert fork and blotted her lips with a napkin. "We both want you to win the SunCoast Run."

Now she was talking.

"I could be your partner. If you let me rally, I'll pay all your expenses. Gas, food, lodging. The race will give us a chance to get to know each other better."

Was she humming the wedding march? Fitting him for a tux? Designing her own gown? If she knew he had less than a hundred dollars to his name, she'd be hightailing it out of the church.

No woman wanted to marry a poor man. His ex-girlfriend, Lila Miller, had shouted those words at the top of her lungs at a Fourth of July company picnic. Her tirade had included "louse" and "loser" and lots of embarrassment.

Absently, he ran his fingers along the edge of the dessert plate, feeling like a lowlife for even considering letting Kimmie Thorn pay his way. He was this side of broke, however, and in need of cash flow. If the race went as planned, he could pay her back from his winnings and recoup his dignity. If she just weren't so damn hot . . .

He sucked in a breath. "I can't afford any distractions, Kimmie."

"You won't even know I'm in the Jag until we stop for the night," she promised, crossing her heart.

Not know she was in the Jag? Rhett was already sweating bullets. Even if she were dressed in burlap with a paper bag over her head, he'd still feel her presence. He'd be hard the entire trip and unable to work the clutch.

Looking for one last roadblock to discourage her, he said, "You might have to share your seat with a mechanic."

Her green eyes widened. "Two butts in that leather bucket?"

"I need a navigator more than I need an investor." Which wasn't entirely true.

She rested her elbows on the table and her chin on one palm. Her reply, when it came, shocked the hell out of him. "You'd better pick a beanpole, Rhett Evans. I'll not share the seat with a man with a curly tail."

His jaw dropped as she arched one brow. "Unless you want me to sit on his lap and—"

He sliced the air with his hand, his tone as sharp as the stab of his jealousy. "No lap sitting."

His thoughts went to Sam Mason, a mechanic who lived in Gulf Cove, but hadn't raced for several years. Over time, Sam's keen sense of direction and quick diagnosis of a stalled engine had been dulled by Jack Daniels. The man was known to drink his lunch and dinner. Rhett wondered if Sam could remain sober for the four-day rally with the right incentive. He'd have to give the fellow a call. Sam was a skeleton of a man.

"Can you pack four days into one overnight bag?" he asked.

"An overnight bag and a very large purse. V-strings don't take up much room, Rhett."

Rhett pictured Kimmie on stage, her tight butt in less than nothing. It was going to be a long, trying trip.

"Then you can come along."

"You won't be sorry." Her smile spread, as did her legs. Just enough to catch his eye under the table.

"Come back to the hotel with me," he invited. "We can celebrate your investment in the rally."

Kimmie shook her head. "My investment involves our future, not sweating up your sheets."

Her words set him back. He was suddenly confused. "I thought you wanted me as much as I want you."

"I want you, Rhett," she agreed. "But I want you for life."

If she knew how he'd gambled his life away, she would never have stayed for dessert. He ran his fingers through his hair. "We can take it slow." Difficult for him to say, when his body wanted hard and fast and deep.

Kimmie touched his forearm with her fingertips. "Slow and safe. We'll need separate hotel rooms."

Separate rooms? "One room is cheaper."

"I won't sleep with you until after we're married."

The odds were against their exchanging vows. "Why not?"

"I'm a virgin."

A virgin? Mother Mary!

The image of centerfold Kimmie in a white wedding gown gave him blue balls.

Mick Wilcox hated whiners. Especially when that whiner was a man. A man seated close beside him on a barstool at Chugger Charlie's.

"Hardly seems fair you got to dance with TZ Blake and I didn't, Ox," the man known only as Skinner griped.

Mick was none too pleased by Skinner's use of his nickname. "Ox" was reserved for family and close friends, not to be spoken by an acquaintance of the past thirty minutes. He looked down his nose at the man. "TZ likes tall, well-built men."

"Well-built, you say?"

Mick caught Skinner pointedly staring at his beer belly and attempted to suck in his gut. With little success. His belly hung over the waistband of his jeans. He shrugged. "Height matters more."

He caught Skinner's frown as the man kicked out his feet from the upper rung on the barstool, his unlaced sneakers barely brushing the floor. When standing, the top of Skinner's head hit Mick mid-chest. Skinner was wiry and bald with a keen sixth sense for sidestepping the law.

It was Skinner's ability to beat police heat on which Mick now focused. "So, are you in or out?"

Skinner sucked down his third beer, then lit a thin cigar before answering. "Too sweet a deal not to have a catch, Ox."

He fanned aside the smoke Skinner deliberately puffed in his face. "No catch. I need a car for the SunCoast Run."

"You want me to supply your wheels?"

"Top-dollar wheels. You're the man with the chop shop."

"Not so loud." Skinner shushed him. "I buy and sell used cars."

Mick scoffed. "Ugly Duckling is strictly a front. I've done my homework. The cars on your lot are all stolen. You repaint, reupholster and retag each out-of-state vehicle. You deal in cash and avoid the IRS. You've never purchased a business license."

Skinner flagged the bartender and ordered another Moosehead. When it arrived he drank deeply, straight from the bottle. "You can't blackmail me."

"Not planning to," Mick replied. "Just trying to cut a deal."

Skinner puffed on his cigar. "You're in need of a vintage model?"

"A true classic."

"I've got a '59 Caddie, a bit rusty, but it runs well," Skinner said.

"Not what I'm looking for." Mick wanted a vehicle that would cause TZ Blake to give him a second look when he took it in for service.

"How about a 1950 Borden's milk truck?"

Mick ducked the smoke ring Skinner blew at his forehead. "I'm not into Elsie the Cow."

Skinner tapped the ashes from his cigar into the pink curve of the conch shell ashtray. "A 1931 U.S. Mail truck?"

"One step up from the Pony Express." A muscle ticked in Mick's jaw. Skinner wasn't trying hard enough to please him. "I need a vehicle worthy of the rally."

"How are you planning to get in the race, Ox? Only nationwide qualifiers get to rally."

The haze from Skinner's cigar blinded Mick. His eyes watered. The cherry-sweet scent made him sneeze. "I've ways of limiting the competition. Once some of the rallyers drop out, their slots are open to the public, to whomever can pay the entry fee."

"I've heard the fee is damn steep," Skinner said.

"I've got the money." Several trips to the pawn shop had secured his rally fee.

Skinner rolled his cigar from one corner of his mouth to the other, the tip burned as brightly as his eyes. "Sounds interesting."

Mick shifted on the barstool. He was a large man, and

the round leather seat supported only one butt cheek. "Interesting enough to join forces?"

"I supply the car and you—"

"Supply the know-how. I've ways of winning this race."

Skinner scratched his jaw. "Not all legit, I'm guessing."

"Never claimed to be a law-abiding citizen." Mick finished off his beer and belched loud enough for the customer on his right to shoot him a dirty look. He belched a second time, just out of orneriness.

"Might be able to locate a '65 Cobra by midnight," Skinner speculated.

"A Cobra?" Mick was impressed. "An aggressive bruiser."

"I'll need time to paint it."

Mick glanced at his watch. The face was cracked, and it was hard to tell the time. "You have ten hours."

"Where shall we meet?" Skinner inhaled, then shot a stream of smoke at Mick's nose.

Mick held his breath until the smoke cleared. "I'll come by Ugly Duckling."

Skinner once again sent smoke Mick's way. "I'll be ready."

"You damn well better be."

Skinner motioned to the bartender. "It's getting late. One more beer and I'll hit the road."

Thoughts of the advancing evening drove Mick's departure. He had a big day ahead of him tomorrow. Reaching into the torn pocket of his jeans, he removed a five-dollar bill and tossed it on the bar. He'd had two drafts. He didn't mind paying for his beers, but he'd decided the bartender didn't deserve a tip. The bartender had paid more attention to the rallyers than to his other customers, which was poor service in Mick's estimation.

Sliding off his bar stool, he hiked up his jeans, towering over Skinner. He reached for Skinner's cigar, and ignoring the man's protest, dropped it in his bottled beer. He then stuck his face in Skinner's own to deliver his threat. "Blow smoke in my face again, little man, and you'll be exhaling it through a different hole."

Chapter Four

The sound of screeching tires drew TZ Blake from under the hood of Rhett Evans's Jaguar. She caught a flash of black before the Sting Ray skidded sideways toward All Tune and Lube. Her heart clenched at the imminent collision. She nearly choked on the chocolate Hershey's Kiss she'd just swallowed.

All around her the scent of burned rubber seared the morning air prior to the loud crash that buried the sports car beneath a stack of retreads. In the aftershock, the tires bounced off the Sting Ray's hood and rolled across the pavement, knocking into the gas pumps, then toppling over.

TZ and Rhett took off at a run, rounding the side of the building just as Cade Nyland climbed out of his car. His chest heaved beneath his navy polo. He was wild-eyed and angry as hell.

"Some entrance," Rhett said, reaching Cade first. "Are you all right?"

"I'll live." Cade raked his hand through his hair and blew out a breath. "Lost my brakes."

On a highway going seventy he could have lost his life. Her hands remained damp and her heart had yet to slow. "When did they go soft?" TZ asked.

"I started pumping them a half mile from the garage."

"Let me check for damage." She reached into the pocket of her baggy cotton overalls for a second Hershey's Kiss as she rounded the Vette and looked it over. The tires had provided a cushion against the cement wall. "Minor dents and dings that can be pounded out without much problem. Major scrape over the back right wheel well. Perhaps a touch-up paint job."

She dropped to her hands and knees, then onto her back and scooted beneath the Sting Ray. Her assessment came quickly. The brake line had a hairline slice, just deep enough to leak fluid. It was clean cut, razor-blade straight.

Cade Nyland would not be happy.

TZ frowned over her own misfortune. If he didn't rally, neither did she. Her future was suddenly looking as dark as the skid marks left by his Vette.

She wiggled from beneath the car and straightened her overalls. "Leak in your brake line," she informed Cade.

Cade straightened, his expression tight. "How bad a leak?"

"It needs replacement."

His twilight gaze turned midnight dark. "Something you can fix?"

TZ shook her head. "I don't have the parts in stock. They would need to be specially ordered. It could take a day or two to have them delivered."

"Damn." Cade slammed his hand on a retread, then

started to pace. "Not a good way to start my day."

TZ felt as rotten as Cade. On a sigh she started removing the tires from the Sting Ray. Rhett assisted. Cade went after the runaway tires near the gas pumps. Once all the tires were restacked, the three headed for the garage.

"Problem with your Jag?" Cade asked when he spotted the XKE in bay three.

"Unforeseen oil leak," Rhett replied. "TZ replaced the oil pan."

"A part I had in stock." She snagged a clean cloth from the rag bag and wiped a spot of grease from its bumper. "You're all set."

"Thanks for the quick fix," Rhett said appreciatively. "Can I run an account until after the rally?"

The account would only be outstanding for a week. "Sure, no problem." She patted the hood. "Good luck with the rally. Drive safely, Rhett."

Rhett climbed into the Jag, his gaze on Cade. "Hope to see you at the starting line."

Cade shrugged. "You never know."

TZ jammed her hands into the pockets of her overalls. Maybe the garage wasn't meant to be hers, after all. She glanced at Cade. He looked as disappointed as she felt. "There will be other races—"

"None like this one. It's the final race of the season."

"Perhaps next year—"

He shook his head. "I've won all eleven races up to this point. I wanted the twelfth. No other rallyist has won an entire year of races. I wanted to be the first."

"Have you been rallying a long time?" she asked.

"Since I was twenty. Before that I did off-road racing. My grandfather taught me speed meant nothing without

49

skill and strategy. Rayburn took me to classic car shows, and we pored over scrapbooks of his past rallies. Rallying appealed to me, also, and after an accident confined my grandfather to a wheelchair, I restored a GTO Judge—"

"The most feared and respected muscle car of its time," TZ quietly acknowledged.

One corner of his mouth curved slightly. "Inexperienced and full of myself, I entered a straightaway racer in the Rockies Rally. To the Coloradans' amazement, I didn't flip the car off the mountainside. I ended up placing twenty-eighth out of a hundred. With each rally, I lowered my score, came closer to the winner's circle. My grandfather bought me the Sting Ray after my first win. I've driven the Vette in every race since." He slapped his palms against his blue-jeaned thighs. "Up until today, that is. I'd wanted this win for Rayburn."

TZ watched as he moved to the entrance of the garage and stared out into the sunlight. A light breeze ruffled his hair, the dark strands shadowing the grim set of his jaw. He swung his arms, his biceps flexing. The barbed-wire tattoo appeared to bite into his skin. After scuffing the toe of his boot across a deep crack in the cement, he walked back toward her.

Directly behind Cade came Halo, the garage cat. The one-eyed, one-eared, three-legged cat with a stubby tail had awakened from his nap and now stalked Cade as if the man were a mouse. Halo's low hiss brought Cade around. The cat was about to use Cade's leg as a scratching post.

"Don't pet him—" TZ was about to warn, but Cade had already dropped down beside the cat.

"Looks like you've used up eight of your nine lives,"

Cade said as he scratched Halo's good ear. "What's the other cat look like?"

"He wasn't in a cat fight," TZ told him. "He tangled with a cement truck. He was a long-time neighborhood stray who jaywalked."

"You saved his life?"

"My aunt, actually. She witnessed the accident. Elise rushed him to the emergency animal hospital. After a three-hour surgery and a thousand prayers, Halo became our shop cat. He's very protective of the property."

Halo was, however, making fast friends with Cade.

TZ watched as the scrawny cat wound around Cade's big body, emitting a purr that sounded like a choked engine. Halo took to people, but people seldom took to him. He wasn't the prettiest kitty in the pet store window. Most customers pretended not to see him.

Halo rolled onto his back, and Cade scratched his belly. "Such a warrior." He gave Halo a final pat on the head, then stood.

Halo made one final pass around Cade's booted feet before hobbling back to the office and his cat bed.

Cade blew out a breath and shifted his stance. "Do you know anyone who might be willing to rent me a classic car? Anyone at all?" He paused, seconds passing, before he jabbed a finger at her. "You have a Mustang!"

She took a step back and held up her hands. "Hit the brake, rally man. The Mustang's temperamental." She never knew if it would start or, worse, roll to a stop on a main street. They would be lucky to make it out of town before a piston misfired or the carburetor needed adjustment.

"It's my only option, TZ."

"Rally rules don't hold you to driving the Vette?" she asked.

"I can qualify with any classic car." He glanced at his watch. "We don't have much time."

TZ sighed, turned on her heel. "If you're sure . . ."

He was on her heels in a heartbeat. "Positive, sweet cheeks."

They left the garage through a side door, then crossed an empty field knee-high with violet and crimson wildflowers. Lavender wafted on the sunshine. The scent reminded TZ of her aunt, warm and fragrant.

To the west, a group of young boys raced around a playground with swings, teeter-totter and a set of monkey bars that resembled a skyscraper. Elise had commissioned an architect to design those monkey bars. Once completed, she'd donated the small park to the city. Although Elise had never married, she had loved children. Especially scruffy little boys.

"TZ!" the group called and waved to her in unison.

She waved back.

"Nine-forty." Kyle Richards, a thin boy in need of a haircut, gave her a thumbs-up.

"Gotcha." TZ returned the sign.

Fifty yards from All Tune and Lube, TZ directed Cade to a separate two-car garage. She had parked the Mustang in the main garage directly following her aunt's death, but had moved it soon after. A loose wire had the horn honking at all hours of the night, bringing local law enforcement to the garage, guns drawn. When TZ had forgotten to set the emergency brake, the Mustang rolled into the hubcap display, denting the metal caps. The car never seemed to be where she'd left it.

"My personal retreat," TZ told Cade as she unlocked the garage door and shoved it upward. The door rattled on its rusty rollers and started back down. Reaching over her head, Cade gave it a second push, which locked the door in place.

TZ stepped inside and flipped on the light switch. Cade stood behind her, so close in fact, she could feel his breath on the back of her neck. Faint and warm and minty.

"Right over there." She motioned toward a tarp-covered vehicle.

Cade pulled on the tarp, and the '67 Mustang was revealed. He whistled low. "She's a beauty, down to the skunk stripes, even with the gash in her door."

TZ ran her fingertips along the white racing stripes. "My aunt once drove the Mustang in several rallies."

"Then you have racing in your blood."

"More oil than racing," she corrected him.

He rested a hand on the hood. "What's her horsepower?"

"V-8 engine, with a four-speed manual."

"Pony's got gallop." He circled the car. "How's she handle?"

"A highway burner."

"How about in town?"

"Has a bit of a vibration."

"Start her up," he requested. "Let me judge the rumble."

TZ pulled the key from her bib pocket. Opening the car door, she slid onto the seat. A mere twist of the key and the Mustang bucked.

"Pony's got soul." Cade smiled as he slid onto the passenger seat.

"And a wild pulse." Her bottom had already begun to

tingle from the thrust and hum of the engine. It wasn't unpleasant, just distracting. And mildly arousing. Miles of stimulation would have her on the edge of her seat.

From the corner of her eye she caught Cade running his hand over the eyebrow, the rise at the center of the dashboard, admiring the slope. His wide shoulder brushed hers as he leaned forward and studied the instrument layout. The contact set her nerves hopping. The top of his head dipped near her chin. His hair was clean and shiny and slightly damp at the ends. A shower-in-the-morning man. Drawing in a shallow breath, TZ inhaled the scent of Polo. The urge to kiss the back of his neck stole her next breath.

She licked her lips and bent a little closer. They were cheek-to-cheek. He emanated a heat so carnal she grew hot.

A sudden blast of air through the air vent cooled her off. The air also hit Cade. Startled, she jerked right, just as Cade snapped left. The back of her head hit him square in the nose.

Crack! The impact of skull against cartilage had Cade seeing stars. His eyes watered as splinters of pain shot across his cheekbones.

"Oh no! Are you all right?" TZ slid across the carpeted driveshaft tunnel that ran between the seats. Her hip ground into his groin. Her face was pale; her expression one of concern.

He rubbed the bridge of his nose. "You're a hard-headed woman, TZ Blake."

She settled on his lap as if he were a car seat. "What can I do? Get ice? A Band-Aid? Call 911?"

He curved his free hand around her hip. "You can sit

still." The roll and press of her bottom brought a new kind of pain. A stirring pain that pulled tight and hard and would soon prove embarrassing.

"Is your nose broken?" she asked, nose-to-nose with him.

He continued his examination. "It doesn't feel broken."

"Out of joint then?"

"I'm not mad, sweet cheeks."

"I'm so sorry." She leaned back slightly. "The surge of air startled me."

"It felt as if someone had blown in my face."

"Did you accidentally hit the outside air switch?" she asked.

He shook his head. "Didn't touch a thing, I swear."

"Must be another loose wire."

"Anything serious?"

"Nothing to keep us from the rally."

He breathed easier. "That's a relief."

TZ traced his nose with the tip of her finger. "Does it hurt?"

"I've hurt worse."

"You look as if someone punched your lights out." She skimmed her finger under one eye, then the other. "You'll have two shiners by morning."

"I can do raccoon for a day or two."

She stroked the side of his face, her thumb lingering at the corner of his mouth. "A kiss would make it better."

Cade covered her hand. "It's my nose, not my mouth, in need of healing."

"I'll start with your mouth and work my way up."

TZ's lips were a hairbreadth from his own. Hers was a full, flirty mouth meant to be kissed until tongues tangled and she moaned his name. The woman had flame. He had a feeling one kiss would ignite stroking and stripping and backseat sex.

Cade couldn't allow wild and crazy to distract him from the rally. "Sorry, sweet cheeks, kissing's bad—"

"But chocolate's good." Her eyes suddenly laughed at him, and her smile spread wide as she pulled her hand free. She then withdrew a Hershey's Kiss from the pocket of her overalls. Unwrapping the foil, she pressed it between his lips. "Consider yourself kissed."

The rich chocolate melted on his tongue. TZ had played him once again. He'd expected lips and received candy. A sweet, dark Kiss. Relief or disappointment? He felt a little of each.

Patting his cheek, TZ wiggled off his lap and returned to her seat. "Back to business. Do you want to rent my 'Stang?"

Rent? Cade nodded slowly. "How much?"

"Yours for a mere five grand."

No way in hell. "You're taking advantage of me."

She smiled a slow smile. "You'll know when I'm taking advantage of you, and this isn't it."

"Three grand," he countered.

"Four," she shot back.

He glanced at his watch. He had one hour before the rally. Little time to negotiate. She had him where she wanted him, and she knew it. This was his very last compromise. "You've got a deal."

She held out her hand. "My check, please."

"First the keys."

"You're planning to drive?"

"It's *my* rally."

"It's *my* car."

"You're not a registered driver," he informed her.

"As your mechanic, I've qualified for the race."

"You're qualified to change fan belts and tires, not to shift gears."

"What if something were to happen to you?"

Did she plan to break his kneecaps with her monkey wrench? Stab him with a screwdriver? "Trust me, nothing will."

She jabbed a finger near his sore nose. "You'd best not have a heavy foot."

He captured her hand, a soft, nicely manicured hand for a mechanic. "I promise not to ride the clutch."

She still wasn't convinced, he could see it in her eyes. "I'm a good driver, TZ. No parking or speeding tickets. I don't tailgate and always use my turn signals."

She sighed and tossed him the keys.

He then reached in his shirt pocket and handed over her check. "Twenty thousand down, the remaining four once we reach Key West."

"Win or lose?"

"A deal's a deal. You'll get ten percent of my winnings should we place first." He patted the padded dashboard. "Let's get a move on. I don't want to miss the starting gun."

TZ exited the vehicle. "Pull the Mustang around to the gas pumps. Free fill on All Tune and Lube."

"Much appreciated." Cade crossed to the driver's seat. He straightened the rearview mirror, only to have it tilt slightly. Loose screw? He'd have TZ tighten it before they hit the road.

The Mustang rumbled as he backed it from the garage.

Definite punch, definite power. The vibration made him sweat. It was the hum of foreplay.

TZ watched Cade pull up to the pumps. He looked good behind the wheel. He drove the 'Stang as smoothly as the Sting Ray. He had a strong, masculine touch.

Cutting the engine, he hopped out of the car. "Tools? Tote? I'll pump while you pack up."

TZ headed to the office. Her assistant, Scott, would be arriving shortly for work. She scribbled him a note, reminding him of the rally and his need to feed Halo. She patted the cat on the head. "Protect the garage. I'll be back soon."

She changed clothes in the women's rest room, slipping out of her overalls and into baggy black shorts and a loosely fitting white top. She settled for tennis shoes and left her hair in a ponytail.

The mirror reflected a face free of makeup and grease smudges. She thought of Cade and his sore nose. All because of a blast of air.

The memory of Cade and the Hershey's Kiss drew her smile. He'd sat all tense and uneasy until she'd produced the chocolate. He had a great-looking mouth—firm, yet nicely curved, befitting the hard lines of his face. Cade was carnal. She'd known in her heart that if they'd kissed, they would have landed in the backseat and missed the starting gun.

She blew out a breath. Time to get him out of her head and prepare for the rally. The Mustang would prove a challenge.

Hanging her overalls on a hook on the back of the bathroom door, she locked up the office then returned to the garage and lowered two of the bay doors.

"Let's push your Vette into bay three," she called to Cade.

He met her at the retreads. "Why don't you sit and steer while I push."

She was perfectly capable of pushing. "Put the vehicle in neutral and steer from the car door. I've got your bumper."

The hard lines of his mouth drew even tighter as his gaze lit on her lips, her breasts, then lowered to her hips. He waved her forward. "Guide me into the garage."

TZ knew he was no longer looking at her as a mechanic. He was momentarily viewing her as a woman. One of the weaker sex.

She'd show him weak. For ten years she'd labored like a man. Today would prove no different from any other. She valued her strength. Throwing her entire one hundred and twenty pounds into the task, she shouted, "Move it or lose it."

She nearly ran over his foot. His scowl deepened, and his eyes darkened to midnight blue. "Have it your way."

He then put so much muscle into his push, he left TZ running to keep up. Just ahead, they faced a sharp turn into bay three. Without brakes the vehicle would take out her display of fan belts. "Slow down!"

Cade Nyland had super powers. The Vette slowed so quickly TZ slammed into its bumper. She rubbed her right thigh, knowing she would bruise. She wondered how often Cade wore a cape and stopped runaway trains.

"Your Vette will be safe in the garage," she told him. "I'll start the repairs when we return."

"Where do you get your auto parts?" he asked.

"From Action Auto. Any objections?"

He dipped his head, and she swore he smiled. "None whatsoever." He then reached across the driver's seat, hefted an athletic bag from the passenger side and slung it over his shoulder. He further collected a compass, stopwatch and several road maps. "Ready to rally?"

"I'll get my toolboxes."

Cade beat her to her workbench. He grabbed the two silver boxes and she snagged air. "Travel tote?"

"By the front door."

She thought to beat him to the small leather bag, but doubted she could outrun him. The man had a long, powerful stride. His arms full, he turned and said, "Let's hit the road."

"As soon as I lower the third bay door," which she proceeded to do. Locking it behind them, she grabbed her straw purse and followed Cade to the Mustang. A Mustang that had rolled around the gas pumps and now sat facing All Tune and Lube. Cade walked slowly toward the car. His face was pale beneath his tan. "The car was in park."

"It's best to set the emergency brake," TZ said. "If the pavement slants, the vehicle rolls." It had rolled across a parking lot and down a side street just last week.

Glancing at her watch, she noted the time. Nine-forty, and not one second after, the DeFreeze Ice Cream Truck cruised Gulfbreeze Boulevard, its bell ringing, calling to the children.

"TZ! TZ!" The group of boys from the playground rounded the corner of the garage at a dead run. They pushed and shoved and tripped over themselves to reach her.

"Who wants ice cream?" She'd asked that same question every day for the past five years. Ever since the day she'd caught Kyle Richards standing on the curb, his hands in his pockets, watching the DeFreeze truck pass him by. Though his parents held their own in the rising economy, they couldn't afford the little extras. TZ supplied the treats.

"There's ten of us today, TZ." Kyle scuffed the toe of his worn tennis shoe, the one without the laces. "Is that too many?"

The boys held their collective breaths as TZ surveyed the group. The children ranged in age from six to twelve, all of them scruffy, most of them in need of a bath.

"How many scoops?" she asked as the ice cream truck pulled off the main road and onto the easement in front of the garage.

"Since there's so many of us, one scoop will do," Kyle said.

"A-ah, Kyle, you promised us two scoops." A husky boy with a Crew Cut thumped his friend on the shoulder, hard enough that Kyle rocked forward, then caught himself.

TZ thought the kid looked like a miniature Marine.

Kyle narrowed his eyes on Crew Cut. "It's not my money."

"Who are you?" TZ asked the larger boy.

"Kid Quick." The boy raised his chin and puffed out his chest. "I plan to be a boxer."

"He also drinks Strawberry Nesquik," Kyle informed her, and the other kids snickered.

"Put 'em up." Kid Quick raised his fists, angered by the snickers.

"No one fights on my turf," TZ said firmly.

Kid Quick looked contrite. "I'd never hurt my friends, honest."

61

"I'll hold you to that," TZ said as she unzipped her straw bag and drew out her wallet. She fingered several bills. "I have just enough for two scoops each."

The boys whooped and jumped around like pogo sticks. TZ handed the money to Kyle. "Go treat your friends to some ice cream."

"How about you, TZ?" Kyle asked. "Butter pecan? I'll split my scoops with you."

Her heart warmed. Kyle had so little, yet he shared all he had. "Not today, big guy. You enjoy for both of us."

His smile was wide, with two teeth missing. "Thanks, TZ."

"Hold on a minute." Cade Nyland crossed to the group. He stood tall and intimidating as he looked over the children, one by one.

"Who are you?" Kyle was first to ask.

"Cade Nyland." He held out his hand and Kyle shook it.

"What happened to your nose?" Kid Quick studied Cade's face. He then dropped his chin and weaved side to side. "Ever heard of ducking and dodging?"

"I was caught unaware," Cade said.

"Sucker punch," Kid Quick scoffed. "Sneaky bastard."

"Watch your language, young man," TZ softly scolded. Color rose in Kid Quick's cheeks. "Sorry, ma'am."

It was Cade who cleared his throat. "TZ won't be around for several days, guys."

The children's eyes grew wide with the news. Kyle moved to stand protectively before TZ. "You taking her away from us, mister?"

"Only for a short time," Cade assured the boy. "We've entered the SunCoast Run."

"Wow, rallying. That's cool!" A grin split Kyle's thin face.

"That's crap!" Kid Quick frowned. "TZ's our ice cream connection."

Cade chucked Kid Quick under the chin. "Since she can't be here, I'll leave a cash reserve."

Kyle shuffled his feet. "A reserve, huh?"

"I'll leave enough cash to buy your cones until TZ returns," he explained.

"You will?" Kyle's eyes lit up, then just as quickly darkened. "You're kidding, right? No one's ever trusted us with money before."

"There's a first time for everything," Cade said before he shot Kid Quick a man-to-man look. "Protect the funds, Kid."

Kid Quick flushed with pride. "I'm here for you, Cade. I've got Kyle's back."

Cade pulled out his wallet and handed Kyle several large bills. "This should cover two scoops a day."

Kyle clutched the bills as if they might disappear before his eyes. "Thanks, man," he said as the boys pumped their arms over their heads and shouted, happier than TZ had ever seen them.

After the children left to order their cones, Cade nudged her shoulder. "Pony's waiting."

She didn't move. "Thanks for taking care of my kids."

Cade shrugged. "No biggie."

It was big to her, a grand gesture on his part. "I'm surprised Kid Quick hasn't highjacked the ice cream truck."

"He's tough, but not a punk. He'll protect his own."

TZ was amazed. "You got all that from a crew cut and a dirt-smudged face?"

"I'm good at reading people."

She wondered how well he read her.

Together, they walked toward the car. Once reaching it, he held the door for her. "Thanks," she said.

After settling in, she stretched across the seat in an attempt to return the courtesy. To her dismay, the door got away from her, swinging wide, nearly hitting Cade in the groin. He jumped back. The thick cords in his neck worked and a muscle ticked along his jaw.

"Trying to take out the driver?" he asked, none too pleased.

Her gaze shot to his abdomen, then ran down his zipper. Did he really believe she'd tried to debilitate him in order to take the wheel? "The handle slipped—"

"Looked more like a shove," he insisted. "That's twice now, TZ. Once at Chugger Charlie's, then here at the garage. You took out my Vette, and now you almost got me."

It had felt like a shove, TZ silently admitted. But one she hadn't initiated. She sniffed. "If I'd wanted to get you, you would have been gotten."

"Should have worn my cup." He set the toolboxes and their bags on the backseat, then slid in beside her. "Take a quick look at the rearview mirror before we leave. It appears loose."

TZ twisted the mirror right, then left. "It's tight."

He straightened the mirror. "My mistake." He next keyed the engine, and the Pony car kicked into action. "Buckle up. We've fifteen minutes to reach Waterside Mall, register and punch the time clock."

"Don't forget the bank," she reminded him. "I want to deposit my check."

He breathed deeply, forcing a control TZ believed him close to losing. "The bank had better be near."

"Three blocks from the mall."

They hit Waterside with seven minutes to spare. Cade positioned the 'Stang in last place behind a '59 Cadillac. Pink, with a hood the size of an aircraft carrier, the vehicle sported rocket-style fins and jet-age ruby taillights.

TZ counted heads. "There are four people in the Caddie."

Cade nodded. "Some drivers travel light; others with an entourage. Marisa runs with a mechanic, navigator and timekeeper."

As if sensing herself being discussed, the platinum blonde turned and blew Cade a kiss. A grin too brief to be more than a trick of the light softened his harsh features.

TZ blinked, then looked away. Sunlight sliced the windshield. She dug a pair of black cat's-eye sunglasses from her purse and slipped them on. From behind amber lenses, she took in the long line of cars parked bumper-to-bumper amid heat waves radiating off the asphalt. The classics shimmered with illusionary life. Rally fanatics gathered close, catching their reflections in the buffed polish, yet never leaving a fingerprint.

The vibration of the 'Stang had her bouncing on the seat like a Mexican jumping bean. She was as turned on as the highly tuned engine. She glanced at Cade, caught him shifting into first. His worn jeans hugged his thighs as he released the clutch and slowly accelerated. TZ had the wild urge to run her hand down his leg, tracing the muscles and sinew. Lacing her fingers in her lap, she stilled the impulse.

Once the woman in the pink Cadillac punched the time clock and headed out, Cade aligned the Mustang behind the white line. His window was within arm's reach of the boxed clock secured atop a short pole.

"Wasn't sure you'd make it," said a short, thick-waisted man with a badge identifying him as the rally master. "Heard your brakes went out. Is that when you broke your nose?"

"My nose isn't broken," Cade said, but didn't elaborate. "As far as the rally, my mechanic, TZ Blake, rented me her Pony car."

"Walter Brown." The rally master introduced himself. "Rhett Evans mentioned you fixed his Jag's oil leak."

TZ smiled. "Easy fix."

Brown clutched a clipboard to his chest. "Seems you weren't the only two with car problems. All four tires on Eric Klein's Bentley Flying Spur were slashed last night. Those '62 Dunlop tubeless cross plys will be hard to replace. And a midnight caller took a baseball bat to the car windows on Tripp Sawyer's '48 Porsche."

Cade stiffened beside her. "I don't like what I'm hearing."

"Because of the availability of slots," Brown further confided, "we have several first-time rallyists on the course. They can't win the grand prize, but they can gain points and qualify for future rallies."

The rally master poked his head inside Cade's window, noted, then jotted down the odometer reading on the Mustang. "She's got some miles on her."

"She's run in several rallies," TZ told Brown. "She's good for one more."

"Hope she makes it to Key West," Brown said as he

pressed an adhesive number one hundred on the bottom corner of the front windshield.

A click and a swoosh, and the windshield wipers swung left, swatting Brown's hand. The rally master jerked back and rubbed his red knuckles. "Careful, Nyland."

Cade held up his hands. "Didn't touch the switch."

Brown didn't look convinced. Slapping a manila envelope onto Cade's wide palm, he finished with, "You've two minutes to scan the route instructions, punch the time clock and hit the road."

"Hard course?" Cade asked the man who'd designed the SunCoast Run.

"It will test your skill," Brown stated. "Should no team cross the finish line within the allotted course time, the prize money reverts to the rally fund. Only a trophy will be awarded." He stepped back, away from the car. "Good luck, Nyland. Watch your rearview mirror."

"Will do," Cade said before tearing open the manila envelope. He quickly scanned the thick set of directions before handing them to TZ. "The course starts fast. First checkpoint is Oakes Farm, south of town." He pointed to a yellow legal pad. "You'll need to start a log. Mileage must be monitored between each speed change segment and between checkpoints."

TZ's eyes crossed. Dear God, what had she gotten herself into? She had read no more than the first line when Walter Brown handed Cade a time card, then fired a cap gun. "Gun and go!"

Cade appeared as primed as the engine. In one smooth move, he punched the clock, stuck the card beneath the visor and peeled across the parking lot.

TZ clutched the dashboard. "Where's the fire?"

"I barely touched the accelerator," Cade said defensively. "Pony left the gate at an all-out gallop."

Unusual for the Mustang. It often took five minutes to hit ten miles per hour.

"Straight, left or right?" Cade demanded at the mall exit.

Oakes Farm. She had shopped there on numerous occasions. Located on the outskirts of town, the enormous old barn stocked fresh dairy products, organic fruits and vegetables, and a deli that served the leanest cold cuts. Exotic flowers and plants cast color about the weathered clapboard interior, and a small gift shop near the exit housed local arts and crafts.

In the back of her mind she recalled a back route that started residential, then turned industrial. The Mustang's suspension could handle a few speed bumps. Maybe a few ruts. If they got stuck, she could always push.

Her problem lay in remembering the directions. "Take a . . . left."

"You sure?" He drummed his fingers on the steering wheel. "Every other car turned right."

She hadn't noticed. "Are we allowed shortcuts?"

"Two alternate routes per rally. Best time wins."

"Then go left."

He eased the wheel in the direction she'd instructed with the hesitancy of a driving school trainee. He accelerated slowly, his body rigid.

"Speed? Distance?" Cade requested.

A rectangular traffic sign beneath a streetlight displayed the appropriate speed. "Forty," she quoted. "Remain on Peach Tree Lane until we cross Plum Avenue."

"Fruit streets," he mumbled. "Must be running residential."

TZ scrunched up her nose. "For about ten or twelve blocks."

"Marker?"

"Plain old street sign."

Crow's feet etched the corner of his eyes. His jaw clutched as his hand seized the gearshift. "Let me know when we're close."

"Sure, no problem." She glanced out the window. A sign for Wig World Warehouse claimed its address on Plum Avenue, less than one block ahead. "Right. Go right at the light."

Cade downshifted, swore.

TZ clutched the strap of her seat belt.

The Mustang cornered on a squeal and a screech, and what sounded like a high-pitched giggle. TZ thumped her head with her palm to clear her ears.

"Stop winging it," Cade ground out. He reached across her, flicked open the glove compartment and whipped out a map. He shook it under her nose. He then handed her the compass. "Read the directions, align the checkpoints with the map and give me the proper coordinates. Use the compass; it's helpful. Magellan used one to navigate the world."

She should have paid more attention in history class.

"From this point on, I want our route in rally code."

"Rally code, huh? I'm not sure—"

"Get sure. I need color. Yellow, thirty. Blue one-point-one."

"This means?"

He cut her a sharp look. "Drive at thirty miles per hour;

69

a course change occurs in one and a tenth miles."

Rally code was a language unto itself. "Do you prefer primary or pastels?"

"You're about as funny as a master cylinder leak. I need a navigator, not a comic."

She was a mechanic. "Give me a few minutes to get warmed up."

"I need you white hot, right now."

She took a deep breath and visualized their course. "Yellow, forty-five. Blue . . . East End Road."

His nostrils flared. "Exact distance?"

"Approximately three miles."

"Be specific. Odometer readings are within a tenth of a mile. Note them on the travel log."

"A log to be shared with the rally master?"

He shook his head. "For our use only."

Thank God. In that case . . . Collecting the colored pencils from the manila envelope, TZ started her log. A color-coded log with stripes and plaids and nothing but whole numbers.

Her mother would have loved her artwork.

Chapter Five

TZ Blake was doodling. Cade was certain of it. What she was drawing he couldn't quite tell. But it involved a lot of detail. More detail than was necessary for a travel log. Her doodles left him as uneasy as the dirt road ahead.

How could she call this a shortcut? The road they now traveled skirted the industrial district. On both sides of the road, cement buildings belched brown smoke. Even with the windows rolled up, the foul scent of a refinery forced him to breathe through his mouth. Road ruts the size of craters caused the Mustang's suspension to bounce wildly. The vibration of the vehicle at such a slow speed rattled his bones. He swore the Mustang had groaned on the last pothole.

"Hang on," Cade said between his teeth as the 'Stang bore down on the deepest rut yet. Without warning, the Mustang cut sharply to the left. He lost control of the wheel.

His instinct was to protect TZ from slamming her nose

on the dashboard. She dipped, and he tried to catch her. His aim was off by a good six inches. Instead of her shoulder, he cupped her left breast. A soft, firm breast that filled his palm. Her heartbeat quickened beneath his fingertips.

"Copping a feel, rally man?"

He swore, damned the rut and made a mad grab for the steering wheel. His apology was waylaid as the vehicle skidded sideways.

Thrown off balance, TZ twisted, grabbed air, then denim, high on his thigh. Her fingers scraped the metal on his zipper. Her palm pressed his sex. His hips strained upward against the seat belt like a rodeo bull trying to toss its rider.

"Get your hand off my groin!" He hit the brake and the car rocked like a hobby horse. "Grab me again, woman—"

"And you'll *what*? Squeeze my breast?"

"I didn't do it on purpose."

"Neither did I." She fell back on the seat. "I bit my tongue on that last bump."

Cade turned toward her. "Tasting blood?"

She glared back at him. "You'd like that, wouldn't you?"

"I'd call it just reward for this shortcut."

She stuck out her tongue at him.

"Real mature, TZ. How old are you, twelve?"

"I'll be thirty in three days."

Hard to believe. "Walter Brown will want to throw you a party. Cake and presents."

"No need," she replied. "Rallying with you is the ultimate gift."

"Cut the sarcasm, sweet cheeks." He ran his hand through his hair, then asked. "When was the last time you drove this route?"

He caught her swallow. "Six months ago."

"You haven't been back since?"

"Didn't want to get stuck . . . again."

Cade ground his teeth. "If I have to push—"

"You won't," she assured him. Then, pointing ahead, she directed, "See that blinking yellow light?"

He followed her finger, squinted. "That tiny blinking light on the horizon?"

"It's not that far away, actually. Oakes Farm is about five miles ahead."

"*About five?* Looks more like ten." Shifting into first, he eased the Mustang along the sandy shoulder of the road. He prayed the sand remained compact. Sugar sand could suck a tire to China.

Two miles farther and the dirt road connected to freshly paved asphalt. The battered orange construction signs faded in the rearview mirror. Green fields soon replaced the factory smog. Off to the east, a weathered red barn was cast in a sun-yellow haze.

"Oakes Farm?" he asked.

A huge billboard came into view, advertising the farm. "Straight ahead," TZ said.

He rolled the stiffness from his shoulders. "Must we depend on signs for locations?"

"That's why they're posted."

It was going to be a hell of a long race.

With no other vehicles in sight, Cade gave the Mustang gas. He shifted through second and into third, listening to the Pony gallop. The speed limit was fifty, and he pressed fifty-five.

He glanced over at TZ. She sat stiffly, her ankles

73

crossed, her legs pressed tightly together. Her kneecaps were white. "Problem with my driving?"

Color rose on her cheeks. "Problem with the pony's pulse."

He understood. "The vibration's pretty intense." Arousingly intense. His sex swelled with each mile. He was uncomfortable as hell. He forced his thoughts back on the race. "Our time, TZ?"

She glanced at her watch. "We're closing in on eleven-thirty."

"Be specific."

"Eleven-twenty-seven and eight, nine, ten seconds."

He nodded toward the thick manila packet of rally instructions. "How much time did the rally master allow from Waterside Mall to Oakes Farm?"

From the corner of his eye, he watched her flip through the packet. He clenched his jaw. "Should be right on top."

She found the information on the cover page. "Ninety minutes."

"We have two minutes to reach our destination."

"We'll never make it"

He shifted into fourth. "Oh yes, we will."

On the back road with no other traffic, the speedometer hit sixty. TZ cleared her throat and suggested, "You might slow down just a little."

He glanced at the dashboard. "Speed limit's fifty."

"You're ten miles over the limit, and the speedometer isn't quite accurate."

"Isn't accurate?" he groaned. "How fast am I going?"

"Seventy." If not eighty. "I'd watch my rearview mirror, if I were you. Sirens, flashing lights. Burly county deputies."

He immediately hit the brake, then downshifted. "Damn, I don't need a ticket."

TZ had a stack of law enforcement warnings. Some were her fault; others, she blamed on the Mustang. The gas pedal stuck at the most inopportune times, usually with a police car in sight. The engine would rev as if wanting to race, and the horn always honked, taunting the cop to write the ticket. More than one officer had suggested TZ take the Mustang off the road. Most recently, she'd taken back streets to her destinations.

She sighed. Their rally destination was just ahead. To her surprise, they arrived at Oakes Farm within the allotted time. Cade punched the time card at the designated checkpoint, then parked the Mustang between a turquoise '55 Thunderbird and a silver '52 Daimler Dart.

He set the emergency brake, then stretched. "Break time."

TZ released her seat belt and kicked out her legs. The juncture of her thighs still tingled from the hum and shimmy of the engine.

"You coming?" Cade asked.

Coming? She blushed.

He nodded toward the weathered barn. "I'll buy you lunch."

TZ sighed, relieved. He hadn't realized every cell in her body was charged for sex. She slipped from the Mustang. "Lunch sounds good."

She felt his gaze on her. "You look unsteady."

Her legs were wobbly. "I'm fine, really."

He didn't take her at her word. "Let me help you."

Two long strides and he was at her side. Taking her by the elbow, his large hand curved completely around her arm as he led her toward the barn. His palm was rough, slightly callused, as it rubbed the soft skin of her inner arm. Her nerve endings danced to his tune. She allowed his touch until they reached the deli counter. Once there, she pulled free.

"I'm steady," she informed him as she scanned the enormous blackboard menu that hung over the deli case. "How long do we have to eat?"

Cade's jaw worked. "You didn't check the instructions?"

When had she had time? "I can go back to the car and—"

"We have one hour." The information came from behind them, from a man so thin he looked like the walking dead.

Recognition came slowly. TZ blinked in surprise. "Sam Mason? I haven't seen you in forever."

Once an acquaintance of her aunt Elise, Sam shook hands first with TZ, then with Cade. "I was recruited for the rally," he told them with a smile.

"So was I." TZ returned his smile. "Who's your driver?"

"Rhett Evans." He jammed his hands in the pockets of navy pants worn two sizes too large. "He's paying me to stay sober."

TZ knew of Sam's drinking habit. It was a problem she'd witnessed firsthand at her aunt's garage. Hand in hand, Sam and Jack Daniels had taken a nosedive into the oil pit.

"Sober, you're a fine mechanic," she reminded him.

Sam shrugged, the bones in his shoulders sharp against the thin cotton of his navy, green and white plaid shirt. "I'm giving sobriety a four-day run."

"Care to join us for lunch?" TZ asked.

Sam looked around the room, found Rhett Evans flagging him down. "Looks like Rhett's ordered for me. Guess I'd better join my team."

TZ glanced in Rhett's direction. Kimmie Thorn sat to his left, dressed in a tailored white blouse and pleated skirt.

"Three in the Jag?" she asked Sam Mason.

"Tight squeeze, but not uncomfortable," Sam replied. "Kimmie's cute, but quiet. She hasn't uttered a word since we left the mall."

Chatty Kimmie silent? Her friend couldn't even stay quiet through a church service or during a movie. Kimmie looked up and caught TZ's stare. She smiled her most innocent smile.

TZ lifted a brow. Kimmie was out to win her man.

Sam nodded to Cade, then patted TZ's arm. "See you later, girl."

She caught his hand and held it between her own. "Let me know if you need anything, Sam. Anything at all."

Sam nodded. "I can see Elise in you."

"Good luck." TZ's heart warmed as she watched him leave.

"Ready to order?" Cade prodded her back to the menu. "Time's a tickin'."

For a woman who never watched the clock, this monitoring to the second was already driving her crazy. "Eat and run?"

"So to speak," he replied. "You can socialize tonight at the Hawaiian luau."

TZ scanned the menu, then gave her order to the teenage girl with spiked orange hair who stood behind the glass counter tapping her pencil against a notepad. The girl's eyes were brown, made darker by black mascara and an outline of kohl. Several piercings marred her olive skin: a tiny silver arrow speared her left eyebrow, as did a safety pin the corner of her mouth.

She wore a gray T-shirt inscribed with SIXTEEN GOING ON THIRTY. Her jeans had more holes than a slice of Alpine Lace Swiss.

"Bean sprout salad and a chocolate-chip brownie," TZ decided. "And a raspberry lemonade, please."

The girl nodded, then turned to Cade. Despite her youth, she looked him over as any adult woman would a grown man—with a whole lot of interest. "How about you, Ace?"

TZ caught his slow grin. "Roast beef on rye."

"Rare?" The girl lifted her brow, the arrow shooting toward her hairline.

"As thick and pink as you can slice it."

He'd charmed the girl to dimples, TZ noted. She was pretty when she smiled. "Your drink?"

"Large Coke," he replied.

"Gotcha." She tore their order from her notepad. "Move down to the pick-up window. Your food will be ready shortly."

"Roast beef?" TZ almost gagged as they moved along the glass counter. "You eat *meat?*"

Cade stepped up behind her. "Don't you?"

She turned to face him. "I'm a vegetarian."

"Nuts and berries. Food that belongs in a hamster cage."

"You are what you eat." She looked him up and down. "You're built like a side of beef."

"You've the attention span of a ferret."

"I can concentrate."

"On anything but the rally." He cocked his head, curious. "What turned you off meat?"

She knew the exact moment. "When my second-grade class took a field trip to a local farm, and I realized steak had a heart." Her lips twitched. "After the trip, I made posters and picketed the dinner table. My parents disowned me when we had company. I can still see my mother's face, red as a tomato, the day I uprooted her prize roses and planted a vegetable garden."

"What's your favorite veggie?" Cade asked.

"Eight-inch cucumber."

He rolled his eyes. "Bananas your favorite fruit?"

"Hard, not yet ripe."

"No surprises there."

Their food, when it arrived, was exactly as TZ had ordered. Cade, however, received a mountain of food on the house. Beside his inch-thick roast beef sandwich, so pink it still mooed, his plate was piled with sides of cole slaw, macaroni and potato salad and a bag of Fritos. An extra-large Coke filled his tray.

"Enjoy!" The girl waved to him.

TZ caught him winking at the girl. A slow, sexy wink with just the hint of a smile. A wink that caused the tough-looking teen to blush.

Still watching him over her shoulder, TZ bumped into the corner of a weathered picnic table. Her lemonade sloshed onto her sprout salad. She grimaced. Another bruise and soggy sprouts, all because she couldn't take her eyes off Cade.

The man's X-rated wink should be outlawed.

"Sixteen Going on Thirty gave you enough food to feed three people," she said once they were seated.

"Take all you want." He offered his plate.

"Thanks, Ace." She helped herself to everything but his sandwich. She then unwrapped the brownie and took a big bite.

Cade's eyes widened. "You eat your dessert first?"

"Always have. I never save the best for last."

After she'd polished off the brownie, she dug into her salad. "Didn't take you for a big eater," he commented while sipping his Coke. "Beneath your baggy clothes—"

"My clothes aren't baggy."

He leaned across the table, lowered his voice. "I've seen how tightly your skin fits your bones. Nice fit, by the way."

"Fast metabolism," she informed him. "I can eat whatever I want and burn it off in a heartbeat."

He leaned back and continued to watch her eat. An easy stare that made her heart quicken. She shifted on the bench; scuffed the heels of her tennis shoes on the wooden floor. She was already burning up more calories than she was taking in. She reached across the table and scored a second helping of Cade's potato salad.

"Did you happen to notice our next checkpoint?" he asked.

She didn't meet his gaze. "A place down the road apiece."

"How far *apiece?*" he pressed.

She thought hard. "I think it was a brainteaser."

"Think or know, TZ?"

She looked up slowly, her gaze settling on his mouth. The firm masculine line no longer smiled. Hard and unrelenting, he remained silent, awaiting her response.

She awaited the softening of his lips, which remained as taut as the lengthening silence. No matter how hard she tried, she couldn't look away. With a mouth that divine, he had to be a good kisser. He'd create want and need. Command submission. Deliver pleasure. Bring his woman to climax on a breathless moan.

She shook her head. The Mustang's vibration had made her horny. There was no other reason for her musings. Her heart slammed, then beat with a mating rhythm. She was definitely burning up calories.

"TZ, are you listening?"

She hadn't been. "To every word."

He shoved his tray aside and rested his elbows on the table. She caught the flex of his tattoo. The man meant business. "You need to take the rally more seriously."

"I thought I was."

"Not by my definition of the word."

She jabbed her fork in the macaroni salad. Several noodles spilled off the plate. "Spell it out, Webster."

"Stop guessing mileage and landmarks. Be alert and anticipate each color-coded checkpoint."

She chewed, swallowed, dabbed her mouth with a paper napkin. "I got us to Oakes Farm without mishap, didn't I?"

He blew out a breath. "Your shortcut didn't follow the main route. We didn't make record time. Other teams beat us here."

"We're no longer one hundredth."

"We need to be first."

She needed to confess her inability to read a road map. Yet the look in his eyes didn't welcome confessions. He wanted results, not excuses. She wiggled her thumb. Hitchhiking was still an option.

"Time to hit the road." The rally master moved through the crowd, heading for the rear exit.

TZ finished her sprout salad in two big bites. She looked longingly at the Fritos she had yet to sample.

"No doggie bags," Cade said as he stood, snagged both trays and headed for the trash containers. "You can't eat, give directions and keep a log all at the same time."

Multitasking? She could try, couldn't she? Unfortunately her chance at snacking had just been dumped in the garbage.

Once outside, the rallyers gathered around the rally master, awaiting his go-ahead to punch the time clock and continue with the next leg of the race.

A loud chug and sputter drew the crowd's attention from Walter Brown to the red '58 Bug-eyed Sprite coming up the lane. In TZ's opinion, no other car had a cuter face. Its ear-to-ear grinning grille, bulging headlights and round rump gave it an engaging character. The two-seater appeared more clown car than racer and was occupied by a wide-shouldered driver and a passenger whose face was barely visible over the dashboard.

"Mick Wilcox and Skinner," Brown muttered. "Better late than never."

Mick parked the Sprite within an inch of Brown's knee-caps. Stickers reading HORN BROKEN, WATCH FOR FINGER and SHOW ME YOUR HEADLIGHTS plastered the rusted bumper. Two of the four hubcaps were missing.

"Glad to see you could join us," the rally master said to the two men sitting in the car with the windows down.

Mick thumped his navigator on the side of the head with his open palm. "Skinner got us lost."

Brown looked skeptical. "So soon in the race?"

"It's not worth rehashing," Mick said, grunting. "We're here now and plan to eat."

"The other teams are ready to head out," Brown told him.

Mick shrugged. "We'll catch up. I'm not leaving without lunch." The Sprite rocked as he exited the vehicle. He hiked up his pants and sauntered toward TZ. "How's it going?"

She hadn't expected his attention. "Trying to keep up with the competition."

He glanced back at his partner. "At least you're not in last place."

"We started last," she reassured him. "I'm sure you'll make up time."

"We'd be sitting first if Skinner had gotten the Cobra he promised. Shady dealings. The man can't keep his word." He looked down at her, his big body blocking the sun. "Floored, the Sprite only hits forty."

"Have your mechanic check the fuel filter."

"Thanks. I'll mention it to Skinner."

"TZ, we need to go." Cade nudged her shoulder.

Several yards from the 'Stang, the owner of the pink Cadillac entered Cade's private space. Her platinum hair was geometrically cut, sharp against her features. Dressed in a short black dress with a kicky hem and rhinestone sandals, the woman looked more cocktail party than rally driver.

"Hello, Cade." She brushed up against him.

"Good to see you, Risa." He nodded to TZ. "My mechanic, TZ Blake."

"Marisa Ashton-Lord." The woman gave her full name

as if TZ should recognize it from the society section of the Sunday newspaper.

TZ scanned sports, read the comics and her horoscope. She didn't have time for black-tie dinner parties, fundraisers and charity auctions.

She stepped back, leaving Cade to Risa's touch. The blonde ran her finger down his cheek. Gold and silver rings decorated her finger from knuckle to nail. TZ wondered if she could bend her finger.

"Good God, Cade, what happened to your nose?" TZ heard Risa ask.

"Long story, and I'm short on time," he replied.

"Will I see you tonight?" Risa pressed.

"I'll be around the hotel."

"Care to have a drink in my room?"

The woman went after what she wanted, TZ noted. In this case, Cade. TZ turned to catch his answer.

The man winked. A lethal wink that, without promising, hinted at the *yes* side of maybe. "Let's see how the day shakes out."

Risa rose on tiptoe and kissed him full on the mouth. "More where that came from," she said before returning to her Caddie.

"Old friend?" TZ asked once they were out of earshot.

"I've known Risa for ten years," he replied.

"Single?"

"Divorced, three times."

Quite a track record. TZ refrained from reciting *until death do us part.*

"Risa married for money," Cade said casually. "She likes older men, established in their professions. Her first husband was a building contractor; her second, an investment broker; her third, a real estate magnate."

Risa went for richer over poorer. She upgraded faster than Microsoft. She'd also looked at Cade as if he were a prime piece of real estate. TZ couldn't see the connection.

She pursed her lips. "You're her . . . boy toy?"

His nostrils flared and his tattoo flexed. "No key in my back. I don't wind up for any woman."

"Risa wants you."

"She's wanted me for a long time."

Reaching the Mustang, he helped her into the car. He cut off her stretch to open his door with, "I'll get my own door, thank you."

TZ dropped back on the seat and watched him circle the hood. Tall and well-filled out, he looked pure male animal, a little intimidating and far too self-assured for her liking. She knew men well. Cocky and carnal were female magnets.

He stopped to straighten his side-view mirror. "I'd like a look at our travel log."

TZ froze. Not a good request. The log was not to rally specifications. Cade wouldn't appreciate her doodling. Not one darn bit.

To save her hide, she separated the one-page log from the rally packet and shoved it under her seat just as Cade climbed into the car. He keyed the engine, and the Pony bucked. The vibration set her teeth on edge.

He glanced at his watch, then at her. "Walter Brown will soon be giving us the white flag to punch the time clock and go. You've just enough time to review the next leg of the race while I study the travel log."

TZ flipped through the remaining pages in the packet.

"I don't see it. It's not with the directions."

It took three, four, five seconds for her words to sink in. He curled his hands over the steering wheel and squeezed. His knuckles turned white. "The log doesn't have feet. It couldn't just walk away."

She spread her hands wide. "Walked or ran, trust me, it's gone."

Cade didn't believe her for a second. "Where's the log, TZ?"

She waved the packet under his nose. "Take a look for yourself. It's nowhere to be found."

He took the pages and fanned them with his thumb, once, twice. No sign of the log.

Beside him, TZ sighed heavily. "I worked so hard on that log. I pray the stats aren't lost."

He prayed so too. The scuff of her foot on the floor mat caught his eye. Was she stretching or had she just kicked something under the seat? He planned to find out.

He tossed her the packet, aiming for her knees. Just as he'd planned, several of the pages slipped free and landed at her feet.

"Sorry . . ." Which he wasn't in the least.

He made a dive for the pages, as did TZ. They bumped shoulders, then heads. He grabbed her ankle, and she clutched his wrist.

"What are you doing?" Her voice rose, cracked.

He shook off her hand and leaned even lower. "Helping to collect the pages. Some, I see, slipped all the way under the seat."

"Damn." He heard her expletive, then caught her pained expression when he straightened with the log. Her heel print marred its edge.

She made a grab for the paper, crumpled one corner, before he jerked it beyond her reach. "I want to see your perfect stats."

She scrunched up her nose. "Maybe not all that perfect."

They certainly weren't. They were the far side of adequate. Totally unreadable. Downright unacceptable.

His anger pricked with a violence he hadn't known since the bar brawls of his youth as pink bunnies, yellow stars and two stick figures riding in a Matchbox car jumped off the page at him. One of the figures had a big head. He recognized the detailed caricature as himself. Stripes and plaids decorated the borders. He ran his finger down the mileage stats. The column of even numbers didn't coincide with the odometer reading. Tenth-of-a-mile tallies weren't even noted.

TZ Blake was about to lose her colored pencils, if not her life.

"I can explain," she said as she shuffled papers on her lap.

He crushed the travel log into a ball. "There's no justifiable reason for such foolishness."

"I'm not good with statistics," she said. "I—"

"Doodled," he growled low in his throat. "And *colored!*"

"Colored rather prettily, I might add." She cocked her head. "Did you recognize the caricature?"

"The man with the big head?"

"Inflated ego. Thought you might recognize him." Her color was as high as his anger.

He couldn't figure for the life of him why she was so mad.

"Perhaps I should have limited my drawing," was weak for an apology.

"Perhaps you're too damn impulsive," he countered.

"I fly by the seat of my pants."

"When you're wearing pants, sweet cheeks."

"Back to the tight butt contest?"

A contest he'd never forget. Tanned skin, slim waist, sleek curves. The memory brought Cade's anger to heel just as Walter Brown rested his elbow on the edge of the driver's open window.

"Cade, TZ. You're presently in eighty-seventh place," the rally master informed them as he took down the odometer reading.

Eighty-seventh place! Cade ground his teeth. They might as well be last. He'd hoped to be in the top fifty after the first leg.

Brown pushed away from the car and pointed toward the time clock situated near a row of mailboxes just beyond the parking lot. "Punch and go."

Disgusted by their rally standing, Cade tossed the balled travel log into the backseat. He hooked his seat belt and waited until TZ fastened hers. He then slammed the Mustang in reverse. Gravel shot from beneath the tires, spraying like shrapnel.

"Temper, temper." TZ gripped the dashboard. "Don't take your anger at me out on my car. Find your happy place."

The image of TZ in her hot-pink boxers flashed through his mind once again. Cade blew out a breath. He refused to allow her to invade his happy place, which, until he'd met her, had been the winner's circle of the SunCoast Run.

"Directions," he demanded. "Which way do we go?"

She studied the brainteaser. "Go east on State Road Eighty until we reach Sucker Punch."

"Sucker Punch?" Cade frowned.

"That's the brainteaser. Whoever reaches the location first deducts thirty minutes from their time."

Cade could use the deduction. "Mileage?" he asked as they pulled up to the four-corner stop.

"No markers or miles," she answered. "Additional directions will be handed out at Sucker Punch."

"Great, just great." He turned right at the stop sign, heading east, back toward the Gulf Coast beaches. He shifted into second. "Any ideas on the brainteaser?"

"You're asking *me?*"

He cut her a look. "We're a team, TZ."

"I'm feeling a real connection with you, rally man."

"Sarcasm won't locate Sucker Punch. Get serious."

Sun streamed through the windshield and windows. Cade lowered his visor, while TZ reached into her straw bag and snagged a pair of sunglasses. Mickey Mouse sunglasses, with black rims and rodent ears. His face tightened. Her idea of serious differed greatly from his.

"Sun too bright?" she asked, mistaking his tight expression for sun in his eyes. "I have other shades," she offered.

"Besides the Mouse?"

"I've Winnie the Pooh and Tigger too."

He had no desire to look like a bear hunting a pot of honey. "Anything more adult? Nike, Oakley, Killer Loop?"

She dug deeply into her bag. "Mirrored Ray-Bans?"

"Thanks." He took them from her, slipped them on.

They drove several blocks in silence with TZ wracking her brain, and Cade studying every sign and storefront.

89

"Perhaps Sucker Punch is a gym," she finally suggested.

He slipped a pack of Doublemint from the pocket of his jeans, offered her a stick. She took two to his one. "Too obvious. Walter Brown is evasive." He unwrapped his stick and popped it in his mouth.

Three miles down the road, TZ pointed to Extreme Sports. Marisa Ashton-Lord's pink Cadillac and Rhett Evans's Jaguar were parked against the curb, just off the main road. "Care to stop?" she asked. "We might not be first, but if it's the brainteaser, you'll need to get your ticket punched for this leg of the rally."

Cade rolled his shoulders, then shook his head. "Doesn't feel right." His gut said to keep driving.

Thump, thump, thump. The sound broke his concentration as the Mustang tilted right. His stomach sank. He cursed the rally gods. Lord, it couldn't be . . .

"Flat tire, front passenger side." TZ confirmed his worst fear. "Pull over."

Cade steered the 'Stang into the empty Dairy Queen parking lot.

"Cut the engine and set the emergency brake," TZ said as she tossed her sunglasses onto the dashboard and shot from the car.

He did as she asked, his mirrored Ray-Bans joining Mickey Mouse as he climbed from the car and moved to the trunk where TZ had already removed the jack, lug wrench and one of the two spare tires. "Let me help."

She shook her head, her ponytail bouncing. "Not on your life, rally man. This is where I earn my money."

He made a grab for the tire, but she hip-checked him, pushing the tire beyond his reach. Dropping to her knees, she set to work. The lug nuts flew off with the twist of her wrench. The woman belonged on a pit crew for a national racing team.

Her struggle with the final lug nut soon became a struggle of wills as he bent to help her. "Let me—"

She glared at him. "I don't need—"

He leaned over her shoulder, and placed his hands on either side of hers on the wrench. "Yes, you do."

The lug nut didn't stand a chance against their combined strength. It spun right off.

"Thanks," she mumbled as he removed the flat tire and she secured the spare.

Cade ran his hand over the ruined tread. With his second pass, his palm brushed the head of a nail, a rusty three-inch nail that punctured the inner tire. Once he'd pulled it out, he held it up for TZ's inspection.

"Caused its share of damage." She wiped her brow with the back of her hand as she returned the lug wrench and jack to the trunk. "Let's take the tire with us. I'll patch it tonight."

He placed the flat beside the remaining good tire. He glanced at his watch. Ten minutes had passed in his race against time. They needed to hit the road.

TZ, however, wasn't ready to move on. She pointed to the Dairy Queen. "I'm hot and thirsty and want a chocolate shake."

He couldn't deny her. She had changed the tire in record time. "I'll get it while you clean up. There's hand sanitizer in my athletic bag."

Cade was at the ordering window when he heard TZ's shriek. He spun around, anticipating another disaster. What next?

He caught her hopping up and down like a madwoman

before she took off running toward him. She wore a smile and a smear of grease on her left cheek. She didn't slow as she got closer. His heart kicked. She was about to jump his bones.

He braced himself as she leaped high, locking her arms and legs around him in a body-clutching hug. He cupped her sweet butt, savored the press of her full breasts against the flat of his chest, liked the feel of her against him.

"All this for a chocolate shake?" he breathed against her hair.

She threw back her head and laughed. He liked the sound, as husky as it was happy.

"*Look!*" She pointed to his left.

He turned with her still wrapped around him. "Where?"

"See the tiny store wedged beside the Dairy Queen?"

Her ponytail swung, blocking his view. He couldn't concentrate on the sign with her wiggling against him.

TZ read it for him. "Lolli's Pops! Home of the Sucker with Punch. We hit the checkpoint, Cade. Sucker Punch is a candy store."

Chapter Six

Tex-Mex jalapeno, crab apple, choke cherry. A major nasal wallop. Cade screwed up his nose at the combination of tart and tangy scents. The candy store was definitely unique. Displayed on counters, hung on walls and stuck in deep bins, thumb-size to four-foot lollipops invited hour-long licks. He watched from the doorway as TZ made the rounds of every flavor. Apparently the chocolate shake hadn't filled her up. She was going for more sweets. He prayed their next stop wouldn't be a dentist's office.

"Over here, Nyland."

Hearing his name, Cade glanced toward the far corner of the room. Seated in the shadows was rally master Walter Brown, sucking on a large spiral lollipop.

"Pickle and vinegar." Brown waved the treat at Cade.

Not his first choice of flavors, Cade decided as he crossed the room. "Good to see you, Walter."

"I'm surprised to see you," Brown returned as he glanced at his stopwatch and jotted down the time. "I thought my brainteaser would keep everyone on the road for hours."

Cade dropped onto an empty chair at Brown's table, then nodded toward TZ Blake. "Call us good at mind games," which wasn't the least bit true. The candy store had been found by accident, not through skill and strategy. Cade didn't give a damn how Sucker Punch had been discovered, only that it had. Thanks to his mechanic, he would be able to scratch thirty minutes off his race time.

Cade caught the rally master eyeing his lucky charm. "You and TZ prove an interesting team."

Not so much interesting as arousing, Cade silently corrected. TZ's excitement over locating the checkpoint had left a permanent imprint on both his mind and body. He could still see her flushed face; the flash of success in her light blue eyes. The feel of her legs wrapped around his waist and the squeeze of her thighs about his hips, had turned him on. Big time. When he'd cupped her derriere, he'd grown hard. Her slow slide down his body had nearly set off his sex sequence. While TZ had danced around him, then dashed ahead, it had been a long, painful walk across the parking lot for Cade.

"Look who just arrived." Brown nodded toward the door.

Cade turned to find Rhett Evans, Kimmie Thorn and Sam Mason entering Lolli's Pops. The mechanic looked worn to a frazzle.

Rhett strode toward Cade. "We had two blown tires outside of Extreme Sports."

"One blown tire outside of Dairy Queen," Cade returned.

"Nail?" Rhett asked.

"A beauty of a three-incher."

"Carpenter nails. Someone lost a box, and we paid for

it ten times over." Rhett scanned the store. "Did TZ change your tire?"

Cade nodded. "That's what I'm paying her to do."

Rhett grinned, a secret grin meant to annoy. "Did you pay full price for her services? Mechanic and navigator?"

"I never put a price on winning."

"Rich kids never do." Rhett's voice held that old familiar envy Cade had come to recognize over their years of competitive rallying. "By the end of the rally, you'll wish you'd bargained her down."

Bargained TZ down? She was worth every penny. Rhett liked mindgames, which Cade refused to play. Leaning back on two legs of his chair, Cade ignored Rhett, refusing to defend his silver spoon legacy. Though he'd never hidden his family's wealth, neither had he advertised it. Only Marisa, Rhett and Walter Brown knew his background. Cade hoped to keep it that way. He valued his privacy. He hated the fact that Rhett's jealousy rode his bumper in every race.

Rhett eyed Cade's nose. "Did TZ punch you?"

"Is she a known slugger?"

Rhett shrugged. "I thought you'd made a move on her and she'd taken you out."

"Wishful thinking on your part?"

"Always hopeful."

"Rhett!" Kimmie called to him from across the room. She held up a bag of Super Blow Pops. Rhett nearly tripped over his tongue to get to her.

Several rallyers had entered the shop and Brown went to speak with them, leaving Cade alone at the table. He eased the front legs of his chair back onto the floor.

"Check out these suckers," TZ said as she dropped

onto his lap and shoved two dozen lollipops in his face.

Did she think him a chair? There were three empty ones shoved up to the table. Cade inwardly groaned as her bottom pressed into his groin. As naturally as breathing, he clasped her hipbone.

"Hold still," he said as he snatched a paper napkin from its holder and wiped a smudge of grease from her cheek.

"All clear?" she asked.

He nodded, so close to her, he could see the golden flecks in her blue eyes, the freckled bridge of her nose, the thickness of her dark brown lashes. Pretty, very pretty.

He eased back, and she rocked deeper into his groin, raving over the lollipops, oblivious to his own rise of excitement.

"Unripe berry, sour cream and black olive," she ticked off several flavors from her selection.

Cade shifted on the chair, trying to work her off his groin and onto his knee. "Makes my mouth water."

"They're not that bad." She turned, driving her shoulder into his chest. "Care for one?"

"Thanks, but I'll pass."

"Your loss, rally man."

Definitely his loss of sanity, Cade realized as TZ settled her bottom squarely on his zipper. Metal teeth scraped his sex. He grimaced. He needed to start wearing underwear. Gripping her hips, he lifted her off his groin. "It's time to hit the road."

She glanced down at his groin, caught the hardness of his sex, then met his gaze with a knowing grin. "I'll go pay for the suckers."

Cade glanced at his watch. "Make it quick."

Kimmie arrived at the cash register just as TZ pocketed

her change. "I need something for my mouth," Kimmie said.

TZ turned toward her friend. "Why is that?"

Kimmie sighed. "I've made an agreement with Rhett. I get to rally, but I'm not allowed to talk during the race." She held up a bag of Super Blow Pops. "I do, however, plan to lick and suck, and blow his mind."

"You'll drive him into a ditch," TZ said. "How's Sam Mason holding up?"

Kimmie gnawed her bottom lip. "A little shaky. He had a hard time changing the two blown tires. He dropped the tools and barely had the strength to lift the spares. Every time I tried to comfort Sam—pat his shoulder, hold his hand—Rhett went ballistic."

"Rhett sounds territorial."

"How about you and Cade?" Kimmie asked.

"Cade is Cade. Intense, focused, aiming to win the race, while I'm sitting on the edge of my seat, all tingly and turned on."

"Be careful, TZ," Kimmie warned. "Cade's restless and you're impulsive. The backseat is close at hand."

"No sex in the 'Stang," TZ said.

Kimmie glanced at Cade, standing near the front door, talking to Marisa Ashton-Lord. "Slam-bam with that man would satisfy you into next year."

TZ had to agree. However, the rally meant more to Cade than any backseat boogie. She might tease him a little, but she wouldn't act on her attraction. The man was a handful. One flirty kiss would lead to sex. She needed the rally win as much as Cade. Cold hard cash would have to be her gratification.

Grabbing her bag of lollipops off the counter, TZ

headed toward the door. "See you tonight, Kimmie."

"Ready to ride?" Cade asked when she approached.

She glanced from Cade to Risa. "Whenever you are."

"Give us a minute," the blonde requested, licking her lips as if Cade were a six-foot sucker.

"Take all the time you need." TZ squeezed around Risa, nudging the woman closer to Cade.

"We'd need a whole night for what I have in mind." Risa's words trailed TZ out the door.

The parking lot was packed with antique cars, carefully spaced so no doors would be nicked, no bumpers dented. TZ wound her way toward the Mustang.

"There's no damn jack in the trunk!"

She eased around the spacious bowling-alley rear deck of a '68 Pontiac GTO and headed toward Mick Wilcox, standing beside his Bug-eyed Sprite. His face was as red as a stop sign. Sweat poured off his forehead, as much from the heat of the day as from his obvious frustration.

"What's the problem?" she asked.

Mick swiped the back of his hand across his brow. Sweat sprayed like a sprinkler. TZ edged back a step. "My mechanic forgot to check the trunk for tools before we started the rally. I've a freakin' flat tire and no jack."

The back passenger tire was so flat, Mick must have been driving on the rim. "You can use mine," TZ offered.

"You mean it?" Mick looked as if she'd handed him the rally trophy.

She glanced toward the door of the candy store where Risa and Cade remained engaged in conversation. Catching up on old times, no doubt. She had five, maybe six minutes. "Let's make it fast."

She jogged to the Mustang, popped the trunk and removed the jack. She returned in record time. "Need some help?"

Mick shook his head. "Skinner can manage from here."

Short, wiry Skinner slid off the hood of the Sprite, stubbed out a thin cigar and immediately got to work. He worked fast, but not fast enough. TZ handed her lollipops to Mick and became Skinner's right hand. She worked with speed and proficiency, counting down the minutes before Cade arrived. The flat came off, and the spare went on. Two lug nuts to tighten and they were home free.

"What's going on?"

Cade Nyland's voice brought her around. "Blown tire," TZ informed him.

"I can see that." He stood directly behind her, legs splayed, his hands on his hips. "And you're . . . what?"

She was eye level with his thigh. "Lending a hand. Mick didn't have a jack, so—"

His eyes narrowed. "You offered *ours?*"

"My jack, from *my* Mustang."

He tipped her chin up with one finger. "Helping hands aren't part of your job description. You need to be available to me, and I'm ready to hit the road."

TZ handed the lug wrench to Skinner, then got to her feet. She and Cade stood close. She met the fire in his gaze head-on. "You weren't ready ten minutes ago. I chose to be useful while you whiled away the time—"

"I don't while."

She poked him in the chest with a dirty finger. "You were whiling."

He snagged her wrist before she could jab him a second time. "While you aided the competition."

"Lighten up, Nyland." Mick Wilcox returned TZ's lollipops. "We didn't take advantage of her."

"We appreciated her help," Skinner added as he set the jack on the ground by her feet. "We owe you one, TZ."

She bent, grabbed the jack, then with her head held high, walked around Cade and back toward the Mustang. She'd stored the jack by the time he joined her.

"No more roadside assistance," he said quietly, but firmly. "Mick could have walked to the Mobil Station two blocks south."

"There was a jack in my trunk two cars north."

His jaw worked. "You don't need to help their team move up in the standings."

"Move up?" She wiped her hands on her shorts. "Mick and Skinner are in last place."

"Their status could change during any leg of the rally."

TZ glanced back at the Sprite, no more than a rusty bucket of bolts. "Definitely our greatest threat."

Cade's nostrils flared.

TZ narrowed her eyes.

"Cars to the time clock." Walter Brown's voice boomed through a megaphone. He waved to Cade. "You're in forty-second place. Watch for your spot to gun and go."

TZ tapped her foot. "They'll be waiting until sundown if you don't apologize."

"Apologize? For what?" he growled.

"For getting on my case."

He looked at her as if she'd lost her mind. "I'm paying you to be my mechanic, not to service other engines."

"It was only a tire."

"A tire this time, a fan belt the next."

"Perhaps I'll overhaul an engine tonight."

His utter stillness caused her to rethink her need for an apology.

"Don't try me, sweet cheeks."

"Try you?" She licked her lips as she looked him up and down. Then raising herself on tiptoe, she pressed close. Her handful of suckers slapped his cheek as she stroked his whiskered jaw. "Isn't that what Risa plans to do?"

Dropping back on her heels, TZ moved to the passenger door.

Cade entered the Mustang slowly.

Once they snapped their seat belts, he started the engine, then glanced her way. "I'll need coordinates for the next checkpoint the second we hit the main road."

TZ studied the directions to Stone Crab Harbor. They appeared to be written in Latin. She flipped open the map, angled it left, then right. She shook the compass and the arrow spun wildly. She wasn't Magellan.

She mentally pictured Georgia to the north; Key West to the south. According to the instructions, members of the rally committee were posted to punch their time cards at both a bridge and Interstate Ten.

What kind of bridge? TZ wondered as the Mustang merged with the southbound traffic. Highway overpass? Or beaver dam?

"Directions, TZ," Cade pressed.

TZ closed her eyes and prayed with the conviction of a nun.

North, south, east or west? Point a cosmic finger! When she finally opened her eyes, her gaze was drawn to the instrument panel. Goosebumps skimmed her spine. She shivered. The left turn signal was silently blinking.

Blind faith. "Left at the next street," she directed.

Cade accelerated, made the turn. "How far on this road?"

"Until we hit a bridge near the interstate."

His tattoo flexed. "That's it? No further details?"

Those were the details she could decipher. "Afraid so."

"Brown has really made this rally difficult," Cade ground out.

"Damn tough," she agreed, folding the map.

His hands tightened on the wheel. "Watch for the bridge."

Several miles passed in silence. The afternoon traffic had grown heavy with beachgoers, and cars were backed up, bumper-to-bumper. Rounding a long curve in the road, TZ caught sight of Marisa Ashton-Lord's pink Cadillac, Rhett Evans's Jaguar and several other classic cars, all motoring below the speed limit. Relief penetrated her bones. They weren't lost. They might not be in first place, but she and Cade were on the right road. That in itself was a blessing.

Twenty minutes later, an overpass came into view. Two lanes soon split into four, and traffic picked up speed. The rallyers raced toward the bridge.

The Mustang kept pace. TZ patted the dashboard, silently praising the car for running smoothly.

Her praise came too soon.

With a clear shot to pass a SUV, Cade maneuvered left. "Damn," he muttered as the steering wheel suddenly locked. His biceps bunched as he wrestled with the wheel. "Car's got a mind of its own."

The engine quieted, and the vehicle slowed, rolling to the right and coming to a stop on the dirt shoulder. A muscle in Cade's jaw ticked wildly as several classic cars whipped by.

He swore softly as Wilcox and Skinner chugged past in their Bug-eyed Sprite. "Back to last place." Climbing out of the car, he circled the hood, waiting for TZ to join him.

TZ eased out the passenger door. The 'Stang was sitting at a slant with a deep ditch to her right. Not one for heights, she cautiously looked down. Water poured from a drainage pipe, widening into a stream at the next cross street. Trees and heavy vegetation swept its banks. Ducks both swam and perched on enormous lengths of wood. Sunlight caught the flash of twisted metal beams partially submerged near the water's edge.

Wood? Metal? She shaded her eyes with her hand and gazed further downstream. Dilapidated, and barely visible against the afternoon sun, an old railroad bridge spanned the banks. She knew the moment she saw it, the bridge was their next checkpoint.

She pointed south. "Cade, look, our bridge."

He looked, yet his expression when he turned to her was dark and skeptical. He shook his head. "It's too far off the beaten path."

"You said Walter Brown was evasive," she reminded him.

"Evasive, not devious."

"It wouldn't hurt to take a look," she insisted. "There's a dirt road that runs along the bank, then skirts the bridge."

"Have you forgotten the car rolled to a stop? We're going nowhere fast."

She edged along the 'Stang until she reached the hood.

She popped it open. "Get back in the car while I check the engine. I'll signal when to start her up."

TZ checked every visible wire. All appeared secure. The battery had plenty of water, and the oil stick registered eight quarts. She glanced over at the bridge, and, on a hunch, called to Cade, "Give her gas."

The engine turned over with a rumble and a shimmy. They were back in business. Her hands shook as she slammed the hood. It seemed strange the car would die so near the railroad bridge.

Car's got a mind of its own, Cade had said. She bit down on her bottom lip. Too ludicrous to contemplate.

She motioned Cade to pull forward. He crept along the shoulder of the road until the passenger door was within her reach. He shoved it open, and she slid onto the seat.

Her thoughts remained on the dilapidated bridge. "Take the dirt road, rally man. You have nothing to lose."

"What about the overpass?" he asked.

"It's not our checkpoint," TZ persisted as Marisa's pink Cadillac and Rhett Evans's Jaguar passed them in the westbound lane, backtracking.

Cade blew out a breath. "What the hell?"

He drove with great care, slowing to a crawl as the road narrowed even farther, now no more than tracks in the tall grass. The grass brushed the belly of the 'Stang, her hubcaps and bumper. TZ swore she heard a faint giggle, as if someone had been tickled.

Their situation wasn't all that funny.

Rusted yellow signs near the base of the bridge warned caution, and to proceed at one's own risk. Cade came to a stop and looked up. "The bridge is hanging by two railroad ties. It's not safe, TZ."

She rose on her knees and leaned out of the car window. The air was damp, filled with the scent of rotting wood. "The road less traveled," she muttered, craning her neck.

A sudden flash of blue caught her gaze from behind a row of bushes. She pushed farther out the window. A man's shirt? A pair of pants? She stretched farther. Her hips rocked, and she was suddenly off-balance. Her feet came off the seat. The ground rose up to meet her . . .

Cade ducked, but not before TZ's tennis shoe grazed his chin. She'd nearly gotten his nose, once again. She dangled out the window; damn close to biting the dust. He'd hate to see her pretty face bruised. She wouldn't look good as a raccoon.

Diving across the seat, he made a grab for her shorts. He caught her by the waistband. His fingers curled between flesh and elastic. Her shorts were baggy, and rode low on her hips. He tugged, and the dip in her spine and high curve of her bottom were soon bared to him. He caught a wisp of satin as her shorts slipped even lower.

He sucked in his breath and jerked back, drawing her with him. He landed on his left hip with TZ sprawled facedown on his lap. Her shorts were at her knees, her bikini briefs exposing her sweet cheeks.

He groaned as she pushed herself up on her hands and arched her back. Her bottom brushed his cheek. The satin felt cool against the heat of his mouth. He expelled his breath over her left buttock.

"Like what you see, rally man?" Her tone was light, teasing.

Too damn much. His male animal wanted to howl and mate, while his inner gentleman ground his teeth to the gum. He took the upper hand and swatted her butt. "Bottoms up, TZ."

She wiggled her bottom, scooted off his lap, and he slid back behind the wheel. She pulled up her shorts. The elastic snapped at her waist.

He ran his hand through his hair. "You should try wearing shorts that zip and snap."

"If I did, you'd never see my panties."

Such a tease. "No more leaning out the car window."

"I was balanced."

"You were about to eat dirt."

"I was about to tell you there's someone in the bushes just ahead."

"You sure?" He didn't see a soul in the tall brush.

She nodded. "Get a little closer, and you'll see."

Cade eased the car forward, skirting the bridge as he neared the dense scrub. He hit the horn, announcing their arrival. To his amazement, Walter Brown, along with rally committee member, Paul Royer, emerged from the bushes.

TZ bounced on the seat. "I'd never say *I told you so.*"

"Such restraint," he returned as he pulled to a stop. He caught a glimpse of Brown's '65 Rolls-Royce hidden within a circle of cabbage palms.

Royer was first to speak. "We were about to pitch a tent and set up camp."

Brown joined Royer. "Cade, TZ, you're first to arrive."

Royer craned his neck in the direction from which they'd come. "First, and possibly last."

Cade withdrew the time card from beneath the visor and, reaching out the window, punched the time clock. "What if no one else passes this way?" he asked.

"Teams will be penalized," Brown replied. "How did you find us?"

"TZ navigates with her nose to the ground."

"You've been successful thus far," Brown stated. "The checkpoints will only become more difficult as the days progress."

The man *could* be devious, Cade decided as he shifted into first. "Later, gentlemen."

"The interstate is just ahead," Brown informed him. "Timekeepers are posted to take odometer readings."

"See you at the luau," Royer called as they pulled away. "The pig's been roasting in the pit since early morning."

Cade nodded and TZ choked. "It's not Porky the Pig," he said. "You won't starve. There will be sweet potatoes, poi and tropical fruit."

A hint of a smile edged her mouth. "Yum, bananas."

The thought of her eating a banana, along with the vibration of the 'Stang, had him shifting on the seat. He could barely work the clutch. The gears ground unmercifully as he slammed through first and into second.

TZ placed her hand over his. "Easy, rally man, you're stripping the gears."

Stripping . . . His mind shot beyond the gears to backseat heat. To naked bodies, pulsing readiness and slippery leather.

He shook his head and turned his mind to the rally. Where was his control? Over the years, ice had run in his veins, and his nerves were pure steel. Yet TZ Blake distracted and disturbed and drove him crazy. He needed to focus.

Just ahead, two timekeepers stood on the shoulder of the access road that fed into the interstate. Once the men noted their odometer reading, Cade accelerated and blended with the traffic. Stone Crab Harbor was sixty miles south.

Beside him, TZ shifted on the seat. "Mind if I listen to the radio?" she asked.

He most certainly did. "Most rallyers drive in silence."

"I'm not most rallyers."

She definitely wasn't. "Enjoy the scenery, TZ."

"One palm tree looks like the next."

"Count mileage markers then. This leg runs sixty miles."

She snagged the yellow legal pad and a black pen. "I'll get an odometer reading."

He shook his head. "No need, we're five-point-three miles into the leg. Do the subtraction."

"I was never good at math."

She leaned toward him then, and he leaned toward the window. He caught mischief in her gaze as she rested her chin on his shoulder. He shrugged, and her chin rose and fell with the motion. He rolled his shoulder, and her face drew even closer. Damn if she wasn't breathing against his neck. Deep, slow breaths that raised the hair on his neck, along with his sex.

Her scent drifted to him: vanilla spice and woman. She had him right where she wanted him, where she could tease and he couldn't touch. She was in control and loving it. He cleared his throat. "Get the reading and get back on your seat."

"Got it," she said, so close to the corner of his mouth her upper lip brushed his lower one.

"It helps to write it down."

She dropped back on her seat and swatted the yellow pad against her thigh. "Are we there yet?"

"Does it look like we've reached the hotel?"

She wiggled on the seat. "Bucket-seat butt."

An active woman confined to a car was not conducive to a smooth trip. "Find a way to entertain yourself."

She began to hum "Good Vibrations" by the Beach Boys.

Cade stuck his finger in his ear to block the sound. TZ was off-key. She was also slapping her thighs to the beat in her head. Her humming grew louder. Annoyingly loud.

That's when he started to whistle. Softly at first, just to drown out her humming. Soft didn't work with TZ Blake. He puckered his lips, blew louder, the sound as shrill as a referee's whistle. He checked the rearview mirror to see if dogs were chasing the car. His ears began to ring . . .

Hum. Whistle. *Honk!*

Joining in, the horn honked, once, twice, then with the blare of a security system warding off a burglar.

Cade's lips froze, and his whistle died.

TZ swallowed her hum.

The beeping, however, went on for the next mile. The passengers in every car they passed waved or blew kisses. While he thumped the horn with his palm, TZ knelt in the floor well and checked the wires beneath the dash.

He was going deaf, Cade decided as TZ dropped back on her seat, covered her ears and shouted, "No loose wires."

No reason for the honking? It didn't make sense. The noise shredded his last nerve. He'd sell his soul for a pair of earplugs.

The honking stopped as quickly as it had started. He and TZ released a collective sigh of relief. They looked at each other. Cade lifted a brow, and TZ nodded her agreement. The silence that followed lasted all the way to Stone Crab Harbor.

Chapter Seven

Stone Crab Inn was luxurious, Kimmie noted as she walked across the pink marble floor to the reception desk. She'd discreetly slipped Rhett Evans her credit card for check-in, which he'd reluctantly pocketed.

Behind the desk, floor-to-ceiling mirrors captured their double image. She inched toward him and primped just a little. They made a handsome couple: he in his black silk shirt and tailored slacks; she in all white. Virgin white. While Rhett filled out the registration forms, she unbuttoned the top two buttons of her blouse, then a third. A naughty virgin, she thought, smiling at herself in the mirror.

As if sensing her actions, Rhett turned and nearly fell into her cleavage. His gaze heated, along with his face. He was short on breath as he handed her one of the room keys. "Two adjoining suites."

"Adjoining?" she asked.

"I'm always hopeful."

"Cross your fingers into tomorrow if you like, but the door remains locked," she said with a finality that made him sigh.

She slipped her arm through his and snuggled against his side. Her breast brushed his arm, and her hip pressed his thigh. He was tall and solid, and a good man to lean on. A fine future husband.

Their reflection in the mirrors portrayed them as lovers or honeymooners, but they had yet to kiss. One look at his mouth, and she'd known Rhett would be a good kisser. Men who smiled as often as he did kissed the best. Smiling made his mouth mobile.

"Where's Sam?" Rhett asked.

"He decided to stay with the car and service the engine early," she replied.

"The Jag shouldn't need any repairs."

"He said he wanted to check the muffler. You drove over the curb twice today. Remember?"

Rhett dipped his head. "You distracted me."

She sure had. From the corner of his eye he'd watched her lick and smack her Blow Pops. In the five seconds his gaze had left the road, the Jag had rolled onto the median and crushed a row of petunias and poppies.

Minutes later, the popping of an enormous pink bubble had caused the vehicle to jump the curb, nearly talking out a row of parking meters.

Kimmie had screamed, Sam had shuddered, and Rhett had sworn. She'd meant to distract him, not damage his car. She hoped Sam Mason would give the Jag a clean bill of health.

She took Rhett's hand. "Let's check out our rooms."

They took the elevator to the third floor.

Her suite was plush. Decorated in navy and mauve with touches of turquoise, the room invited guests to stay longer than one night. She kicked off her white leather thongs and crossed the carpet to the sliding glass doors that opened onto the balcony.

Low tide lapped against the shore as the Gulf captured the sun's slow descent in a spray of gold against blue. Several couples walked hand-in-hand along the boardwalk, while others lounged in beach chairs by the pool. Near the sailboat rentals, colored lights and a neon sign invited travelers to have a Climax at Chico's Chickie Bar. A combination of alcohol and liqueur, Climax was a potent drink. One of those this-is-so-good-I-can't-believe-I'm-getting-this-drunk variety.

Kimmie sighed. Definitely a Kodak moment.

Rhett came up behind her. He ran his hands over her shoulders and down her arms, lacing his fingers with hers. He nuzzled her neck, then kissed her ear. "There's something special about this evening. I'm feeling the pull of a mystical force—"

"Sure it's not your hormones?" she asked.

"I believe in romance."

Leaning against him, she tilted her head until she could see his face, shadowed by the setting sun. "Your idea of romance is whatever will separate me from my panties."

He pulled back and released her hands. "I'm hot for you, Kimmie. I like the chase, the catch and the sex. I don't, however, favor commitment."

Classic case of love versus lust. She admired his honesty, however misguided. She planned to touch his heart before she ever touched his zipper. "I need it all, Rhett," she said softly. "The vows, the wedding bands, the partner for life."

"No compromise?"

She touched his arm lightly. "All or nothing. I'd never settle for second best."

She could hear his protest coming. "I'm a man with—"

"Needs. I understand completely." She took him by the arm and led him toward the door. "You *need* to get ready for the luau. You also need to locate Sam and check on the Jag."

His brow furrowed. "You've twisted my words."

"Better than tangling your sheets."

He looked reluctant to leave. "Sam and I need to divide closet space; toss a coin to see who gets which bed."

"Bet you take the one nearest the window," she said.

He looked surprised. "Why's that?"

"That's the bed I'd choose. I love to wake to sunlight streaming across the bed."

He swallowed. "So do I."

"That's mystical, Rhett. Morning, fresh and dewy, and golden." She reached around him and opened the door. "A member of the rally committee will be coming by my room shortly with a selection of sarongs for the luau. I need to shower before he arrives."

"Wear something yellow or gold," he requested.

She'd been thinking white, but a little color would set off her blond hair. "Pick me up at seven."

Rhett glanced at his watch. He had two hours before he returned for Kimmie. In that time, he needed to locate Sam Mason, select a Hawaiian print shirt and Climax twice at Chico's Chickie Bar.

He walked down the quiet hallway. Quiet, until the

elevator doors swished open and TZ Blake and Cade Nyland stepped out.

"*One room?*" Rhett heard TZ question.

"The hotel is full. Full, as in no room at the inn," Cade replied in an exasperated voice. "I hadn't realized my partner, Jay Wright, would cancel his reservations when he couldn't rally."

"Problems, children?" Rhett crossed his arms over his chest and looked from TZ to Cade. He liked TZ and would do anything to help her. Cade could drop dead, and Rhett would step over his body. Nyland was one arrogant bastard. He was admired by men and desired by women. He was financially stable in a world that shook like an earthquake beneath Rhett's feet. Justified or not, if he could take Cade down a peg, Rhett would hand TZ the hammer.

Cade's look told Rhett to mind his own damn business.

TZ, however, sought his assistance. "I need a place to stay."

"We have a room," Cade said flatly.

"With one king-size bed." Her ponytail swung, and her eyes flashed. "Unless you plan to sleep on the couch—"

"Like hell." Rhett caught the anger in Cade's gaze; heard the frustration in his voice. "I'm the driver. I need a good night's sleep."

"Then I'll take the couch, and nap in the car tomorrow."

Cade went utterly still. "Not an option."

TZ bounced on her toes. "You're not the boss—"

"I'm the driver, and I call the shots."

Rhett studied TZ and Cade. Rigid, unmovable and demanding, Cade held his ground, while TZ hopped from foot to foot, a bundle of nerves.

Was it anger or attraction that zinged between them? Rhett went with attraction. Sparks shot between them like hot little darts. He grew warm in their crossfire.

Rhett smiled to himself. He had a solution to their problem, one Cade would hate, which made his suggestion all the sweeter. "TZ is welcome to share Kimmie's room."

"I am?" TZ looked hopeful.

"You're not," Cade asserted.

"Kimmie would love to have a roommate for the night," Rhett assured her.

"I'm there." TZ jumped at the opportunity. "Which room is hers?"

"Suite three-ten," Rhett said.

"Hold on a minute," Cade cut in. He looked more upset than the situation warranted. No man got that ticked off unless he'd gone territorial, which amused Rhett to no end. "I want TZ close. During the rally, we do things as a team."

TZ dodged his nearness. "'Team' does not include bed buddies."

Cade ran his hand through his hair. "Sleep, that's all I'm after."

"Yeah, right." Rhett coughed into his hand.

Cade shrugged. "Believe what you will."

TZ bit down on her bottom lip, hesitating. "What about the luau?" she asked.

"You can come with Kimmie and me," Rhett was quick to suggest. "We'll meet Cade on the beach."

"That works," TZ agreed. She blew Cade a flirty kiss. "Later, rally man."

She'd gone from biting her nails to sweet tease in less than three minutes. Rhett watched her bounce down the hall. She was free-spirited and sexy, dancing just beyond Cade's reach. She was also one smart woman in his opinion. Teasing Cade on the road or in public was less dangerous than behind closed doors.

"Stay out of my business."

Cade's dark tone had Rhett looking for the nearest exit. "Noted," Rhett replied. "No hard feelings?"

Cade's answer was in a hard look as he turned and headed down the hall to his suite.

Rhett watched him leave. Misery loved company. If he couldn't get Kimmie in his bed, he'd keep TZ out of Cade's, too.

Mick Wilcox and Skinner entered Stone Crab Inn under the watchful gaze of the doorman. "The man looks like he's smelling onions," Mick grunted as he hiked up his jeans and proceeded to the reception desk. He sniffed the collar of his shirt. "My shirt's clean. Hell, it's only the second day of wear."

"You've worn the same clothes for two days?" The lady from the pink Cadillac looked down her nose at him.

Marisa Ashton-Lord. He recognized her from the rally. The bitch had cut him off on State Road Eighty, beating him to Lolli's Pops. Her entourage had laughed at him: three pretty boys with kiss-ass smiles.

She stood to his left, smelling like a newly minted bill. New money from marrying old men, Mick figured. She had a face shaped by plastic surgery and Botox and a body starved of food. There wasn't a hair out of place, nor a wrinkle in her little black dress.

He liked his women with meat on their bones and a smile on their faces. Moneybags was so boney, she'd jab a man to death during sex. She was the type who posed through life in designer outfits and full carat diamonds. Nothing mattered to her beyond whom she saw, and who saw her. Mick wasn't impressed.

"I wash once a week at Suds and Duds," he told Marisa. "It takes seven days to save up my quarters for the machine."

Her gaze widened and her mouth gaped. It was probably the most human she'd looked in years.

"Ms. Ashton-Lord," the man behind the desk said. She quickly composed herself. "The suite you requested is available. Shall I ring for a bellhop?"

"Please do." She leaned toward the man, lowering her voice. "Did you receive my list of requests?"

"All taken care of, ma'am. The champagne, caviar, candles and chocolate-covered strawberries will be delivered at eight P.M.," he assured her.

Mick edged a little closer. "Party in your room tonight?"

"Eavesdropping?" she asked coolly.

"Hard not to hear when we're standing so close."

She took two steps back, froze him with a look. "Private party."

Mick understood. "Hope the guy dresses warmly, otherwise you'll freeze his balls."

"You crude man!" she said.

"Excuse me, sir," the man behind the desk interrupted. "If you're looking for work, personnel is down the hall on the right. Both maintenance and food prep have positions available."

The woman looked Mick up and down. "Definitely not food prep. He'd eat the profits."

"I'm not here for a job," Mick gritted out. "I'm with the

rally and in need of a room. My money's as green as yours, lady."

"Get out the coin counter," Marisa told the man behind the desk. "No doubt he'll pay in change."

She turned on the heel of her rhinestone sandals and crossed the marble floor. Her skirt swished, brushing the back of her legs. Toothpick legs and no ass, Mick thought. Her spine was as stiff as her profile. The woman was a snob. Money couldn't buy a personality.

In her haste to escape him, she walked straight into a potted fern. Taking her temper out on the defenseless plant, she swatted the fronds leafless. If it were up to him, she'd take her broom and flying monkeys and return to Gulf Cove.

"The woman's got a major hate-on for you, man," Skinner said as he came to stand beside Mick.

Mick made a gagging sound. "She makes me want to puke."

Skinner scanned the reception area, the thickening crowd of guests lined up to register. "Just don't lose your lunch here. Not on my boots."

Mick glanced down. Skinner wore an old pair of combat boots newly polished. "My stomach's settled." He leaned against the reception desk. "Let's get a room. I want to clean up before the luau, maybe change my shirt."

Skinner scratched his chin. "I could use a shave."

Mick sniffed. "And a shower. I'm not the only one who smells like yesterday's laundry."

Marisa Ashton-Lord wanted to run, not walk, away from Mick Wilcox. Running would, however, create a scene, and she despised scenes. Scenes detracted from her image. Image meant everything to her.

She took the elevator to her suite. Once inside, she leaned against the door and caught her breath. Wilcox was the crudest, most disgusting man she'd ever met. A bear of a man, he smelled as if he'd just come out of hibernation. His hair was matted and greasy, and he had tufts growing out of his ears. A grizzly had fresher breath.

His sidekick, Skinner, was wiry with darting eyes that sought trouble. She was certain he had a criminal record.

She wished she'd never spoken to Mick. He would consider their exchange an invitation to approach her again. If they crossed paths, she'd be forced to ignore him. He was an embarrassment. She never made small talk with the common man.

She crossed to the dresser, looked in the mirror. Her reflection was frightful. She had bits of fern in her hair and all over her dress. Scheduling a hair appointment this late in the day would take a heavy bribe and even larger tip. But it would all be worth it when she saw Cade Nyland. She wanted to look her best for him.

She located the telephone on the dry bar, and after going through reception, was connected to his suite.

"Nyland," his voice was deep and strong and pure male animal.

"It's Risa," she said. "I'm planning a small get-together in my suite following the luau and wanted to extend you the first invitation."

She held her breath as she awaited his reply. "Sorry, Risa, I'd planned to turn in early."

She'd planned to turn him on with her new lingerie. A

lacy, French, blue gown that showed more skin than satin. "Come for one drink."

She twisted the phone chord as the silence stretched on. "Please, Cade." She hated to beg, but she would go down on her knees for this man's attention.

She heard him sigh; could picture him running his hand through his hair. "Just one, Risa. It's been a long day."

It would be a longer night. She'd wanted Cade since the day she'd laid eyes on him. He was wild and restless with a hard body and eyes the color of midnight sex. She grew wet just thinking about him.

She longed to experience the bad boy whose fortune matched her own. Sleeping with money was the most stimulating thing she knew.

A knock on her door ended her conversation with Cade. "I'll see you at the luau," she said. "We won't stay long, just make an appearance, then return to my suite."

"See you downstairs," he agreed.

She hung up, high on anticipation and the hope that one night with Cade would lead to several more.

At the door, a member of the rally committee presented her with a rack of Hawaiian sarongs from Hilo Hattie's, an exclusive dress shop at the hotel. She had an eye for fashion. The cognac-colored silk with peach hibiscus would bring out the brown of her eyes, and the glow of her skin. Topaz at her ears, neck and wrist would shimmer in the torchlight and speak of her wealth.

She hoped Cade was counting the minutes until they met for dinner as avidly as she was.

Cade Nyland stood by his bed, embraced by silence, but no TZ Blake. He missed her energy, her craziness, however off-the-wall. She could bring a room to life. He cursed Rhett Evans and his interference in a situation that could have easily been settled without his help. The man had stuck his nose where it didn't belong. Next time Cade would silence him with more than a look.

He crossed to the television and turned it on low. Maybe the noise would distract him from dwelling on TZ's absence. For whatever reason, the idea of one room, one bed, had sent her running like a scared rabbit. She'd covered her ears and refused to listen. He didn't understand her fear of him. Hell, she'd blown him a hot kiss before heading toward Kimmie's suite.

Contradictory woman. Still confusing as hell. One of these days he'd take her public tease to the privacy of their room. Then he'd see what made her tick. But all in good time. There wasn't any hurry. When they made love . . .

Made love. He scuffed his boot across the carpet, blew out a breath. Double damn and triple hell. When had that possibility come to mind? Taking his mechanic to bed broke his rally code. He'd never had sex during a road race. While wild and crazy might add to the excitement of the race, his primary goal remained the finish line. SunCoast Run was for his grandfather.

He'd planned to hit the sack early, with or without TZ. He'd also planned to sleep, no matter what Rhett Evans might have insinuated. The luau, a quick drink with Risa, then bed. Of his night's entertainments, the last seemed the most appealing.

He needed a shower and a change of clothes. He'd selected a Hawaiian shirt from the rally rack to be worn with navy slacks. He checked his watch. He had time for one more preparation: a way to guarantee he'd get TZ's attention at tonight's festivities.

Torchlights cast flames and shadows on the sand. The beach glowed warmly beneath a pitch-dark sky. An enormous tent dominated the shoreline, north of the roasting pit. Palm fronds had been freshly cut and woven together to make windbreaker walls. The tent poles were decorated with ti leaves, heleconia and red ginger.

Cade took it all in. An authentic luau from the *Aloha* to the orchid leis, right down to the hula girl sculpture at the entrance of the tent. Two buffet tables were decorated with traditional center table runners of ferns and flowers, and edged with raffia hula skirts. The rally committee had gone all out.

He scanned the tent for TZ Blake. There was no sign of her auburn ponytail. Risa waved to him from the makeshift bar. She was dressed more for a fashion shoot than a relaxing dinner on the beach. She wore gold tone spike-heeled sandals when everyone else was barefoot. Her jewelry glittered; her hair and makeup were flawless. The woman didn't comprehend casual.

He passed Kimmie and Rhett on his way to the mai tais and hors d'oeuvres. "Where's TZ?" he casually asked.

"She'll be here shortly." Kimmie's eyes shone, as if she had a secret.

Cade wasn't fond of secrets. "Care to share more?"

Kimmie laughed. "She'll be very . . . entertaining."

Entertaining? Lord, what was she up to?

He didn't have to wait long. Sounds of Polynesian drums and Pacific Island music reached the tent, followed by ten Tahitian dancers. The hula performers moved through the crowd, drawing approval and applause.

One hula dancer caught his eye and held his gaze. TZ Blake in her natural grass skirt, coconut bra and white orchid lei was a sight to behold. She had been born to hula. Damn, but she could move a grass skirt. The woman had a little South Pacific in her blood.

She swayed toward him, her hair down, wild curls about her shoulders. Her skin was flushed and glowing in the torchlight. Her eyes shone with fire and mischief. "Aloha, rally man," she said when the music ended. "You can blink now."

"Aloha, sweet cheeks. Nice coconuts."

"Nice Hawaiian shirt." She pulled lightly on his sleeve. "The black on blue matches your eyes."

"Hey, girl, nice dance!" Kimmie came to stand beside TZ.

"You're a natural," Rhett agreed.

She damn sure was. "Care for a mai tai?" Cade asked.

TZ shook her head. "Club soda with my meal. I don't drink."

"You're just naturally high?"

She smiled. "Kites have nothing on me."

Across the tent, rally master Walter Brown picked up a microphone and spoke. "Welcome, everyone. Please find a seat. Dinner will be served shortly."

"Where do you want to—" Cade started to ask TZ, only to have Rhett cross him a second time.

"We'd planned to sit by Brown." Rhett snagged Kimmie's hand and TZ's elbow and guided them away from Cade.

Cade followed the sway of TZ's grass skirt as she found a seat between Kimmie and the rally master. A hollowness settled in his belly that had nothing to do with hunger. He had no claim on TZ's time, except as his mechanic, but he would have enjoyed her company at dinner.

"Cade?" Risa tugged on his arm. "Where shall we sit?"

He scanned the tent for two seats. The only ones remaining were on either side of Mick Wilcox and Skinner. A look of disgust crossed Risa's face. Cade nodded to the men as he pulled out Risa's chair next to Wilcox. He then rounded the table and took a seat next to Skinner.

"I've lost my appetite," Risa said tightly.

Cade was hungry, but not for food. Once seated, he glanced again toward TZ. The torchlight caught the richness of her auburn curls, the sweet curve of her shoulder. The roundness of her coconuts. Her head was bent, and she nodded at something Brown had said. Brown patted her hand and smiled.

As if she felt his eyes on her, TZ looked up. She didn't smile or frown, only stared. Cade returned TZ's stare until Risa rubbed her sandal over his bare foot. The heel spiked his big toe. He lowered his gaze, then met Risa's across the table. Her eyes were hot and wicked. She arched her brow, a hint of a smile on her lips as she slid her foot higher, so far up his pant leg she could count the change in his pocket.

He drew his leg back, uncomfortable as hell. She pouted, still in the mood for games that he refused to play.

"What do you think of the hotel?" Mick asked Cade.

"Comfortable room. Nice view." His stay would be a lot more pleasant if TZ were sharing his suite.

"Great water pressure in the shower." Mick sniffed his forearm, then leaned a little closer to Risa. "I love the smell of hotel soap, don't you?"

Her nostrils pinched, and she fanned her face with her hand. Cade knew hotel soap couldn't compare to the hundred-dollar-an-ounce Perfection she sprayed so lavishly.

Continuing the conversation, Mick scratched his chest. "I'm into these Hawaiian shirts. Might even buy a few for the road."

"Buy them in a larger size." Risa averted her gaze. "Your buttons are stretched to the limit, and—and—"

Mick looked down. "And *what*? You can see the hair on my chest? My six-pack abs?"

"That's no six-pack, it's a keg," Risa said tightly. "You should have worn a T-shirt underneath."

"I'm available and advertising, lady. I'm a neon sign for nasty."

"Neon or color blind?" Risa asked. "An orange-and-green print shirt with red shorts—"

"I've got the legs for shorts."

"Hairy tree stumps—"

"Are better than toothpicks."

Risa look ready to kill, and Mick wasn't ready to die.

Cade figured they needed to retreat to their corners and take a breather. They'd gotten in more hits than fifteen rounds of boxing.

He passed Mick a platter of crab cakes, knowing food would silence him for a time. "Eat and enjoy."

Mick took the hint. However, instead of passing the platter back to Cade as he'd expected, Mick set it down in front of himself, and began eating directly from the silver tray.

Risa's "Dear God" didn't detour Mick from his feast.

Two crab cakes went into his mouth instead of one. His cheeks became as puffed as the crab cakes.

"Save room for the main meal," Skinner warned Mick.

"I'm not a pig," Mick mumbled, his mouth full. He'd left one lone crab cake on the platter.

Music drifted to Cade, and he noticed a small group of men playing guitars and ukuleles by the buffet tables, where the servers cut and sliced large portions of meat. He smiled at the hula dancer who brought him his food: a plate filled with roast pork, Lomi salmon, poi, sweet potatoes and edged with slices of pineapple.

"Oh, my!" He heard TZ's squeal of delight, and looked up to catch her excitement. She'd received his gift.

TZ couldn't believe her eyes. She'd been debating how much pineapple she would have to eat to still the growl in her belly when the most delectable fruit basket, along with a box of chocolate-covered caramels, was set before her. She tore open the attached envelope and read the card. *Enjoy, sweet cheeks. Cade.*

The assortment was almost too pretty to eat. Almost. From a deep wicker basket, daisy-shaped pineapple flowers were topped with melon balls and grapes. Fat strawberries bloomed with centers of cream cheese, and clusters of cherries were stacked on thin sticks. Slices of honeydew curled over the basket edge like greenery. Her very own edible flowers.

She sought Cade across the room. He grinned at her. And she grinned back. "Thank you," she mouthed.

He nodded, then turned back to his own meal. A meal he was sharing with Marisa Ashton-Lord. The woman hadn't taken her eyes off Cade, TZ noted. TZ had fought the urge to do the same. The man was just too sexy. He'd tied his hair back, and even his two shiners couldn't detract from the hard planes of his face. If anything, black eyes made Cade look more bad boy than ever. People assumed he'd gotten into a fight. And won. He'd kept them in the dark, neither acknowledging nor denying their assumptions.

"Can I have a pineapple flower?" Kimmie asked. "They are so pretty. Who sent them to you?"

TZ lowered her voice to a whisper. "Cade."

"He knows you're a vegetarian?"

"I told him at lunch just as he ordered a roast beef sandwhich so rare it could have walked off his plate and returned to the herd." She opened the box of caramels and selected one. "Cade gives good chocolate."

"The man's got hungry eyes. Bet that's not all he's great at giving. How are you going to thank him?" Kimmie asked.

"I don't do nudie thank-you cards."

"Too bad. Cade looks like the type who would take his time opening the envelope, easing out the card, then reading the message over and over."

TZ swallowed. "He scares me, Kimmie."

"Scares as in *boo* or tummy flutters?"

"Flocks of butterflies," TZ admitted.

Kimmie bit into a pineapple petal. "Do you plan to net the butterflies or the man?"

"I'm not sure yet. Mixing sex and the rally—"

"Would make for a hell of a ride."

"We'll see." TZ nodded toward Rhett, who was engrossed in conversation with the rally driver on his left. "How's it going, Virgin Kim?"

"The man's more interested in sex than a lifetime with

127

me," Kimmie said on a sigh. "I don't believe in one-night stands, and I don't want to end the rally with a broken heart. As far as the costume party Wednesday night, I'm going as a nun, 'cause Rhett's getting none."

TZ grinned. "You'll drive the man to prayer."

"Prayer is good, an altar would be even better. I want to walk down the aisle with him at the end of the rally."

Kimmie had focus, TZ gave her that. She, herself, didn't know if she were coming or going when it came to Cade. She was bewildered by her reaction to him. And she had no idea how he felt about her. The man was too controlled, too focused on the rally to give her much thought. Yet he'd gone all tense and annoyed when she'd opted to stay with Kimmie and not with him.

In truth, TZ was more afraid of her feelings for Cade than she was afraid of Cade himself. If she made a move, and he retreated, his rejection would devastate her. Better to keep things light, she decided. That way no one got hurt. Especially her.

Her stomach growled, and TZ returned to the caramels. She then sampled a strawberry filled with cream cheese. Thirty minutes elapsed, and she couldn't believe she'd eaten the whole thing. Her stomach ached, and she needed to stretch her legs.

Excusing herself, she left the tent and started down the beach. She walked to the edge of the torchlight and stared into the Gulf. A soft breeze ruffled her hair and grass skirt. She curled her toes in the wet sand.

"Keeping company with the night?"

Cade. She hadn't heard him approach. "I like the quiet."

He moved to her side. "So do I."

The darkness embraced them in a comfortable silence, which TZ eventually broke. "The caramels and fruit were delicious."

"Can't have my mechanic going hungry." Another short silence, followed by, "Have you settled into Kimmie's suite?"

She was far more settled and comfortable than she'd be with him in the same room. She could breathe with Kimmie. With Cade she'd be holding her breath, expectant and apprehensive. Curious and wanting. That was no way to get a good night's sleep. "Kimmie's my closest friend," she told him. "This isn't our first pajama party."

"How's she doing with Rhett?"

"What do you mean?" As if she didn't already know.

He shrugged. "I've got eyes, sweet cheeks. The more Kimmie pushes him away, the harder Rhett pants. She wants him, but on her terms. What's she want beyond a ride to Key West, a ring?"

Damn, but the man was observant. "I'm not certain—"

"Sure you are, but you're too good a friend to break a confidence. I respect that."

He crossed his arms over his chest, and cut her a glance. A long glance that TZ felt all the way down to her toes. His gaze burned as hot as the torchlight as it drifted over her coconuts and down to her bare belly. He reached over and rustled her grass skirt. "What's underneath?"

Keep it light. "Bruises and tropical-print panties."

One corner of his mouth curved. "Care to compare bruises?"

She quelled her impulse to flash her right hip and thigh. "My bruises can't compare to your shiners."

"Prove it."

His curiosity got the better of her. "One peek," she agreed. She then parted her skirt just above her knee.

"What caused your bruise?" he asked.

"I slammed into the bumper on your Vette."

"My Vette, my fault. A kiss would make it better." There was a raw edge to his voice that made her shiver.

"Honestly, there's no need—"

"Yes, there is."

Before she could argue, Cade had dropped to one knee. He brushed back the grass skirt until her entire thigh was visible to his gaze. She grabbed onto his shoulder, held fast so as not to fall. His body was tight and hot, and muscle packed. She curled her fingers in his shirt as his thumb gently circled her bruise. She felt the circular motion in her belly; all the way to her nipples, which had puckered beneath her coconut bra. Her nails scraped his shoulder blades as she pulled him closer.

Her heartbeat quickened as his hand fell away, soon replaced by the heat of his mouth. When he kissed her bruise, he did it slowly. A light press of his lips, a flick of his wet tongue, a slight rub of whiskers on her tender skin. Strands of his hair escaped the leather tie and skimmed her thigh, soft and electric. A hint of Polo rose on the breeze. A breeze that did nothing to cool his hot, healing lips.

Her body went liquid, and her mind blank, as his tongue swept wide, wetting the inside of her thigh, licking higher still, nearer and nearer the demarcation line of her panties. A tiny bit higher, and she'd be lost to the dark magic of his mouth.

A touch of panic edged her pleasure. She hopped back,

barely keeping her balance on the sand. "A-all better," she stammered as she straightened her grass skirt. So much better, in fact, she was certain the bruise had completely healed.

Cade rose slowly, brushed the sand from his knee. His gaze was dark, his breathing deep as he took a dangerous step toward her. "Your other bruise?"

TZ took a quick step back. She wasn't about to let him kiss her hip. "Will heal just fine on its own." Needing to be free of the seductive darkness, she licked her lips, and said, "It's getting late."

He glanced at his watch. "It's barely eight o'clock."

"While it's still early," she corrected, "I need to go back to the hotel, change my clothes and check on the 'Stang. I've a flat tire that needs to be patched."

"Don't stay out too late," he said. He jammed his hands in the pockets of his slacks. "See you in the morning, sweet cheeks."

"Night-night, rally man."

Chapter Eight

TZ saw Cade long before he saw her. And it wasn't even morning yet. She'd returned to her suite, changed her clothes and set out to service the Mustang before bed. She'd waited patiently at the bank of elevators as they climbed floor by floor, slow as snails.

Lights blinked and a soft gong sounded as two doors swooshed open simultaneously. TZ stepped into the elevator closest to her. She was about to punch the button when she heard a giggle.

Kimmie? If so, she needed to tell her friend where she was headed. She stepped back, only to find it wasn't Kimmie. It was, however, a man and woman, arm and arm, and extremely chummy. A couple she knew.

It was Cade and Risa.

TZ's stomach sank. Cade was turning in, all right. Turning in with Marisa Ashton-Lord.

Her heart slowed to a dull ache in her chest. How quickly Cade had forgotten what she would never forget.

The memory of his mouth, the wet flick of his tongue, the scrape of whiskers on her thigh were still vivid, while he, apparently, had already moved on to the platinum blonde.

There was no competing with money. TZ had lived through days at the garage when she hadn't had two quarters to rub together.

Kimmie had called Cade a loner and a heartbreaker.

With Risa on his arm, he wasn't alone.

TZ's heart, however, felt the impact of seeing him with another woman. She hurt.

She entered the elevator and hit the garage button with more force than was necessary, imagining it Cade's nose.

All the classic cars had been parked on the lower level of the garage complex. Several mechanics were servicing engines as she searched for the Mustang. She was certain Cade had parked the car between a curvy '52 BMW sedan and a streamlined '70 tour de force Citroen SM. The 'Stang wasn't there now, however. The parking place had been vacated.

TZ studied the lay of the lot. It slanted, somewhat, and the Mustang was known to roll. It had yet to roll with the emergency brake set. She'd been certain Cade had set it. Yet anything was possible.

She started to walk, slowly, then more briskly, winding between cars, searching for the 'Stang. There were a hundred parking spaces to cover. Several minutes passed before she spotted the vehicle, parked near the exit, as if ready to drive away.

TZ approached the car and circled it twice. She ran her fingers along the racing stripes. The engine felt warm to the touch, as if it had been recently driven. She knew that neither she nor Cade had taken the vehicle out. No one had an extra key. And the 'Stang was a difficult car to hot-wire.

She rubbed her forehead, narrowed her eyes. Thought hard. She hadn't a clue as to how the car had rolled as far as it had without a dent or scrape or someone seeing it move.

She pulled a spare key from the pocket of her jeans, hopped into the Mustang and fired the engine. She needed to find an all-night gas station that could plug the flat. The nail had penetrated the inner tire; she couldn't patch it with the kit from the trunk.

The night was cool, and TZ left the windows rolled up. Before she had gone more than a mile from the garage, the scent of lavender filled the interior, wrapping her in a warm hug. The fragrance grew stronger, as if it were a perfume worn on skin.

TZ glanced at the passenger seat, expecting to find someone sitting beside her. She saw nothing, but felt a presence nonetheless.

TZ slowed the 'Stang and pulled onto the easement. The car idled with a wild pulse. She could almost hear a heartbeat, could almost sense someone breathing. Where had the scent come from? Lavender . . . her aunt Elise's signature scent. TZ had recognized the light fragrance early in life and held it in her memory to this day. She missed her aunt more than she'd ever thought possible.

She tilted the rearview mirror to check the traffic behind her. Few cars traveled the road. On a sigh, she turned the mirror back to its original position, then relaxed on the seat.

She wished she had someone to talk to.

That *someone* came silently. Ever so slightly, the mirror

angled left, then lowered. Amid a gray haze, a faint image formed. A recognizable image if TZ believed in ghosts, which she hadn't until that moment. But there was no denying the pale face that smiled gently back at her. It was her aunt Elise!

TZ went hot, cold, then hot again. Her breathing came in short, quick puffs. Her fear must have frightened her aunt, for no sooner had she appeared, than she disappeared.

Within seconds, the rearview mirror straightened to its original position, and the lavender scent faded. TZ felt very much alone. She covered her heart with one hand, trying to calm the beat that kicked against her ribs. It took several minutes for her pulse to slow.

Wishful thinking? Hallucination? Or had she truly seen her aunt? She wasn't certain, might never be certain. It had happened so fast, and nearly scared the daylights out of her. Her reaction hadn't been particularly welcoming. Especially to a beloved relative.

TZ shook her head and returned to her original purpose: patching the tire. She eased the Mustang back onto the road. The vehicle rumbled and shimmied, and TZ swore, beneath the vibration, the faintest hint of a heartbeat lived in the car.

This was not something she planned to share with Cade. He'd think she'd lost her mind. Besides, he was too busy with Risa to dwell on a Pony with soul.

TZ cast several looks in the rearview mirror as she drove to the gas station. Would her aunt make a second appearance?

* * *

Cade's appearance in Marisa's suite was a mistake, he realized as soon as he stepped into her room. Candles burned, casting a seductive glow across her king-size bed. A lavish cart with a silver bucket of iced champagne, a tray of hors d'oeuvres and chocolate-covered strawberries had been wheeled near the bed. A wisp of blue satin lay at its foot.

Damn, he cursed himself ten times over. He should have turned down Risa's invitation. He knew she was interested in him.

But he hadn't expected to be the only driver invited to her all-night party.

"Dom Perignon?" she asked, stroking the magnum of champagne with the tips of her blood-red fingernails.

Cade thought of TZ and her preference for club soda. A few bubbles went a long way.

"One glass," he agreed. She handed him a fluted glass, bubbly and cold, then pressed a chocolate-covered strawberry to his lips. "Decadent."

He took one bite, thought of TZ and her Hershey's Kiss. "No more, thanks," he told Risa when she offered him a second sampling.

She ate the remainder of the berry, slowly, seductively, her tongue lingering at the corner of her mouth. She kicked off her shoes and leaned into him then, invading every inch of his private space. She traced the buttons on his Hawaiian print shirt before she undid the top three. "Get comfortable. Relax, and stay awhile."

He placed his hand over hers. "One drink, Risa."

"We've a magnum to savor." She rubbed her knee along his inner thigh. "Did you enjoy the luau?"

Cade widened his stance, shook off her knee. She was

too close to his boys for damage control should her knee rise with her anger. "The food was good, the hula performers—"

"Cheap tricks in dried grass skirts. Any woman with any class wouldn't be caught dead swaying like—"

"The hula is an art, Risa," he said softly, yet firmly. "I enjoyed the entertainment." TZ Blake's performance was a memory he'd take to his grave.

"I could entertain you."

Before Cade could stop her, she'd untied the knot on her sarong and let it drop. She stood before him in lacy taupe panties and an inviting smile. He nearly dropped his glass of champagne.

She was lovely, if a man liked thin, anorexic women.

"See anything you like?" she asked as she ran her fingers over her small breasts, concave abdomen and narrow hips. Her fine bones looked as if they'd break beneath a man's weight.

Without meaning to, he compared Risa's body to TZ Blake's. While Risa was pale and delicate, TZ had an aura of strength. Her muscles were toned, and her skin glowed with health and time in the sun. While Risa openly pursued him, TZ moved beyond his reach. A little too far for his liking.

Earlier that evening, he had kissed her bruise, then nuzzled high onto her thigh, swirling his tongue near her tropical-print panties. Had panic not edged her pleasure, he would have satisfied TZ right there on the sand, surrounded by darkness and surging waves.

Risa's cool sophistication paled compared to the heat of TZ Blake.

When Risa slid her fingers inside his shirt, Cade stilled

her hand. "You know my rally code," he reminded her. "No sex on the road—"

"We're in my room, Cade, not tearing down some highway. We have a whole night ahead of us." She wiggled her hand free and reached for his belt. "I want to please you."

Risa couldn't please him when his mind was on his mechanic. Risa did, however, have lightning-fast fingers. She'd unbuckled his belt and pulled it through the loops before he'd snagged her wrists. Enough was enough. Bending down, he retrieved her sarong and draped it over one thin shoulder. The fabric fell over her breasts and covered her hips.

He met her eyes, now cold as the champagne. "Not tonight, Risa."

"Then, *when?*" Her voice was a willful whine. "After the rally?"

He stepped back and set his glass of champagne on the dresser. "It's not going to happen. Ever."

She looked stunned. "You winked, smiled—"

"But never spoke of sex."

"You're a walking billboard for getting it on," she said, angry and shrill. "Any time, any place, anywhere."

"I'm selective, Risa," he said evenly as he slid his belt back through the loops and buckled it once again. "If gossip has built my life into one giant orgasm, the climax ends here. Tonight I turn in alone."

"You bastard!" He was halfway to the door when a pillow hit him in the back. He turned, only to be pelted by a round of cheese canapes. Then by chocolate-covered strawberries.

The lady had a temper. Reaching for the door handle,

he jerked the door open, then shut it quickly. Through the wood, he heard every name she hurled his way. She cursed like a sailor. Surprising for one who prided herself on snooty self-control.

He shook his head. It was time for bed.

"Woman problems?" Sam Mason asked as he walked toward Cade. The mechanic looked so tired, he appeared ready to draw his last breath.

Cade brushed pastry crumbs from his shoulder. "Nothing I can't handle."

Sam coughed, a deep-in-the-chest cough that shook his entire body. Cade grew concerned. "Do you need anything, Sam?"

Sam looked grim. "I've sworn off whiskey. I need to find a way to tire myself out instead of passing out. Guess I'll just walk the hall until I turn in for the night."

"I'm in three-fifteen if you need me," Cade told him.

Sam patted his shoulder. "Thanks, son." He took a step, stopped. "TZ should be up shortly."

Cade's nostrils flared. "Up shortly? From where?"

"Last I saw her, she was under Marisa's Caddie," Sam told him. "That Nancy-boy mechanic Risa hired couldn't tell a sparkplug from a piston. None of the other mechanics would lift a finger, but TZ, bless her heart, finally came to his rescue."

"She did, did she?"

"She's always helping others, never thinking of herself."

Or apparently thinking of him, and his earlier reminder that she service only the 'Stang. Her helping hands were at it again!

"Thanks, Sam. See you in the morning."

Cade moved down the hallway, stopping at the bank of

139

elevators. He took the first one available to the garage level. He immediately spotted a group of mechanics around the hood of the pink Caddie. They were all bent, waist deep in the engine.

He recognized TZ before she saw him. Baggy blue jeans covered a bottom that wiggled with each shift in her stance. As she talked and instructed, she wiped her hands on her hips, over denim worn thin from both work and wear. Grease smudged her thigh and her left buttock. Her hands were black to her wrists.

Cade breathed deeply, trying to keep his temper in check. As quietly as possible, he moved to stand directly behind her. He braced his legs wide and crossed his arms over his chest. That's when he cleared his throat.

"Damn!" TZ turned so fast she bumped her head on the raised hood. The chrome bumper backed her knees, and she had no means of escape. A dark blush stole across her cheeks. "Busted."

The mechanics turned as one, a perfect chorus line of grease smudges and guilty expressions. Cade met TZ's pale blue stare. "You shouldn't be down here this late and with all these men."

"I'm merely one of the guys."

"Then I'm incredibly gay."

She rolled her eyes. "Your sexuality means nothing to me."

"Your working on the Caddie means a lot to me. Looks like you've been busy."

She set down her wrench, placed her hands on her hips, lifted a brow. "Apparently, so have you. Thought you'd last longer, Quickdraw. Only one bullet in your clip?"

Quickdraw? Bullets? He didn't understand, but apparently the other men understood perfectly, given their bowed heads and hidden smiles. "You can explain yourself in our suite," he said.

She shook her head. "I've work to do here. Go reload."

Reload? Cade's utter stillness drove the mechanics to motion. The two on either side of TZ nudged her forward. "You've done plenty. We can finish without you," Risa's mechanic insisted. He held out his hand. "Thanks, TZ."

She shook it, smiled. "Anytime, Winston Henry."

Winston Henry? After years of rallying, Cade hadn't known the man's name, yet TZ had learned his first and last in one short evening. The thin, blond man, dressed more for tennis than servicing an engine, looked smitten by her mechanical skills.

"Let's go, *now*," Cade directed.

She held up one finger. "Give me a sec—"

"Second's passed." He bent, drove his shoulder into her stomach and tossed her over his shoulder.

She hit him on his back, his butt, his thighs. "Put me down!"

She had punch, Cade had to admit as her fists struck with a vengeance. But nothing he couldn't handle. He swatted her bottom to shut her up. "Enough, sweet cheeks. You're making a scene."

"There's no one around," she hissed.

"The scene's with me, and I'm not liking it one bit."

He stopped at the bank of elevators and took the first one to the third floor. The mirrors in the elevator reflected their image: Cade standing tall, one hand on the back of her knees, the other on her buttocks, while TZ squirmed and wiggled, all flushed, her eyes flashing.

141

On the third floor, her breathing grew shallow. "I can't breathe."

"Stop squirming, and air will reach your lungs."

"I can walk now."

He continued down the hall. He wasn't ready to set her down.

"Stop! You've passed Kimmie's suite," TZ said, her voice alarmed.

"You'll be staying with me."

"No way in—"

He stopped so suddenly, she swallowed her words. Very, very slowly, he allowed her to slide down his body. He wanted to feel her against him, her thighs, belly and breasts as they stroked him, shoulder to calf.

The sensation of man against woman quieted her. Her cheeks grew warm, this time from awareness and not anger. She gripped his shoulders, curling her fingers into his shirt, clinging, holding him close.

With her face now a hairbreadth from his, she scrunched up her nose and sniffed the collar of his shirt. "You smell like chocolate and cheese."

Cade hid his smile. "Scents from a farewell party." His farewell to Risa.

She released him. "Must have been some send-off."

"You wouldn't have wanted to be there."

"I wasn't, I was in the garage—"

"There you are! I've been looking everywhere for you," Kimmie said as she and Rhett stepped from the elevator and approached them at a brisk pace.

"Anything wrong?" TZ asked.

"I wanted to be sure you had a key to our room," Kimmie said. "I didn't want you waiting in the hall."

"She won't be needing a key. She's staying with me," Cade said with a finality that caused both Kimmie and Rhett to take a step back.

"Are you certain?" Kimmie asked TZ.

"Damn certain," Cade spoke for TZ. "She needs a keeper."

Kimmie's eyes widened as she looked at her friend. "What did you do?"

"She serviced another engine," Cade answered.

"Is that so bad?" Kimmie asked.

Rhett wrapped his arm around Kimmie's shoulders. "TZ broke a rally commandment, *Thou shalt service thy driver's engine, and none other.*"

"That's simply unfair," Kimmie retorted.

"The rules were established long before today," Cade told the women. "I abide by them." He then nodded to TZ. "Get your overnight bag from Kimmie's room. I'll wait for you."

"You could wait in your room," TZ insisted as she took out her plastic room key and inserted it in the lock.

"You have five minutes before I come after you."

"It might be locked," she tossed over her shoulder.

"I've knocked down heavier doors."

"A rally driver built like a linebacker. Just my luck," TZ muttered as she disappeared into the room.

"You'd better be nice to her," Kimmie warned, looking both pleased and a little anxious. "Or you'll answer to me."

"And, uh, to me also." Rhett coughed into his hand. He didn't look as ticked off as Kimmie. If anything he looked uneasy at interfering in Cade's business once again.

"We both need a good night's sleep," was all Cade would answer.

"Sleep we will," TZ said as she stepped from the suite, clutching her overnight bag.

Cade caught the glance exchanged between TZ and Kimmie as TZ passed her friend and preceded him down the hall. Kimmie had winked and TZ had winced. Obviously, she dreaded sharing his suite.

Cade dreaded having her so near and not being able to touch her. He flexed his fingers. Tonight restraint and reserve would lie between him and TZ Blake.

He followed her into his suite. Dark greens, tropical blues and a touch of purple brought the room to life, along with TZ's presence. The space felt suddenly warmer, suddenly brighter. He watched as she swung her leather tote from side to side, uncertain where to settle it for the night.

Cade nodded toward the dresser. "There's plenty of room—"

"I don't plan to unpack."

She looked ready for flight. He needed a distraction to ground her. "Now's as good a time as any for you to explain 'Quickdraw.' "

She scrunched up her nose. "I'm not feeling inspired."

He pursed his lips. "We can stand here until you do."

She dropped her bag at the foot of the bed, averted her gaze. "My, um, comment referred to sex."

What the hell? "Sex?"

She nodded. "You and Risa."

His eyes narrowed. "You saw us? When?"

"When you came out of the elevator and headed toward her suite."

He hadn't seen her. "Where were you, hiding behind a potted plant? Why didn't you say something?"

She edged along the far side of the bed. The side farthest from him. "I was entering the elevator, heard laughter and stepped out. I thought it might be Kimmie. When I saw the two of you, I didn't want to interrupt—"

"There was nothing to interrupt."

TZ took a deep breath, swallowed. "You looked like lovers."

"My time with Risa was short."

"That's what I figured."

Realization hit him below the belt. "Quickdraw..." She thought him a slam-bam man. "There's no quickdraw in my blood," he said to set her straight. "Never has been, never will be. When I take a woman to my bed, we spend the night, not an hour. One shot in the dark isn't satisfying. I go for the slow burn. My kisses, my touch, my penetration, all slow until the moment of climax. A climax that drives me deeper and faster, and singes our skin."

He paused and studied TZ with male satisfaction. She stood so still, he'd have thought her a statue if not for the wild pulse at the base of her throat.

He slapped his hands against his thighs. Then smiling to himself, he pulled down the navy bedspread and patted the mattress. "Firm," he noted. "I'll face the window, and you can face the wall. The bed's large enough that we won't meet in the middle."

"We'd better not," she finally managed.

He pointed toward the bathroom door. "It's all yours. Go change."

She bent quickly and snagged her overnight bag. "You don't sleep in the nude, do you?"

"Only if my woman does."

"You're safe with me, rally man. I sleep in a long T-shirt."

"And panties, TZ. Wear your panties."

Kimmie paced outside Cade's suite for fifteen minutes after TZ's departure, concerned for her friend. "Should we have insisted TZ stay with me?" Kimmie asked Rhett.

He shook his head. "Cade doesn't take well to demands."

Kimmie sighed. "I'm sure she'll be fine."

"As will I, if you'll join me in my suite for an after-dinner drink."

Kimmie wasn't so sure a drink was all Rhett was offering. "I don't think that's a good idea."

Rhett patted his stomach. "I'm so full, I'm uncomfortable. I want to lie down and relax."

"I won't relax on your bed."

"The room has chairs, Kimmie. Come sit and tell me about yourself," he encouraged. "We'll get to know each other better."

Getting to know each other was important. "I'll join you for a little while."

Pleased over her agreement, he directed her to Room 316. "This way."

As soon as they entered his suite, Rhett crossed to the mini-bar and poured two tumblers of brandy. He set both tumblers on the nightstand, then climbed onto the king-size bed. He stretched out on his side while Kimmie pulled a club chair next to the headboard. She sat on the edge of the chair, crossed her legs and slowly pumped her left foot. Rhett's gaze lit on her T-strap sandals, sandals she'd slipped on once she'd left the luau. The dainty ankle wraps made her feet look small and sexy.

She felt his gaze lift to her sarong, travel the long slit in the yellow silk that bared her calf and thigh, then higher still, to her bare shoulders. She looked good and knew Rhett liked what he saw. His gaze was hot and bright, and appreciative.

"Must you wear the hibiscus behind your right ear?" he asked.

Kimmie fingered the bright red flower. "I'm available, Rhett. Worn behind my left ear, it would mean I'm taken. You could change my status at any time."

He blew out a breath. "I don't know you well enough."

She smiled. "Ask me anything you like."

He reached for his brandy, took a sip. "How long have you lived in Gulf Cove?"

"All my life."

"Do you work?"

"For my parents."

He lifted a brow, but she wasn't ready to talk hamburgers and fries. He took the hint. "What do you do for fun, besides tight butt contests?"

She spent sixteen-hour days at Burger Joe's; that didn't leave much time for play. "I like to read, and I love to make up stories."

"Bedtime stories?"

Kimmie swirled her brandy, momentarily thoughtful. She believed marriage was based on love, compromise, and spicy sex. Fantasy was such a turn on. Though she wasn't ready to sleep with Rhett, she could hold his interest without having to take off her clothes. She would show him creativity could be delicious.

"Would you prefer Dr. Seuss, *Tales from the Crypt* or a naughty fairy tale?" she asked.

Rhett chuckled. "X-rated Disney? Where Aladdin rubs more than his lamp? Or Mickey gets hickeys?"

She licked her lips, a slow sweep of her pink tongue that left her mouth moist. "Perhaps you'd prefer sinful? How about 'Sally Does the Rally'?"

"She's no Snow White," he said as he finished off his brandy.

And she took her first sip. The brandy warmed her belly. She smiled to herself. For all her innocence, she was about to do it to him, down and a little dirty.

She watched as he snagged the corner of the deep purple comforter and drew it to his chest. After plumping the pillow behind his head, he said, "I'm tucked in and ready for my story. Put me to sleep, sweetheart."

Kimmie clicked off the light on the bedside table. The room settled into a seductive darkness.

"Once upon a road race," she began, "Sally saw Stan across the crowded dining room at Bricker's Roadhouse, a restaurant where rallyers and groupies dined on barbecue ribs, then later tasted one another. Sally wanted a closer look at the man with the bad-to-the-bone attitude and go-to-hell stare.

"He, however, hadn't given her a second look. When he entered the bar, she left Bricker's and waited in the parking lot for his departure. Several other groupies were gathered there also, seeking a driver who didn't believe in two hands on the wheel after midnight.

"After a plate of ribs, several shots of whiskey and bragging rights to a first-place win, Stan found his way outside. He caught Sally leaning against his classic car, her arms raised over her head, her blouse hiked beneath her breasts, and her low-rise jeans riding below her navel. She was dark and sensual, with a veiled gaze and full mouth that could suck the life from a man."

Rhett clutched the comforter with both hands. "What a way to die."

"Stan was filled with the devil, as aroused as he was angry. Classic cars were to be respected, not used as back rests. 'If your ass isn't Turtle Wax, get it off my car,' he growled.

"Sally wiggled her bottom. 'I can buff more than your car, if you're interested.'

"Stan liked casual sex—no names, no phone numbers, no cuddling. 'Interest me,' he said.

"Sally was fascinated by his '68 Charger, a vehicle with a massive torque that rocked the car in a way she hoped to imitate when they made love.

"She motioned toward the backseat. 'Join me.'

"Stan slipped in beside her. The night was as hot and sultry as Sally. She made it even hotter by rolling up the car windows. The air was charged with restless anticipation."

Rhett blew out a breath, his nostrils flared and his cheeks flushed. He patted the mattress. "Come sit by me, Kimmie."

"And finish my story flat on my back? Not on your life. Just relax and enjoy my bedtime tale. Are you feeling sleepy?"

"Are you kidding? My whole body is awake."

Rigidly awake. Beneath the comforter, the bulge in his pants told a story all its own.

"Beneath a smattering of stars and a sliver of a moon, Sally whispered in his ear, 'You are not allowed to touch me, but I can touch you. Close your eyes, big guy. Don't open them again until you've cum.' "

Kimmie glanced at Rhett. He'd also closed his eyes, living the story right along with Sally and Stan.

"Leaning close to Stan, Sally nuzzled his chin and cheek, teasing him with sex talk. Her mouth brushed against his, corner to corner, light and teasing. Then she bit down on his bottom lip, so hard, in fact, his blood surged straight to his groin. His sex swelled and throbbed, and he nearly rose off the backseat.

"Sally's tongue slipped through Stan's teeth, and he sucked it into his mouth. Her taste was smoky and dark, and utterly sinful. The thrust and jab of their tongues intensified, until he submitted to her dominance. She kissed him long and hard, and as deep as any penetration.

"Sally wanted to taste Stan further. Her teeth scraped the strong line of his jaw, now set in a concentrated effort to control his climax. His erection strained for her."

A muscle jumped along Rhett's jaw. His teeth clamped tight as Kimmie stroked him with nothing more than her voice. "Sally nipped the lobe of Stan's ear, hard enough to leave her mark. Pleasure followed his pain as the tip of her hot, wet tongue soothed its sensitive shell. He shivered with desire as she blew moist heat into his ear."

Goose bumps rose on Rhett's arms.

"She next pressed her lips against Stan's throat. His scent, warm and woodsy, reminded Sally of sex in the forest beneath the late afternoon sun. While breathing against his pulse point, she began unbuttoning his shirt.

"Stan's neck pulled tight and the tendons of his shoulders flexed. Her nails scored his nipples as she spread back the silvery silk. Stan had a nice chest, lightly muscled, but hairless. Sally knew hair didn't grow on steel.

"Stan was exposed and vulnerable. Sally was excited and adventurous. Sweat gleamed on his chest and belly.

His blood heated, and every muscle in his body pulled as taut as his sex."

"That taut, huh?" Rhett mumbled, as if in pain.

"The inside of the car grew hot and airless," Kimmie continued. "The windows fogged with a film of passion. His body molded to the backseat as Sally rested her cheek against his chest and spread kisses across his abdomen. Stan tasted slick and salty. Dipping lower, she unsnapped his jeans and gave his belly a flick of her tongue. She then eased down his zipper with her teeth. She freed him from his boxers."

"Tongue and teeth," Rhett mumbled low in his throat. "The man's going down for the count."

"Stan was definitely The Man. His erection was enormous. He was harder, thicker, longer than anyone Sally had ever been with. She grew wet for him, only him.

"Clear moisture beaded the head of his sex. Sally positioned her mouth over him, a light stroke of her tongue, a gentle graze of her teeth, then a deep-throated slide.

"Stan was an iron man. He could last forever . . ."

Rhett Evans's forever ended in the next ten seconds. Darkness blazed and throbbed behind his eyelids. He blinked rapidly, as if awakening from a dream. A near wet dream. "Story time's over," he rasped, drawing on his reserves, and praying he wouldn't embarrass himself. "Go to bed, Kimmie."

"You're sure?" she asked, all innocence and confusion. "You would definitely fall asleep to 'Holly the Hitchhiker.' Hank picks her up and—"

"Thumb toward the door," Rhett insisted.

She uncrossed her legs, then clicked on the lamp on

the bedside table. Cast in a halo of light, she looked like an angel.

His thoughts would shame Satan. "Good night."

"Sweet dreams," she whispered as she rose from the chair and crossed the room to the door. She slipped out without a backward glance.

Rhett sat up, then swung his legs over the side of the bed. He could barely breathe. Kimmie the Virgin had a way with words. He'd nearly fired his bazooka. He wanted her so badly even a cold shower wouldn't erase her story. A story that would have been best told naked, with lights out, and on satin sheets. Sleep would evade him for hours.

He rose, crossed to his suitcase and popped it open. A mystery by one of his favorite authors lay atop his silk boxer briefs. A shower and a good book. The mystery couldn't compare to Kimmie's storytelling, but it might make him sleepy.

It was 3:00 A.M. before Rhett found Kimmie in his dreams. Erotic dreams where he was Stan and she became Sally.

Kimmie Thorn passed Mick Wilcox without a glance in his direction. Her cheeks were flushed and her eyes bright. She looked aroused, but not satisfied. Mick knew she rode with Rhett Evans, but in what capacity he'd yet to learn. If they were heating the sheets, Kimmie wasn't getting her full share of the burn. Perhaps she packed a vibrator— that would give her the release Evans kept for himself. Selfish bastard.

Mick passed Marisa Ashton-Lord's suite just as the door opened and she shoved a cart into the hallway. The front wheels rolled over his bare toes. The ice in the champagne bucket had melted. Water sloshed over the side and onto the carpet. The canapes and strawberries looked flat, as if smashed by a fist. "Party over so soon?" he asked.

"That's none of your business."

"You got dumped, didn't you." He smirked.

"No man walks out on me."

"Apparently he ran, judging by all this leftover food."

Risa gnashed her teeth. "What are you doing on the third floor? Stalking me? Do I need to call security?"

He grunted. "You're not a woman I'd chase. This floor isn't exclusively yours. I'm right next door in three-twelve."

She covered her heart with her hand. "The hotel has gone to hell."

"Which is exactly how you look, like hell." His gaze took her in, from her mussed hair and smeared lipstick, to her disheveled nightgown. "You shouldn't walk into the hallway without a robe. One look at you could scare ten years off a man's life."

"You disgusting little man!"

He scratched his belly, bare beneath his unbuttoned shirt. "Trust me, Ris, there's nothing little about me."

She swayed in the doorway. If she fainted, he'd leave her to her fate. What he wanted was her cart. He nodded toward the food. "Mind if I finish what you started?"

"You ate enough at the luau for ten men."

"I've the capacity of eleven."

She waved her hand, dismissing him. "Take it."

"Mighty neighborly."

The slam of her door indicated how neighborly she truly felt. Whistling softly, Mick pushed the cart to his suite.

He was about to have a private party all his own. A late-night snack readied a man for bed. Chocolate-covered strawberries and canapes washed down with champagne would have him sleeping like a babe.

Chapter Nine

TZ Blake had the best night's sleep of her life. She awakened slowly, with a stretch and a yawn. Still drowsy, she rolled her cheek against her pillow, snuggled more deeply, seeking the warm place that cradled her head so perfectly. Hair tickled her nose, and she brushed it off her face. The ends swung back, thicker this time. She sneezed.

"Need a tissue?" Cade Nyland's voice sounded much closer than it should.

She squinted between the loose strands and found it was his hair, and not her own, that tickled her cheek. Worse yet, she'd used the curve of his neck as a pillow. The shadow of his beard abraded her temple.

A seductive warmth penetrated her oversized T-shirt from shoulder to calf. A man's warmth. His scent enveloped her, a hint of Polo and morning male. Her breasts were pressed against his back. A very broad, muscled back. Bent at the knee, her right leg rested between his two. The hair on his legs felt coarse against her smoothly

155

shaven thigh. Her arm draped his hip, and her pelvis spooned his buttocks. His naked buttocks!

She nearly jumped out of her skin.

Her body spasmed, and her hand flexed. Flexed around his morning erection.

"You've cupped me since six A.M.," Cade informed her with a yawn.

She released him like a hot potato, then scooted across the bed. The sheets were sweaty and rumpled, and three of the four pillows were on the floor. She tugged her T-shirt down and tucked the hem beneath her knees. "*Where* are your pajama bottoms?"

"On the floor with the blanket."

"W-why did you remove them?"

"You have a hot little body, TZ Blake," he said, his voice low and husky. "I lowered the AC twice, and changed sides of the bed three times. It appears you like to cuddle."

She'd found him in her sleep.

She bit down on her bottom lip. "I'm sorry I bothered you."

"No bother." He pulled himself to a sitting position and swung his legs over the side of the bed. He scratched his abdomen. Then, glancing over his shoulder, he smiled, a slow, sexy smile that reached his midnight-blue eyes. "I liked your hand on me. You've got a nice touch."

He'd liked her touch.

She'd liked touching him.

His rigid length would forever be imprinted on her palm.

The wall clock ticked loudly. It was eight-ten. "I'll dress

while you shower," she suggested. "The rally resumes at nine."

Cade rose and walked buck-naked toward the bathroom. TZ dipped her head and blew out a breath. The man had no shame. He did, however, have a rocking-hard body. His long hair brushed wide shoulders that tapered down to a sinewed back, a tight ass and long, muscular legs. A side glimpse of his sex showed him aroused. He was more than a handful. Several inches more.

As soon as Cade reached the bathroom and closed the door, TZ jumped out of bed and made a mad grab for her overnight bag. She unzipped it and chose her outfit quickly: a pair of wide-legged jeans, periwinkle big shirt that hung past her hips and her tennis shoes. With her eyes on the bathroom door, she tore off her T-shirt and dressed. She didn't want Cade to catch her naked.

She collected her hairbrush and tube of toothpaste, but couldn't find her toothbrush. She thumped her forehead with her palm. Stupid, stupid, stupid. Last night she'd left it hanging in the holder in the bathroom. A bathroom where Cade showered.

Did she dare sneak in and grab her toothbrush? If she did, she could be completely packed and out the door, waiting in the Mustang by the time he dried off and dressed.

She took a deep breath and crossed the room. The bathroom door opened easily and quietly. On tiptoe she reached the sink, just as the water cut off and the shower curtain slid back. She heard Cade step from the shower, snag a towel from the rack and snap it open. Her mind screamed "Run," and her heart hit a marathon pace. Her feet, however, refused to move.

157

Reaching toward the mirror, she wiped the steam from the glass with her fingertips. That's when she saw him: his hips wrapped in a towel, his chest wet and his gaze hot and locked on hers in the mirror.

He stood so close, the steam from his body dampened the back of her big shirt. She felt the rise and fall of his chest, heard the deepness of his breathing. The front of his towel brushed her buttocks, and his sex pressed the small of her back.

He was still hard.

She had gone limp. Her legs were barely holding her up.

Cade ran his fingers through his damp hair. He looked predatory and uncivilized. "Trespassing on my shower time?" he asked.

She plucked her toothbrush from the holder and held it up. "My last item to pack."

"You thought to sneak in and sneak out before I finished showering?"

She nodded. "I thought to be quick."

"Not quick enough, sweet cheeks." Leaning forward, he rested his hands on the sink on either side of her hips. She had no wiggle room. "There's a penalty for getting caught."

A *penalty?* "A shove out the door?" she asked hopefully.

He held her gaze in the mirror, bold and decisive, and slowly shook his head. "Towel me off," he breathed near her ear.

Dry him off? The man was delusional.

On impulse, TZ turned slowly. "Head to toe?" she asked.

"A full-body rubdown."

With cool porcelain at her back, she faced his hot body.

She couldn't let Cade intimidate her. Couldn't let him know how one look at his broad chest made her fingers itch.

Instead, she teased him. She was living dangerously, and she knew it. But she couldn't resist. Meeting his gaze, she traced the edge of the towel that wrapped his hips. She fingered the knot until it loosened. She held the ends between her fingertips.

She watched his gaze darken, caught the flex of his tattoo. His nipples puckered, and his six-pack tightened, grew more defined.

Excitement and a touch of panic pressed her forward. In one swift motion, she snatched the towel from his hips and slung it over his head. Keeping her eyes on his face, she rubbed the towel from side to side, as if buffing his forehead.

"What the—"

She stuffed the corner of the towel in his mouth, cutting him off. Then darting under his arm, she shot out the bathroom door. She didn't look back. "I shammy cars, not men."

His deep chuckle followed her into the suite. She tossed her toothbrush in her bag and had one foot out the door when Cade stopped her in her tracks. "Wait for me, TZ."

She slapped her palm against her thigh. "We're running late."

"I'll only be a minute."

Silence settled over the room. With her back to him, she listened to the sounds of his movements as he padded across the carpet and grabbed his gym bag. The slide of the zipper, the selection of his clothes, the soft rustle of fabric against skin as he dressed drew images she found herself longing to witness. But she'd poke a finger in her eye before she'd sneak a peek.

"All ready. Let's go." She jumped when he nudged her from behind. "Give me your bag."

"I can carry it," she insisted.

He snagged it from her hand before she could step beyond his reach. TZ looked at him. He'd tied his damp hair back with a strip of leather. He'd shaved, and the angles of his face were sharp and prominent. He appeared athletic and very male in his gray knit shirt, dark jeans and black Nikes. No matter his attire, there was a restlessness about him that prevented his ever looking respectable.

They reached the elevator bank at the exact moment as Marisa Ashton-Lord and her entourage. TZ took a moment to study Risa, as Risa studied Cade.

Dressed in an off-white pencil-thin skirt and a dune-colored shirt that tied at her waist, Risa appeared as posed and stiff as a mannequin. Turquoise and crystal earrings dangled from her lobes, and a chunky turquoise bracelet banded her wrist. The three-inch heels on her leather sandals spiked the hallway carpet.

"Sleep well?" she asked Cade, her smile tight.

"I'm rested and ready to hit the road," he replied.

"As are we, thanks to TZ," Winston Henry told Risa.

Risa arched a perfect brow. "Thanks to Cade's mechanic?"

Winston nodded. "She changed a few sparkplugs—"

"Something *you* couldn't handle?" Risa pressed.

Heat crept up the man's neck, rising above the collar on his yellow knit shirt and into his gelled blond hair. "Could have, but-but—"

"I offered to help." TZ jumped to Winston's defense. "He knows his business."

"You know the rules." Risa looked sharply at Cade. "Call your mechanic off my Caddie or I'll file a formal complaint with the rally committee." She turned then, and jabbed one long red nail at the elevator button.

With Risa's back to them, Winston glanced at TZ, his expression pained. TZ nodded her understanding. When the elevator arrived, Risa and her entourage stepped in, joining several other hotel guests who filled it to capacity.

"We'll take the next one," Cade said.

The elevator doors closed. TZ swung her arms at her sides, shifted her stance, caught Cade watching her. Dark and assessing, his stare unnerved her. "What?" she finally asked.

"You heard Risa. Stay away from her car."

TZ ground her teeth. "If you'd stayed with her last night, she wouldn't be after me this morning. You could have put a smile on her face instead of that scowl."

"I could have made her smile," he agreed before his gaze narrowed. "However, if I'd spent the night with Risa, I would have lost track of you. Should Walter Brown catch you servicing someone else's engine, we could be penalized, or worse, disqualified."

"It's hard for me to say no."

"It gets easier the more you say it."

She scrunched up her nose. "Was it hard to say no to Risa?"

"We're talking two separate services, sweet cheeks."

"Both give good lube."

"Is that what turns you on? Grease-reducing friction?"

"I also fall hard and fast for a dead battery."

161

Cade looked down, shook his head. "Why aren't you married?"

"I've yet to find a man with oil in his blood, someone who doesn't mind getting his hands dirty."

Cade had gotten his hands dirty on more than one occasion. He'd rather overhaul an engine than sit at a board meeting any old day of the week.

A soft gong announced the arrival of the next elevator going down. TZ preceded him inside. As the elevator descended, he took a moment and studied her profile in the mirrored panels. Her auburn ponytail hung a little below her shoulder blades, sweeping a shirt two sizes too big for her. She wore baggy-butt Levi's that hid her perfect rear. There was no evidence of her bustline, no indentation at her waist.

He preferred her in hot-pink boxers and a crop top or hula skirt and coconut bra. She had a body to stop traffic, to cause a ten-car pileup, yet she chose to hide every curve.

Though she might hide her body, she couldn't hide her face. Anyone who got within five feet of her could see her natural beauty. Free of makeup, her nose freckled, she looked younger than her soon-to-be thirty. Her pale blue eyes revealed her love of life, and when they darkened, her impulsiveness. Her high cheekbones and straight nose were classic. Her flirty mouth teased a man to hardness with the hint of a smile.

She was a man's woman. Working in a job dominated by testosterone, she'd carved a niche all her own. A niche where no man could touch her, unless she wanted to be touched. His grandfather would love TZ Blake.

"Why are you staring at me?" TZ asked, suddenly self-conscious. "Do I have sleep in my eyes, something on my face?"

"You look just fine," Cade assured her.

"Then look at yourself in the mirror and not at me."

"You're easier on the eyes."

"Black eyes, and now bad vision. Must be my day to drive."

Apparently she couldn't take a compliment. "Guess again."

TZ was set to argue when the elevator doors slid open. Chaos reigned in the garage. They both stared, listening to the raised voices, accusations and swearing among the rallyers.

Cade stepped into the fray. "What's happened?" he asked Walter Brown, who paced beside Rhett's Jaguar.

Brown looked harried. "Damaged vehicles," he replied, as disgusted as he was irate. "The cracked crankshaft on Barry Wyatt's '57 Mercedes looks as if someone took a sledgehammer to it. And the automatic transmission on Lyle Lomat's '52 Peugot slips between shifts."

"Major damage," TZ murmured, looking as stunned as Cade felt. "No quick fix."

"How did it happen?" Cade pressed.

Brown ran his hand through his hair. "No one knows."

Cade checked out the ceiling. "Security cameras?"

Brown shook his head. "None at this level. The rally requested private parking, and the hotel didn't anticipate any problems."

"The Mustang . . ." TZ's voice trailed away as she took off in search of her car.

Cade followed her. Her walk became a jog before she broke into a run. He thought she mumbled "It's not where

I left it," but couldn't be certain. Cars didn't move without a driver.

She'd reached the far end of the garage and was backtracking when he spotted the 'Stang. "Two spaces south," he called to her. "Behind the Camaro RS."

As she rounded the Rally Sport, the relief on her face was that of a mother finding her lost child. Cade frowned. "Did someone move the Mustang?"

"No . . ." She sounded anything but convincing. "The car's right where I left it."

He didn't believe her for a second. But why would she lie? "Let's get ready to rally," he said as he unlocked the passenger car door, then circled the hood. "The Mercedes and Peugot will need to be towed. The race will continue with ninety-eight vehicles instead of one hundred."

TZ slid onto the seat. "The drivers must feel awful."

Awful, and angry. Cade glanced over his shoulder, caught the fire in Barry Wyatt's eyes, the tight set of his jaw. On any other day, Barry was soft-spoken and easygoing. Today, however, he burned on a short fuse. Barry wanted answers. Walter Brown could only shake his head, as concerned as the drivers.

Cade wanted the perpetrator caught. Tampering with a classic car was a rallyist's nightmare. It was also a crime. Throughout all his years of racing, he'd never participated in a rally where damages eliminated vehicles. Reaching his side of the car, he tossed their luggage on the backseat then eased behind the wheel. He started the engine. Though he felt badly for those left behind, he was equally thankful when the Pony kicked, ready to run. Cade rolled down his window and waited for Walter Brown.

Twenty minutes and thirty cars later, the rally master

approached them. He held the boxed time clock against his chest. "You're sitting in thirty-first place," he said. "Ready to punch and go?"

Cade nodded. He reached beneath the visor for the time card and handed it to Brown who punched the card and returned it to Cade. Before the rally master could retreat, the driver's side window rolled up and trapped Brown's wrist. The time card dropped onto Cade's lap.

"Nyland, put down the window!" Brown demanded.

Cade tried to roll down the window, but it wouldn't move.

"My hand!" Brown's voice rose as the window cranked even tighter. His face was red, and his fingers wiggled wildly near Cade's face. "You're going to break my wrist!"

Cade put his weight into rolling it down. The window wouldn't budge. He glanced at TZ. "Major problem, sweet cheeks."

TZ leaned across him. He felt the brush of her shoulder against his chest, the jab of her elbow to his ribs, as she struggled with the window.

"Hurry up!" Brown was panicking, his breath fogging the outside of the window. Other rallyers had circled the car, checking out the commotion.

Cade rested a hand on her shoulder and squeezed. "An inch, TZ, give Brown an inch, and he'll be able to slip his hand free."

She thumped the door panel with her palm, then turned toward the rearview mirror. Cade watched her stare at her reflection, as if she had a connection with the glass. A haze formed on the mirror, then TZ's image blurred completely . . .

Cade blinked, drawn back to the raised voices outside

his window. The car was rocking as two drivers attempted to shake Brown's hand free, with little success.

Big Mick Wilcox held up a hacksaw. His eyes looked downright scary. "Let's cut off Brown's hand at the wrist," he suggested.

"Get away from me, you psycho!" Brown took a swing at Mick with his free hand, but missed him by a finger's length.

Paul Royer, one of the rally committee members, swung a hammer at his side. "Want me to break the window, Walter?"

"No broken glass!" Cade said sharply.

"Release the rally master," TZ's voice was so soft, he wasn't sure he'd heard her correctly.

A faint hint of lavender filled the car, and within seconds, the window lowered. Brown jerked his hand free, then shook circulation back into his fingers.

"How's your wrist, Walter?" Cade asked.

The rally master scowled. "Sore enough to slap you with a penalty."

"The window stuck," Cade returned evenly as he secured the time card beneath the visor. "You can't penalize what we can't control."

"This car is a menace," Brown stated. "I've been slapped by its windshield wipers and had my wrist crushed in the window. What's next?"

As if on cue, the car began to back up. The left front tire ran so close to Brown's feet, the man squealed like a girl. Cade hit the brake, then held up his hands. "The car rolled, Walter, I swear."

Brown's scowl darkened. "Your word is becoming less

and less believable. Hit the road, Nyland. Drive safely. This car's an accident waiting to happen."

Cade shifted into first, eased out the clutch. The 'Stang backfired like a bazooka. Black emissions enveloped Brown. He looked like a human smokestack.

Cade slammed into second, then third, only to hit a speed bump near the garage exit. The car bottomed-out with a low groan.

"Slow down." TZ gripped the dashboard.

"Sorry." He downshifted, slowed to a crawl. "Check the directions for the first checkpoint," he instructed as he collected his Ray-Bans from the dashboard and slipped them on.

TZ also sought sunglasses. Rifling through her straw bag, she selected round rainbow frames with emerald lenses. She looked as if she belonged in the Land of Oz. Shortly thereafter, she reached for the manila envelope and map. While she studied the packet of directions, the 'Stang shimmied and shook, leaving Cade as stiff as the gear shift.

Beside him, TZ licked her lips. "First checkpoint . . . if I'm reading this correctly, looks like we're headed for some back-road racing."

"Give me the coordinates," he pressed.

"Take a left. Proceed yellow, twenty. Blue, about . . . six miles."

He drummed his fingers on the steering wheel. "*About*, TZ?"

"Until we hit State Road Eighty-two. That's were we turn country. Run the back roads."

Cade blew out a breath, decided not to call her on her rally terminology. She'd spoken in color-codes, which was a far better start than yesterday when she'd fumbled through the instructions, then colored on the mileage log. "Take down the odometer reading," he said, then gave her the numbers. "We need to be alert and attentive if we're going to rise in the standings. I want to finish the day in the top ten."

TZ wanted to finish the day, period. In whatever manner would get her through the next eight hours. She'd limp along, using whatever crutch possible to get them to their destinations.

The next two hours passed in a blur of palm trees, Florida pines and a single-lane dirt road that curved like a snake. TZ cast sideways glances at the rearview mirror on the outside chance her aunt's face would again materialize. She had caught a glimpse of Elise in the mirror at the hotel garage, when the window rolled up, squeezing Walter Brown's wrist. Even in the grayish haze, her aunt's gaze blazed with hatred. A hatred TZ did not understand.

Beside her now, Cade handled the 'Stang with sure-handed precision. He accelerated and slowed as if born behind the wheel. His looks in the rearview mirror were brief. TZ wondered, if Elise suddenly appeared, how he'd react to the Pony with soul.

Keeping her mind on the rally, TZ guided Cade to each checkpoint: a white-washed church with stained-glass windows where baptisms, weddings and funerals brought together generations of citrus growers; a telephone pole struck and blackened by lightning; and, finally, a herd of cows so far off in the distance they looked like animal pieces on a toy farm.

They didn't, however, pass another classic car. She prayed they were on the right path. She skimmed her finger over the directions she held on her lap. "A sixty-minute chow-down is scheduled at Four Corners."

"Distance?" Cade asked.

More coordinates. She read the directions, then angled the map until north was south. "Yellow, forty-five. Blue, Evacuation Route Twelve."

"Route Twelve runs clear across Pelican Point."

TZ refolded the map. "Go straight," she said with more conviction than she felt. "We're looking for a four-way stop with restaurants on each corner."

They hit pavement six miles down the road, along with a sign for the evacuation route. The two-way traffic had grown heavy as the noon hour approached. TZ shifted on the seat, then cranked down the window. Fresh air blew in, warm and welcome.

A honk, and a swerving flash of pink, caught her eye in the passenger side mirror. Cruella De Vil came to mind as Marisa Ashton-Lord's Cadillac shot by two cars in a no-passing zone, and bore down on their bumper.

TZ whipped around and watched Risa through the back window. "She's going to hit—"

Before she could finish, the Cadillac bumped the 'Stang.

"These aren't bumper cars." Cade's jaw locked.

"That wasn't a love tap," TZ agreed. "Risa wants us to speed up."

Cade refused to go faster. "There's too much traffic. If she's in such an all-fire hurry, she can go around us." He motioned her to pass. Instead of passing, however, Risa rode their bumper; less than an inch separated them.

Cade tapped the brakes, warning Risa to back off.

She ignored his warning. Contrary to rally rules, she nudged their bumper a second time.

TZ reached for the door handle. "Pull over!"

Cade clutched the steering wheel. "I'll handle it."

"As well as you handled Risa last night?" TZ demanded. "If you'd slept with the woman, her Cadillac wouldn't be humping my 'Stang. She's horny and heavy-footed—"

His gaze shifted to the rearview mirror. "And about to hit us again."

TZ motioned him forward. "Pass the car ahead of us."

His eyes narrowed. "Hang on."

She clutched her seat belt as Cade swung the steering wheel left, accelerated. He'd barely crossed the white line when the Mustang spun, doing a doughnut in the middle of the road.

"This isn't a stunt car!" TZ shouted above the rumble of the engine.

"That wasn't *my* doughnut," he shouted back.

Not his? Then whose? The aroma of lavender filled the car, as if someone had lavishly sprayed the scent.

Cade fanned his face. "Did perfume spill in your purse?"

"It's not my fragrance." She knew whose fragrance it was, however. Glancing in the rearview mirror, she found her aunt controlled the car. Amid a gray haze, the faint image of Elise was reflected in the glass. Elise's eyes bore the determination of a woman about to right a wrong.

"Don't fight the wheel," TZ said.

Cade disagreed. "We could go into a ditch—"

Before he could finish, the 'Stang spun a second time. This time, however, it didn't complete the circle. The car did a one-eighty, slowed, then faced the pink Cadillac, which had come to a stop and idled quietly.

The Mustang was anything but quiet; it resonated with challenge. Traffic in both directions had come to a halt. Marisa sat in her car, wide-eyed, her mouth open, before she slammed the Cadillac in reverse, nearly hitting Mick Wilcox's Bug-eyed Sprite. Mick lay on the horn, shook his fist. Risa burned rubber as she slid sideways, then stopped so fast she got whiplash.

The Mustang rolled forward, slowly, stealthily.

"What the hell is going on?" Cade swore as he stomped on the brake. He jerked the emergency brake, but the car continued forward.

"Ride it out." TZ was barely able to speak.

"Are you crazy?"

"We're about to find out."

TZ held her breath as the 'Stang stopped within an inch of the Cadillac's bumper. Once there, the front wheels began to bounce as if pumped on hydraulics. The engine roared as if the accelerator were floored.

"Good Lord . . ." Cade jiggled the key, but couldn't cut off the engine.

Then, as quickly as the Mustang had confronted the Caddie, it spun right and reversed direction. The car eased down the road, picking up speed, until it cruised once again at the speed limit.

TZ dared a glance in the rearview mirror. The glass was clear, almost sparkling, as if recently cleaned. Now, more than ever, she believed the spirit of her aunt inhabited the 'Stang, and that Elise could take control at any given time.

The thought, however, didn't frighten TZ in the least. If anything, she felt oddly protected. She wondered if Cade would feel the same.

Cade reached into his pants pocket for a stick of Doublemint. He offered TZ a stick, and she took her usual two. He then took one for himself, unwrapped it and popped it into his mouth. He chomped down hard.

"Care to explain what just happened?" he asked.

He looked pale and concerned, and irritated he'd lost control of the car. What to say? "The Mustang flexed a little muscle."

"A *little muscle?* The car felt"—he hesitated, searched for the right word—"possessed."

Possessed? Her aunt might not take kindly to his word choice. She counted to ten, then asked, "Do you believe in ghosts?"

He started, paused, grew thoughtful. "I once had a friend who used the Ouija board."

"With any success?" she pressed.

"She swore she'd contacted Elvis."

TZ bit down on her bottom lip. "Perhaps she did."

He looked skeptical. "What's Ouija got to do with the 'Stang?"

She took a deep breath, then blurted out, "My aunt may be traveling with us."

"Your *dead* aunt, here in the Mustang?" He glanced over his shoulder, checked out the backseat, then returned his gaze to the road.

"She's not in her physical form," TZ explained.

He stopped chewing his gum. "What form then?"

Not mincing words, she called it like she saw it. "I believe her spirit's in the 'Stang."

"In the 'Stang?" He reached for the rearview mirror, turned it directly at her. "Look in the mirror, TZ. You've got crazy on your face."

She smiled to herself as she tilted the mirror back toward him. "It's not my face in the mirror."

Cade glanced up, and with one look into the mirror, forgot his name, the rally and the woman sitting beside him. He swallowed his gum. Without conscious thought, he ran a yellow light. A part of him realized the Mustang had geared down, then pulled off the side of the road without his turning the wheel.

Time slowed along with the vehicle as he concentrated on the face in the gray haze reflected in the glass. The face was female, a woman with delicate features, whose gaze was both thoughtful and direct. She shared an uncanny resemblance to TZ Blake.

He rubbed his eyes, cleared his throat, then shifted his gaze to TZ. "Does she talk?"

She shook her head. "Not verbally. Elise communicates through the car."

"You've seen her before?" he asked.

"Only twice. The night I patched the tire, and again this morning when the window rolled up on Brown's wrist."

Cade turned back to the mirror. "Your aunt's riding this Pony."

The corners of Elise's mouth turned up slightly.

"Why isn't she in Heaven?" he asked.

TZ shrugged. "I'm not certain why souls linger. Perhaps lack of resolution or unfinished business." She patted the dashboard. "Elise is with us now, and from all indications, she plans to rally."

"Rally, *and drive?*"

"I hope not. I'd much rather see your hands on the wheel."

"Yeah, me, too."

They sat in silence for several minutes. During that time, Cade cautiously eyed Elise. "I want to win this race," he informed her ghostly image. "Warn me when you want to steer."

The horn honked her agreement, and then Elise vanished.

"How do you feel about our passenger?" TZ asked.

"Surprised, but not spooked," he answered honestly. "Elise is welcome to come along for the ride."

"She's very protective of the 'Stang."

"She also has a temper," Cade noted. "Elise nearly broke the rally master's wrist."

"She handled Risa just fine," TZ pointed out, then poked Cade in the arm with her finger. "Never send a man to do a woman's job."

"Woman? Don't you mean *ghost?* Elise has a definite advantage over us mere mortals." He rolled his shoulders, settled deeper in the seat, actually smiled. "Damn fine doughnut, by the way."

TZ returned his smile. "How about the hydraulics?"

"Hell of a bounce."

"Risa appeared shaken."

"Her entourage looked catatonic."

TZ sighed with relief. "No more bumper cars."

Cade scrubbed his knuckles over his jaw. "It's going to be an interesting race. Expect the unexpected."

Her stomach unexpectedly growled. "I'm hungry. Let's find Four Corners."

They hit the checkpoint in a very short time. Dozens of vintage cars lined the streets near the four-way stop. Rallyers congregated on the sidewalk, selecting where to have lunch.

Walter Brown stood on the southwest corner with the time clock clutched to his chest. Cade got his card punched, then parallel parked between a '70 Alpha Romeo, the poor man's Ferrari, and a '57 Buick Roadmaster the size of a land yacht with some get-up-and-go.

He exited the 'Stang, circled the hood and stepped onto the sidewalk. He took in the four lunch spots. "Where do you want to eat?" he asked TZ. "Spud's Potato Bar, Crab Trap, Sweet Caroline's Crepes, or"—he cast a long, interested look at the last vendor—"Hot Diggity Dog?"

TZ jabbed him in the side with her elbow. "Craving a foot long?"

Her question drew his smile. Several feet from where they stood, three blondes sporting red bikinis, deep cleavage and dark tans served hot dogs from a steaming metal cart. Customers were lined up for a solid block. Business was definitely good.

Cade watched as Mick Wilcox strolled the sidewalk, openly checking out the vendors before he cut to the front of the line. His discourtesy drew hisses and boos, and some shoving. Turning on the line, Mick hawked and spat. Those around him scattered.

Mick then motioned for Skinner to join him. After ordering, the men left with foolish smiles and a dozen fat frankfurters.

Shortly thereafter, two of the blondes scanned the roadway, their radar picking up Cade. They tossed their hair, and their smiles grew suggestive. So suggestive, he felt the sidewalk heat.

Cade winked, and TZ rolled her eyes. "Too hot on the street for me." She then stepped off the curb and crossed with the light. "I'm headed to Spud's," she cast over her shoulder. "Enjoy your weenie, rally man."

Weenie? TZ made him feel five.

He glanced once again at the bikini-clad vendors. The blondes were as hot and mouthwatering as the hot dogs they sold. His gaze then wandered to the crosswalk where TZ Blake in her oversized shirt and baggy-butt jeans headed for Spud's.

No contest. "Hold up, TZ," he called, jogging to catch her. Once he reached her side, he slowed his stride to match hers.

She looked surprised to see him. "No weenie with the works?" she asked.

He shook his head. "Spud's is fine. I'll have whatever you're having, Ms. Potato Head."

Chapter Ten

Mick Wilcox sat beside Skinner on a wide seawall over-looking the Gulf of Mexico. The sun beat down on his neck, and he began to sweat. No deodorant, no cologne and clothes plucked from the hamper. He scooped a hand-ful of ice from his soft drink and melted it on his forehead. The water ran down his face, caught in the creases of his double chin. Almost as refreshing as a shower.

"Meal on a bun, my favorite," he said, grunting as he proceeded to take a big bite of his hot dog. Nothing pleased him more than a frankfurter with extra mustard and onions. He took a second bite before he'd swallowed the first. Damn fine dog.

He glanced across the street at the vendors. Definite hotties. The blondes could cook his dog any day of the week. From what he'd observed, Pelican Point was a laid-back resort with just enough traffic to keep life interesting. He might relocate here someday. Lunch at Hot Diggity Dog would satisfy him into old age.

"You've got mustard on your chin," Skinner told him.

Like he cared. Mick turned slightly and wiped his chin on the shoulder of his black T-shirt. One more stain wouldn't make that much difference. Mustard and butterscotch from his breakfast ice cream sundae looked a lot alike. He then brushed the crumbs off the front of his shirt, smiled around a mouthful of food over the inscription *If You Don't Like What I'm Wearing, Feel Free to Undress Me.* Apparently everyone thought him a sharp dresser.

"Check out the umbrella brigade." Skinner pointed to a plot of sand below.

Mick glanced down. Beneath the shade of a bright yellow beach umbrella, Marisa Ashton-Lord and her entourage had set up for a picnic. Four chairs surrounded a folding table arranged on a circular raffia rug. Their feet would never touch the sand. China, goblets and polished silverware were arranged on a pristine white tablecloth. Mick snorted. A table set for a snob.

Wiping sweat from the back of his neck, he ran his damp palm down his blue-jeaned thigh. The sun dried the worn denim almost immediately. He squinted as Risa's minions unpacked a picnic basket the size of a small diner.

Skinner cocked his head, asked, "What the hell they eatin'?"

"Looks like crap," Mick replied.

"Don't you mean *crepes?*" Skinner corrected.

"Whatever," Mick returned.

"Wine, fruit, cheese." Skinner leaned forward for a better look. "Mighty fancy lunch."

Mick nudged his shoulder, and Skinner nearly took a nosedive off the seawall. His arms flailed wildly. Two of his six hot dogs flew off his lap, and dropped on the sand, several feet from the picnic.

"What the hell did you do that for?" Skinner demanded, his face as red as the ketchup on the hot dogs.

"Just checking your balance," Mick replied.

"And if I'd fallen?"

"Splat."

"You're a real jerk, Wilcox."

"So I've been told," Mick said as he stuffed an entire hot dog in his mouth. He swallowed most of it whole.

From the corner of his eye, he caught several seagulls in flight. Spotting the hot dog buns, they dived like bombers to get their fair share. A dozen more gulls soon joined those squabbling over the largest portion.

Mick watched Risa turn toward the squawking and flapping of wings. Her gaze then lifted to where he and Skinner sat on the seawall. He could almost hear her groan. He was surprised when she left the table and crossed the sand, coming to stand ten feet below him. Her face was tighter than a bad face-lift.

"Careful or you'll wrinkle," he called down to her.

Beneath the noonday sun, her chest rose and fell. The woman was thin as a swizzle stick. A swizzle stick with tits. Her breasts were visible beneath the sheer fabric of her blouse. Mick looked his fill.

In a crisp voice, Risa commanded, "You need to move, you're blocking my sun."

Her sun? The rich bitch thought she owned the sky. "The umbrella's blocking your sun," he returned, biting into his third hot dog.

She sniffed disdainfully. "You're sitting upwind of our picnic."

Upwind? Like a garbage dump? "You calling me white trash?" he said, growling.

She looked at the discarded hot dog buns near her sandaled foot. "If the litter fits."

Litter? Hell, he'd been feeding the gulls, which he planned to continue doing. Removing his fourth hot dog from its bun; he ate it in two bites. He then proceeded to tear the bun in several pieces. A flick of his wrist, and the chunks landed on Risa's toes. She shrieked as loudly as the seagulls, who quickly swooped in to feed.

Mick witnessed his own personal footage of Alfred Hitchcock's *The Birds* as dozens of gulls landed and pecked near her feet. "Go away! Shoo, shoo!" Risa flapped her arms as wildly as the seagulls' wings. Feathers flew as she wove left, then right, stumbling across the sugar sand.

He cupped his hands around his mouth, shouting, "Take your butt where your mouth can't find it."

By the time she reached the beach umbrella, Risa's hair stood on end, and her clothes were as mussed as his own. She no longer looked like a million bucks.

Skinner shifted on the seawall. "Think the gulls will peck her eyes out?"

Brown eyes that flashed hatred every time Risa looked at him. Eyes that labeled Mick white trash. "Nope, but they'll damn sure ruin her picnic."

Marisa Ashton-Lord was furious. There were feathers in her hair, and her blouse was splotched with bird excretion. She was an absolute mess.

Beside her, Winston Henry pulled his yellow shirt over his head. He peeked through the neck hole, his gaze locked on the hovering gulls. "Should we pack up?" he asked.

Risa sniffed. She wasn't about to let Mick Wilcox spoil her picnic. She sat down on her chair like a queen on her throne. She shook out her linen napkin, placed it on her lap. "Keep the gulls away," she ordered Winston.

"Away?" his voice croaked. "How do I do that?"

She plucked a feather from behind her ear. "Flap your arms, squawk, *be a seagull*."

"Be a seagull?" He looked incredulous. "I'm your mechanic, not a birdman."

She looked down her nose at him. "As long as you're in my employ, you'll be whatever I want you to be."

"Risa, please . . ."

"Flap, flap." She clapped her hands.

With a long-suffering sigh, Winston Henry left the shelter of the umbrella and waved his arms over his head.

"Join him," Risa told the other two men who snickered behind Winston's back. "If a gull so much as flies near my umbrella, you're all fired."

While the three men fought off the seagulls, Risa nibbled her strawberry crepe and thinly sliced cantaloupe. She sipped a glass of chardonnay to steady her nerves. She cut a glance to where Mick Wilcox and Skinner still sat on the seawall. Their side-splitting laughter over the three blond men warding off the gulls was hard to stomach.

Wilcox had stolen her appetite. She'd looked forward to lunch alfresco. That was until Wilcox blocked the sun and summer breeze and whipped the seagulls into a feeding frenzy. He was utterly hateful, a true blight on society.

Pouring a second glass of wine, Risa pretended to enjoy herself. She reached into the picnic basket for a pecan chocolate chip cookie. Watching her weight, she broke the gourmet cookie into fourths. It took her four days to eat one cookie. While some thought she was as nutty as the pecans, she believed in savoring. Savoring kept her weight at one hundred pounds.

She bit into the cookie, and smiled. The cookie wasn't as good as sex, but satisfying, nonetheless.

"Risa, my arms are tired," Winston Henry whined. He rolled his shoulders. "Can I stop now?"

A seagull flew by the umbrella, so close, Risa swore it made eye contact.

"Keep flapping," she said, dragging out her meal for as long as she dared.

Sitting silently, she contemplated the fate of Mick Wilcox. She planned to punish the buffoon. No one left Marisa Ashton-Lord to the mercy of seagulls. She just had to wait for the right moment. . . .

Her opportunity came sooner than she'd planned. Once her entourage had packed up the picnic and they'd crossed the sand to her Cadillac, she caught sight of the Bug-eyed Sprite parked two cars ahead of her own. Dented and rusty, the Sprite looked far older than its forty-two years. The back window was cracked; the front windows rolled down.

Rolled down . . . Risa smiled. Paybacks were hell. She crossed her fingers, prayed seagulls liked crepes. She'd eaten very little, and her entourage even less. It had been difficult for the men to eat while flapping their arms. Glancing over her shoulder, she noted Wilcox and Skinner still perched on the seawall. She turned back to the Sprite.

Pressing her finger to her lips, she signaled Winston Henry to silence. She then motioned him to follow her with the picnic basket.

Reaching the Sprite, Risa lowered herself to Mick's level. It felt surprisingly good. She selected crepes, croissants and grapes from the basket, then spread them over the roof and hood of his car. At the last second, she tossed a handful of cookie crumbs on the front seat.

"Run!" she called to Winston as the seagulls landed with a flourish of hungry eyes, snapping beaks and bird droppings.

A car wash and interior cleaning were in Mick Wilcox's future.

Risa felt childishly giddy. Lunch had been delicious.

Across the street, Kimmie Thorn, Rhett Evans and Sam Mason sat in a booth at Crab Trap, waiting for their waitress. Service was slow, and Kimmie was hungry. The aroma of sauteed fish and shrimp had her ready to suck down sugar packets.

"What looks good?" Rhett asked her.

Seated on the same side of the table as Rhett, Kimmie scooted a little closer. Her arm brushed his, and her thigh pressed intimately against him. "You order for me, Rhett."

He lowered the menu, looking uneasy. "I don't know your taste in seafood."

Kimmie touched his forearm. Rhett's warmth penetrated the cool, silky fabric of his indigo shirt. Indigo was definitely his color.

"Trust yourself," she encouraged as the waitress arrived to take their order. "You know me better than you think."

The waitress looked harried. Her red lipstick was smudged, her brown hair escaped her bun and her apron was twisted over her left hip. She cleared her throat, rattled off the daily specials, "Cajun-fried popcorn shrimp and bacon-wrapped sea scallops served with French fries and cole slaw."

Rhett glanced across the table at Sam. "Go ahead, Mason. I'm still looking over the menu."

Kimmie squeezed his arm. "You'll order the perfect meal."

Sam Mason ordered grouper fingers from the kiddie menu. Kimmie understood his need to eat light. Liquor no longer sloshed through his system. Sam was adjusting to solid food.

She smiled at their mechanic. "Holding your own, Sam?"

Sam looked down at his hands. "By the tips of my nails."

"You'll make it," she assured him. "Strong, handsome man like yourself—"

"Strong?" Sam gaped. "Handsome?"

She met his gaze. "There's a quality of agelessness about you, Sam. I see inside you and know your strengths."

"A man of strength?" Kimmie heard Rhett mutter. No doubt he thought her perception of Sam as blind as her love for Rhett. She did, however, believe Sam could remain on the wagon for the SunCoast Run.

Sam looked at her as if he wanted to believe her. She patted his hand, felt the bones beneath his skin. His costume for the party should be a skeleton. It would take little to rattle Sam's bones.

Kimmie had such a short time to fatten Sam up. Even just a little. An additional ten pounds, and his face would flesh out nicely. She noticed his eyes were a little brighter from her compliment. She made a mental note to remind Sam what a good man he truly was.

Sam dipped his head. "Excuse me, I'll be back in a few. I want to review the next checkpoint and brainteaser while I have the time."

With Sam's departure, the waitress tapped her ink pen against her order pad, then pressed Rhett, "Your order, mister? Sometime today."

Kimmie heard him swallow. "I'll have crab legs, and the lady will have..." He paused, pursed his lips. "Oyster stew."

The waitress nodded, moved on to the next table.

Oyster stew? Kimmie sighed. She would have preferred lobster salad with a twist of lemon. Something light and succulent, not slimy in the throat. Swallowing her disappointment, she hugged his arm and said, "Perfect, absolutely perfect."

Rhett looked pleased with himself. "I remembered how much you enjoyed the tomato bisque at Calypso's. Bisque is similar to stew. I thought oysters might—"

"Might what?" Realization hit slowly. "Turn me on?"

He couldn't meet her eyes. "Just a little."

"It will take more than oysters to get me in your bed," she said softly.

"A-ah, hell." He signaled to the waitress, who returned with a make-it-quick look in her eyes. "I'd like to change the lady's order," Rhett informed her. "Make it lobster salad."

Amen! "With a twist of lemon," Kimmie added.

"Anything else?" the waitress asked.

"We're fine now," Kimmie assured her. "I know how busy you are, so thanks for making the change."

"Busy?" The waitress leaned her hip against the table. "I'm busting my hump for change," she complained. "The cook needs glasses, but refuses to wear them. He's sending out orders that don't match the customers' requests. Customers are pissed, leaving me less than a dollar in tips. The day sucks."

"I understand completely." Kimmie reflected on her time at Burger Joe's. "I've worked fast food, and I often felt the days couldn't go fast enough."

"Tell me about it, sister." The waitress actually smiled. "I'll be sure your order goes to the front of the stack. Shouldn't be too long."

"Thanks. We're patient," Kimmie said as the waitress headed for the kitchen.

She turned to find Rhett staring at her. "You're sweet, Kimmie."

"Never hurts to be nice to people."

"I wish you'd be a little nicer to me."

"Nicer? As in agreeing to sleep with you?"

He nodded. "That would be gratifying."

"Gratifying for you, but it would be giving up for me."

"How can you say that? We'd be great together."

"Great for life," she said flatly. "I'm going the distance, Rhett. Ring, church, vows. Keep up or the church bells might ring without you."

"Without me? You'd marry someone else?" His astonishment was almost comical.

"You're my first choice, but—"

"You said you'd never settle for second."

"Then I'd suggest you step up to the plate and state your intentions."

His jaw clenched, stubborn and strong. "I will when I'm ready."

She patted his forearm. "I know you will, Rhett. That's what I'm counting on."

What the hell had just happened? Rhett ran the conversation through his head a second time. Kimmie had a way with words. A way that would land him at the altar surrounded by flowers if he weren't careful.

She was one tricky woman. He refused to think about her with another man. He wanted to be her first lover. Being her last . . . was too far in the future to predict.

He was presently broke. He had his pride. Nickle-and-diming was no way to start a marriage. He'd walk away from Kimmie before he'd live off her money.

Presently, his team was in twelfth place. He was moving up in the standings. He planned to be in the top five by this evening, then running in first on the final stretch to Key West. The winner's circle was his goal. A goal he'd achieve with Kimmie and Sam Mason. He prayed Sam would stay sober.

"Food's up," the waitress said as she set their plates before them. "Told you it would be quick."

Rhett caught several dirty glances from customers who had arrived ahead of them, but had yet to be served.

He knew the reason behind the fast service. The waitress and Kimmie had bonded over fast food. He wondered when Kimmie had waited tables, and if she still slung hash.

"Looks like a lot of food," Sam Mason said of the kiddie plate when he once again joined them.

A lot of food? Rhett counted three fish sticks on the man's plate.

"You can do this, Sam," Kimmie encouraged.

To Rhett's surprise, she reached across the table, picked

up one of the grouper fingers and dipped it in tartar sauce. "Big bite, big guy."

Kimmie feeding Sam? A twinge of jealousy tightened Rhett's gut. He hated the fact her attention had shifted from him to their mechanic. Even from his side angle, the peach-colored blouse beneath her V-neck jumper revealed a lot of cleavage. If Sam so much as lowered his gaze a fraction . . .

To his credit, Sam kept his eyes on Kimmie's face. His trusting, almost appreciative expression changed to a small smile before he took his first bite, then a second.

Afterward, Kimmie took a moment to taste her lobster salad. "Delicious." She lightly touched Rhett's forearm. "You chose the best meal."

Rhett felt momentarily warmed by her pleasure. He liked the way she stroked his arm, the light press of her palm, the play of her fingers along his silky shirt. Kimmie the Virgin. The way she looked at him, as if he were the only man on Earth, both tempted and tormented and left him as hard as Adam when he first took Eve.

With one eye on Sam, Rhett snapped a crab leg with his bare hands. He then removed the crabmeat with his seafood fork and sampled it. It was the best he'd ever tasted. But Rhett would have enjoyed his lunch a whole lot more if Kimmie wasn't feeding Sam.

"Last grouper finger." Rhett watched Kimmie smile at their mechanic.

Sam placed his hand on his stomach. "Honestly, I can't—"

"I'm certain you can," she persisted. "You need to grow up big and strong—"

"For heaven's sake, Kimmie, the man's fifty-two," Rhett

said, his voice tight. "Stop treating him like a toddler. If Sam's hungry, he'll eat. There's no need to force-feed him."

Kimmie looked stricken.

Sam appeared shocked.

Rhett felt an absolute ass. He hadn't meant to sound so bitter, so biting, so damn jealous.

Beside him, Kimmie bit down on her bottom lip. "I'm sorry, Sam."

Sam picked up a French fry. "I promise to clean my plate," he said with a wry smile.

The man was finally eating on his own, Rhett noticed, feeling inordinately relieved. Kimmie was considerate and kind. Such qualities shouldn't drive him crazy. But they did. He wanted her feeding him, not Sam Mason. He wanted her fingertips to brush his mouth, lightly, playfully, teasing him to taste both food and woman. Just one bite . . .

As if reading his mind, Kimmie leaned into him. Her left breast pressed his arm, voluptuous and firm. Her scent was baby-powder soft: fresh and warm and a royal turn-on. "You need to eat, Rhett. We only have twenty minutes to race time."

The woman could crack a crab leg. One squeeze of the seafood cracker, and she stripped the crabmeat with her thumb and forefinger. She then dipped it in warm, melted butter and brought it to his mouth. "Can't let my man starve," she said, as if she had every right to call him *her man*.

In the midst of the crowded restaurant, she traced the seam of his mouth with the tip of her little finger, so sinfully slow, all thought of food evaporated at her touch.

She parted his lips just wide enough to slip the crabmeat inside.

Rhett sucked the butter from her finger, then groaned, low in his throat. His pleasure drew interested and curious stares from his fellow diners. He consumed the crab quickly. A man seated alone at the neighboring booth undressed Kimmie with his eyes, then shot Rhett a knowing look. A man-to-man exchange that branded Rhett one lucky bastard.

Rhett, however, didn't feel that lucky. While the man believed he and Kimmie were lovers, her iron-maiden mind-set kept them holding hands and nothing more. He wanted to feel her soft hands all over his body. He had three days remaining in the rally to convince her to make love with him. If he couldn't . . . Defeat was too depressing to dwell on.

"All finished," Kimmie said as she took her last bite of lobster salad, then blotted her mouth with a paper napkin.

At least she appeared satisfied, Rhett noted as he arranged the remaining crab legs in a chorus line on his plate, just like the Rockettes.

He glanced at his watch. They had ten minutes before the rally resumed. He geared up for the race. "Where are we headed, Sam?"

"Fisherman's Hook, one hundred miles straight down the coastline," Sam informed him. "Checkpoint is City Father's Cemetery. The brainteaser is 'Dead skunk in the middle of the road.' "

Rhett nudged Kimmie. "Let's roll."

She sighed. "Time to button my lip."

He hated to enforce her silence; he liked the sound of her voice, all sweet and sexy. At times, she sounded breathless, as if he stole the air from her lungs. Thank God she'd run out of Blow Pops. All her licking and smacking had left him hard and distracted. He needed his mind on the race and not on Kimmie Thorn. At least for the next few hours.

When she slid across the booth, rubbing against him, he took a heartbeat to enjoy her heat. He held his breath when Kimmie slipped him money to cover the bill, then released it when she tipped the waitress ten bucks.

The woman was generous. Perhaps she'd spread a little generosity on him once the sun set. If not today, then maybe tomorrow. It would be Wednesday. Hump Day.

Chapter Eleven

"We're driving in circles, TZ." Cade pulled to a stop at a traffic light, drumming his fingers on the steering wheel. "We've passed the methodist church once and the Shell gas station twice. Problems reading the map?"

Definite problems. The race had run so smoothly from Pelican Point to Fisherman's Hook, she'd actually relaxed and enjoyed the ride. Enjoyed it until they had reached the outskirts of town, and the city streets became a maze of alleys and dead ends. They had circled the town square like a merry-go-round. As of yet, there had been no sign of City Father's Cemetery. Not even a hint.

TZ was lost.

The map rustled as she peeked around northern Florida. She caught Cade's frown, the bunching of his shoulders, the flex of his tattoo. The long red light gave him time to remove a pack of Doublemint from his shirt pocket, take a stick, then pull two more for her chewing pleasure.

He looked at her over the rims of his Ray-Bans. "A stick for you, and one for Barney."

TZ dropped the map and snagged the gum. Cade's reference to her dinosaur sunglasses made her smile. The dark purple frames were rectangular with violet lenses. Barney's head rose to her right temple, and his tail dipped low, curving near her left ear. "We thank you."

The traffic light soon turned green. The driver in the silver Mercedes directly behind them hit the horn. To TZ's chagrin, the Mustang honked in return. A long honk, as if the car were annoyed. "Easy, Elise," TZ whispered, remembering how much her aunt hated people who honked their horns the moment the light changed.

"Which way?" Cade pressed.

TZ quickly scanned the instructions: Ring around the rosy, pocket full of posies. Flower Power was her only clue. "A little help, Elise," she said softly. When no response was forthcoming, TZ took a wild guess, "Go straight."

"How far?" Cade asked as he shifted into second, eased the car down Hibiscus Boulevard.

"A mile or two." Maybe three. "Until we hit another flower street. With any luck, it's just ahead."

Just ahead turned into thirteen blocks of twists and turns. There wasn't a straight street in Fisherman's Hook. She heard the chug of an engine and looked in the side mirror. Mick Wilcox in his Bug-eyed Sprite tailgated the 'Stang. The Sprite huffed and puffed and emitted exhaust.

"Sprite needs a new emissions system," TZ noted.

"No helping hands," Cade reminded her. "Do you hear me?"

She cupped her hand behind her ear. "Say what?"

"Real cute, sweet cheeks." A block farther, and Cade downshifted, making a sharp turn. "Flower Power. Gardenia Lane."

Gardenia then led into Red Rose Court. They passed several weathered houses with unkempt lawns. "There's an empty lot." TZ pointed to a small plot of grass and weeds, overgrown and littered. A short, white fence in need of paint ran the length of the sidewalk.

Cade parked near the curb, then peered around TZ. "City Father's Cemetery?"

TZ rose on her knees and leaned out the car window for a better look. She felt Cade's wide hand clutch her hip, securing her lower half inside the car. His palm was hard, his fingers long. The curve of his fingertips pressed her abdomen, strong against the softness of her belly. When she shifted ever so slightly, his fingers did also, curving into the crease of her inner thigh . . .

She sucked in a breath, scooted back into the car. "There are small tombstones, wooden crosses and a statue at the back of the lot," she said. "Big and bronzed and covered with ivy."

Cade slid his hand from her hip. "Let's check it out," he said as he withdrew the time card from beneath the visor, then exited the vehicle.

TZ tore from the car. She beat him to the fence. When she pulled open the gate, the hinge squeaked, then broke off the fence post.

Cade read the plaque, then set the gate aside. "*In memory of Martin Hook*. The city has let a lot of grass grow under the feet of its founding father."

She surveyed the lot. "The grass needs to be mowed. Wonder where we could rent a Toro and a weed whacker."

Cade stared at her as if she'd lost her mind. "We're rallying, not maintaining lawns."

She planted her hands on her hips. "Twenty minutes and—"

"I'm not pushing a mower." He put his foot down. Then, taking her by the hand, he pulled her along the stone path.

Tall grass brushed TZ's calves as she stepped over beer bottles and fast food wrappers and followed Cade to the statue. Mold and cobwebs covered many of the tombstones; the crosses were splintered and tilted at odd angles. TZ's heart grew heavy. There was something sad, almost mournful, about the condition of the cemetery. No one should be forgotten in death.

Rally committee member Paul Royer appeared from behind the bronze statue. "This is one scary checkpoint. This place gives me the creeps."

TZ stood quietly, looked around. "It wouldn't be so creepy if someone cleaned up the graveyard, put fresh flowers on the graves."

Cade shifted his stance. "Perhaps there are no surviving relatives."

She kicked a pebble, watching it roll down the path. "Cemeteries need flowers. We should buy some, Cade."

He blinked. "Flowers for people we don't even know?"

"For the founders of a town, long forgotten."

"City maintenance will remember them someday."

"Someday is today," she persisted.

"We're in the middle of a rally," he reminded her. "We're racing against time."

TZ swept one arm wide. "Time has stopped for these people."

Cade jammed his hands in the pockets of his jeans. "The nearest florist has to be miles off the rally route."

Paul Royer cleared his throat. "Actually, there's a roadside flower stand three miles ahead at the four-way stop. The vendor approaches those vehicles that have stopped and offers bouquets of flowers for five bucks."

TZ glanced toward the Mustang, which continued to run even after Cade had cut the engine. "Please, Cade. We'll make up the time later today."

He released a breath, relented. "Sentimental woman."

Seventeen minutes later, the graveyard was ablaze with color. Cade had bought out the roadside vendor. Before they left the cemetery, TZ had spread gerbera daisies, sunflowers, red roses, purple irises and pink and white carnations at each tombstone and cross.

"You've made the heavens smile," Paul Royer told TZ as she collected the decorative bows once wrapped around the flowers.

"It makes me smile, too," TZ said, light-hearted.

"Let's hit the road," Cade called from the end of the stone walk.

TZ waved to Royer, then turned toward Cade. She didn't stop until they were face-to-face, the tips of her tennis shoes touching the toes of his Nikes. Rising on tiptoe, she kissed him on the cheek. "Thank you, rally man."

He looked down at her, his gaze unreadable. Then, taking her by the hand, he led her toward the 'Stang. "Dead Skunk, TZ. Don't ask me to cart around a carcass."

Two hours later, TZ wished they'd see a dead skunk in the road. There were no animals anywhere. A forest fire had swept the land, blackening the earth. They weaved

196

around charred trees and underbrush, so deep in the boonies, power lines no longer edged the road.

The Mustang's wild shimmy had her sitting on the edge of her seat. Sex vibrated between her and Cade, hot and restless. A slide into the backseat with the rally man would take the edge off. Or make her twice as edgy.

Just when she thought they were the last people on the planet, TZ caught sight of the high tail fins on Marisa Ashton-Lord's pink Caddie, along with the long, sleek hood of Rhett Evans's Jaguar. The cars were parked outside a windowless cement building. Graffiti scored the outside, along with lewd drawings that would make the author of the *Kama Sutra* blush. Four Harleys were parked at the corner of the building: three Fat Boys and one Softail, all custom built with lots of iron and chrome and big horsepower.

TZ pointed to a sign that hung by a single hinge over the door. It was riddled with bullet holes. "Roadkill Tavern. We've arrived."

Cade pulled the Mustang next to Evans's XKE. The 'Stang, however, continued to roll forward even with the emergency brake set. It came to a stop within inches of the Harleys. The car's front bumper was so close to the leather saddlebags on the Softail, it appeared to be sniffing out a scent.

Cade turned to TZ. "Does Elise recognize the Hog?"

TZ fell quiet. No . . . it couldn't be. "No one I know."

Just behind them, Risa climbed out of her Caddie and came to stand beside the Mustang. She looked pale and frustrated. "This can't be the checkpoint," she complained. "It's dirty and disgusting, and the rally committee wouldn't subject us to such danger."

TZ rolled down her window. "The checkpoint seems a little obvious."

"Way too obvious," Cade agreed. "Unless Walter Brown wanted us to find it." He looked from Risa back to Rhett, asked, "Anyone seen the man?"

"No one's gotten out of his car," Rhett called from the Jag.

A chug and a sputter, and Mick Wilcox's Bug-eyed Sprite joined the others. He pulled up beside the 'Stang, so close in fact, he nearly knocked over the motorcycles.

TZ swallowed hard. Bikers didn't take kindly to their Hogs falling like dominos.

Hopping from the Sprite, Mick hiked up his pants and approached them. "My kind of bar."

"Guess we'd better check it out," Cade said as he removed his sunglasses and set them on the dashboard. Then snagging the time card from beneath the visor, he opened the car door and climbed out.

"*We?*" Rhett shifted on his seat, uneasy.

Cade folded, then pocketed the card. "Anyone wanting his time card punched."

TZ tossed her Barney shades next to Cade's Ray-Bans and left the Mustang. "I'm ready."

"There's safety in numbers," Kimmie said as she crawled over Sam Mason and slid from the Jaguar. Her departure forced Rhett out of the car.

Dressed in a soft pink jumper and pale peach blouse, Kimmie looked as fresh and innocent as dawn. Rhett looked pure GQ in an indigo button-up shirt and sharply creased khakis. They would stand out like pearls among bike chains in the sleazy bar.

TZ took one baby step toward the bar, and Cade took

one giant step to block her. "Roadkill's a biker bar. Let Mick and me go in and check it out first."

TZ heard Rhett's sigh of relief. She glanced toward the Cadillac, noticing Risa's entourage hadn't left the vehicle. But then neither had Sam Mason or Skinner joined the group.

Mick stuck his thumb toward Skinner and scoffed, "Pure chickenshit. The man's afraid of his shadow."

"He's not afraid, just cautious," Rhett said in defense of Mick's mechanic. "Which we all need to be."

Cade squeezed TZ's shoulder. "Stay put, sweet cheeks. I'll be back shortly."

"I'll be back after a beer," Mick said.

TZ watched as Cade and Mick entered Roadkill. She scuffed the toe of her tennis shoe in the dirt, counted to thirty. A sense of foreboding pushed her to guard his back. "I'm going in."

"Me too," Kimmie agreed.

"Me three," Risa surprised them all by saying.

"Ah, hell, me four," Rhett grumbled as he reached for Kimmie's hand.

The bar was dark and smelled of beer, leather and sweat. Peanut shells littered the floor along with cigarette butts. Two bikers stood at the bar while two others played pool.

Once TZ's eyes fully adjusted to the bad lighting, she found all four bikers staring directly at her. Indecent grins broke out on their harsh faces, and interest shone in their eyes. TZ shuddered. The men spelled trouble with a capital *T*.

She sought out Cade, located both him and Mick Wilcox near a broken-down foozball table, talking to Walter

199

Brown. Bruce Springsteen's "Born in the USA" played on the battered jukebox.

"This is one hell of a checkpoint," she heard Cade growl.

"The bar was uninhabited when I first set up this leg of the rally." Brown glanced toward the bikers, lost all color. "The place isn't safe; we should leave."

"Leave? I don't think so," growled a burly man at the corner of the bar. Dressed in black leather, bald, with a Fu Manchu mustache, he looked dark and dangerous.

Fu Manchu nodded toward the other bikers. A second man in a brown leather vest, his torso marked with tattoos, shoved off the wall, moving toward the rallyers. Mick and Walter Brown stepped back, but Cade held his ground.

"Stay and play." His gaze settled on TZ for a second too long before his pierced bottom lip curled in a sneer. "We'll pop a beer; break open a can of whupass."

Behind him, the two pool players slapped their cues against their palms, then joined the biker with the tattoos. One biker, with shaggy hair that hung to his shoulders, drew a line with the tip of his cue on the dirt floor just behind the heels of Cade's Nikes. "You've crossed the line, you're trespassing," he said.

Big men, with bigger attitudes. TZ stared at Cade, who'd gone perfectly still, then down the bar at Fu Manchu. The man with the mustache held her gaze as he pushed aside a barstool and walked toward the group. He swung a beer bottle by his side. Broken, it could be a deadly weapon. His eyes were light brown and lit with malice. TZ shivered.

The biker had Cade by two inches in height, but Cade

outweighed the man by ten pounds. Ten solid, powerful pounds.

Cade spoke directly to Fu Manchu. "Roadkill is a checkpoint for SunCoast Run. We have no plans to stay."

The biker sneered. "I say when you leave. And in how many pieces."

Cade's body coiled with tangible tension. His eyes had narrowed, and a muscle jerked along his jaw. He looked as mean as the bikers and ready to kick some ass. TZ knew he wouldn't back down, no matter the odds, which weren't in his favor.

"Four against one." Fu Manchu glanced from Cade to the other rally drivers, his look challenging.

Cade shrugged. "I've faced worse." *And won.* His look said *bring it on.*

TZ stepped forward, as close to the biker as she dared. Her heart beat so fast, her chest hurt. She worked to keep her voice steady. "Back off. You're pushing too hard."

"Pushing too hard?" Fu Manchu laughed in her face. "I'm about to knock your friend into next week."

Cade glanced at TZ for the first time since her arrival. His gaze was hard, his midnight blue eyes nearly black. "Go back to the car, TZ," he ordered.

"Stay right where you are, *Tease*," the biker said sharply. "I want you to witness how easily bones break."

"Witness two against four," Mick Wilcox said as he moved to Cade's side. TZ noticed Mick's hands shook ever so slightly.

"What about pretty boy?" The biker jabbed the beer bottle toward Rhett Evans.

"Ah, hell." TZ caught Rhett's low groan as Kimmie nudged him forward. He quickly removed his Rolex and gold signet ring and handed them to Kimmie. "Pawn the Rolex if I go into a coma."

"The old man?" Fu Manchu asked.

TZ turned, found Walter Brown wedged between the jukebox and the wall. The dome of his head was barely visible.

"No fight there," she muttered to herself.

The biker glanced at Kimmie and Risa. "Any fight in Blondie or Stick Woman?"

Mick grabbed Risa by the arm and pushed her toward the door. "No reason for him to snap you like a twig."

Risa rushed for the door.

Kimmie ran her hand along the back of a chair. "Touch one gelled hair on Rhett's head, and I'll smash yours like a pumpkin."

"You've got balls, sweetheart," the biker said, grunting.

"I'm even ballsier." On impulse, TZ inched closer. She stood so near Fu Manchu, her sneakers bumped his motorcycle boots. She lifted her knee. "Care to wear yours as earrings?"

Fu Manchu's gaze darkened. A low hiss escaped his lips. Silence sucked all the air from the room.

"TZ, careful," Cade ground out as he tried to push her out of harm's way.

She shook him off. If she didn't act quickly, someone would get hurt. She knew Cade had to keep his eyes on the bikers. He couldn't afford to miss their move. Taking that into account, she took a quick, steadying breath and motioned to Fu Manchu. "You and me. Let's go, big guy."

The biker shifted his gaze from Cade to her. With a low growl, he broke the beer bottle on the bar. Shards of glass splintered the air. "Bring it on, baby. It's your blood."

"TZ, what the hell? *No!*" Cade shoved her aside, none too gently.

Once she regained her balance, TZ's life hit fast-forward. She launched herself at Fu Manchu. Blindsided, the biker swore and dropped the broken beer bottle as she thumped him in the chest, then grabbed his bald head and bit his right ear. He threw back his head and howled like a wounded animal.

"Damn, woman, you pierced my ear!"

She kicked and squirmed and struggled for breath. Instead of batting her away, the biker wrapped his arms around her until her back cracked, along with her neck. She hung like Raggedy Ann.

As quickly as their fight had started, it came to an end. "Had enough?" the biker growled in her face.

With an audible sigh, TZ relaxed in his arms and giggled. "You're such a bastard, Legend."

Legend? Cade Nyland was ready to deck the son of a bitch. He'd felt a wildness in his blood to protect TZ Blake. His fists clenched, he'd taken his first step when the biker with the shaggy hair had jabbed the tip of his pool cue in Cade's chest and said, "It's ritual."

Ritual, his ass. Jerking the cue from the man, he'd broken it in two. He was ready to rewrite the biker's legend when he'd heard TZ's giggle. A soft, girly giggle that stopped him in his tracks.

What was happening? "TZ?"

"I'm fine, rally man, honest," she said when Legend finally released her. She then proceeded to hug the remaining three men with an exuberance that evidenced strong friendships.

When the bear hugs ended, she turned back to Cade.

"I'm sorry if the guys got on your last nerve. They're not usually such buttheads."

Her eyes dancing, TZ began the introductions. She started with Fu Manchu. "Cade Nyland, meet Legend. He, no doubt, owns this hellhole."

TZ Blake ran with a diverse crowd. A crowd Cade would associate more with himself than with her. He'd nearly fought a man she called friend. He thought of the ritual. She had a strange way of introducing people. When Legend extended his hand, Cade shook it.

"Next"— she pointed to the shaggy-haired biker whose pool cue Cade had broken in two—"meet Hellion."

Hellion nodded, but didn't offer his hand. "You owe me a stick, man."

"I'll buy you two," TZ said soothingly. She then took the hand of the biker marked with tattoos. "This is Rattler."

And Cade understood his name. A tattoo of a diamondback curved across his chest and dipped beneath the waistband of his jeans. The snake's rattles were partially visible just above the silver snap.

"Lastly, meet Bayou." TZ nodded toward the youngest biker, who'd been playing pool. The man had the coldest eyes Cade had ever seen. He'd seen eyes that could ice a man with one stare. Bayou could do it with a glance.

"Bayou is Legend's cousin from Louisiana," TZ continued. "He's also a pool shark. Never play him for money."

Cade turned to Legend. "No pool, but I could use a beer."

"On the house," Legend said as he wandered behind the bar, dug into an icy cooler and tossed Cade a Coors.

With Springsteen's "Thunder Road" vibrating through

the bar, Cade chose a table that had all four legs, then dropped down on a chair. He was close enough to the pool table to keep an eye on TZ. The woman needed a keeper.

"You rack 'em, I'll crack 'em," he heard TZ say.

Once Bayou racked the balls, Cade watched TZ shift left, then right, her jeans pulling tightly over her perfect rear, as she readied for the break.

Her shot hit true. She knocked in the three and six on the break. "Solids," she called, then went on to sink the two, only to miss the five by a fraction.

"Lotta green." Bayou's brow furrowed as he calculated the length of the table for error. He set up his shot and ran the next five stripes. The man could play pool.

"Mind if I sit?" Legend asked, but didn't wait for a reply as he pulled out a chair at Cade's table and straddled it. He popped the tab on his Coors and guzzled the entire can.

"Your dive?" Cade asked.

"I purchased some acreage recently, and Roadkill sits in the center."

"No traffic flow."

"I'm not interested in customers, just land. The property borders two state roads and a main highway. Next year at this time, I plan to have a second Harley-Davidson dealership up and running."

Cade rolled his beer between his palms. "You actually work?"

"Work and ride. Nothing confining. I'm not a nine-to-five, suit-and-tie kind of guy."

Cade smiled to himself. He understood. Truth be told, he and Legend had a lot in common. They didn't belong in a boardroom. When the road called, they answered.

Legend nodded toward the bikers. "The men all work for me. Rattler's my top salesman, Hellion the best motorcycle mechanic in Florida and Bayou's my CPA."

The IRS would never mess with the cold-eyed Cajun.

Cade looked around the bar filled with rallyers. "Sorry we've trespassed on your property," he said.

Legend crushed his beer can in his left hand. "I knew you were coming today," he confessed. "Call us the welcoming committee."

Cade cut him a sideways glance. "Now that you've made us feel all warm and fuzzy?"

Legend rested his elbows on the table. "Watch your back, Nyland. I received an anonymous tip that rallyers would be stopping here today. A bank bag filled with fifties was left on the bar with a request to make the checkpoint *difficult* for you. We came today to see who might show up, not to fight. It's my property, and I don't need a lawsuit." He traced his mustache with his thumb and forefinger. "TZ Blake was the last person I expected to walk into Roadkill. One look, and our ritual began. We got in each other's face, and, unfortunately, yours, since you played hero."

"Your ritual was damned believable."

The biker grinned. "The first time her mother witnessed us butting heads, she called the cops. A policeman pointing a gun at my heart didn't appreciate the explanation that we were just letting off steam."

Cade cocked a brow. "Do you see TZ often?"

"Not often enough. I stop by the garage three, maybe four times a year. Her mother won't let me within ten blocks of their home, so that rules out Thanksgiving and Christmas."

"And birthdays. TZ turns thirty tomorrow."

"She still looks eighteen."

"I took her for a college kid the first time I saw her," Cade admitted.

"She's wild and crazy, but fiercely loyal." Legend studied Cade closely. "She would have protected you if the threat was real."

"Protection is my job."

"Even at four against one?"

"I never calculate odds, only concussions." Cade settled lower on his spine, crossed his arms over his chest and asked, "What are your plans for the money in that bag? More leather?"

Legend pulled at the sleeve on his black leather jacket. "I'm giving the money to TZ."

Cade lifted a brow. "TZ? Why her?"

"It will help pay off her debt on the garage."

"She owes money on All Tune and Lube?"

"Last time I saw her she was close to foreclosure."

"Her debt?" Cade asked.

"No, her aunt's. TZ inherited the garage along with its red ink. She works too damn hard to lose what she loves."

"Generous gesture." Cade hadn't known about her financial situation. Now, more than ever, he had reason to win the rally, for TZ, as well as for himself.

Legend scratched his chest. "How long have you known TZ?"

"Three days," Cade replied.

"And she's already driving you crazy?"

"She could be more focused."

Legend nodded toward the pool table. "She's focused now."

Cade caught a glimpse of TZ over Legend's shoulder. "Pure slop," he heard her say disgustedly, and knew she'd sunk a ball other than the one she'd called. He hoped she wasn't about to lose the shirt off her back. Or worse, her panties.

As if reading his mind, Legend smiled. "She's the only one ever to come close to beating my cousin at pool. He'd never take her money. He only wants her heart."

Cade's eyes narrowed. "Bayou and TZ?"

"Relax, man." Legend chuckled low in his throat. "All of us have hit on her, and she's put us in our place."

Cade sipped his beer. "How did you meet her?"

"The front tire on my Softail went flat just outside Gulf Cove. My cell phone was dead, and I sat on my bike on the side of the road for two hours in the hot sun, waiting for a ride. No one stopped."

"You're no white-haired grandma."

"Hell, neither are you," Legend pointed out before returning to his story. "TZ wasn't afraid of me. She coasted to a stop, and we pulled the tire. She drove me to her garage in a Mustang that vibrated like a sex toy."

"Helping hands," Cade mumbled to himself.

"That's where I made a pass at her and"—Legend laid his hand flat on the table and pointed to a scar near his wrist—"she stuck me with a screwdriver. A damn Phillips head."

Cade winced. "That must have hurt."

Legend rubbed his scar. "Hurt my hand and my ego. I haven't touched her since."

Touching TZ Blake could be a mistake, yet one worth

risking. The woman could play chicken only so long before she was cornered and caught. And taken.

Behind Legend, Cade caught Bayou's scowl, heard his complaint. "Crooked cue, and the felt's in strips."

"Takin' it home," TZ said as she lined up her last shot. Keeping her eye on the eight ball, she tapped the rim around the intended pocket to call the shot. She then sank the ball with a shit-eating grin.

Cade couldn't help smiling.

"What's she to you?" Legend's question turned personal.

Cade answered with the honesty of the moment. "My mechanic for the SunCoast Run."

From the corner of his eye, Cade watched TZ push off the pool table and approach him with a Pepsi in one hand and a fifty-dollar bill in the other. Even with two extra chairs at the table, she dropped onto his lap. She waved the bill under his nose. "I finally beat Bayou at eight ball."

Cade shifted on the chair. If he wasn't careful, TZ would soon realize how happy he was to see her. He rested his hand on her hip, her very sexy hip.

He heard the scrape of Legend's chair as the biker rose. A flash of envy darkened the biker's gaze before he slapped Cade on the back, then shook his head. "Yeah, man, definitely just your mechanic."

"What was that all about?" TZ asked.

"Merely shooting the breeze."

TZ looked him in the eye. "You look at home here."

"I've knocked back beer in bars that make Roadkill look like ladies' night out."

"You would have fought Legend?"

He nodded. "All four men if necessary. I'm not one to back down, sweet cheeks. No one walks my spine."

She bit down on her bottom lip. "I'm sorry I let the ritual get out of hand."

"You stopped it in time. No one got hurt."

"Walter Brown lay down like a doormat." She craned her neck, looking around the room. "Where is he anyway?"

"Last time I looked, he was still hiding behind the jukebox."

TZ glanced over Cade's shoulder. "Brown's still there, but I don't see the time clock. We need to have our time card punched."

"The clock's probably in his Rolls."

TZ sipped her Pepsi. Springsteen's "Hungry Heart" blared on the jukebox. She hummed along. "Ever had a hungry heart, rally man?"

"I've known sexual hunger." He craved TZ Blake, that was for sure.

"I thought Legend was hot until he got handsy."

"He showed me his scar."

TZ blushed. "Friends should look, but not touch."

"They touch when you tease."

"I don't tease."

Oh yes, she did. "You tease like a stripper."

She licked her lips, and her gaze darkened to an impulsive blue. "Want me to strip for you?"

He ran his hand over her hip, squeezed, felt bone and softness. "Slow burn, sweet cheeks. When the time comes, I'll do the stripping. Shirt, jeans, bra and panties."

Chapter Twelve

In the darkest corner of the bar, Rhett nudged his chair closer to Kimmie's. The chair wobbled, uneven, the wood slightly split. He reached for her hands, held them lightly, gently rubbing his thumbs over the back of each.

He needed to apologize for being afraid. He hadn't wanted to enter Roadkill, had preferred to wait in the car. Yet Kimmie had persisted in following TZ into the tavern, which forced Rhett into action. Roadkill was as dark and vile as Hell. The bikers resembled Satan's kin. Especially Legend.

When the bikers had approached Cade Nyland, Cade hadn't flexed a muscle. He'd looked angry enough to chew them up and spit them out, leather and all. Nyland had guts. Rhett admired his bravery.

Rhett, however, hadn't wanted to fight. If Kimmie hadn't nudged him forward, he would have walked out the door and left the fighting to Cade and Mick. Wilcox had surprised everyone. The man with the beer gut and bad manners had stood by Cade, looking nervous but determined.

Rhett hated the fact Kimmie had seen him cluck like a chicken. Strangely enough, he'd wanted her to see him as someone strong and capable of taking care of not only himself, but her as well.

He cleared his throat. "I didn't handle myself well today, Kimmie. I should have been more like Cade, stood up to the bikers with arrogance and attitude. Instead, the only words leaving my mouth were *pu-uck, puck, pu-uck.* I'm damn sorry."

Silence followed his confession. He felt guilty as sin and half a man. With a sigh, Kimmie laced her fingers through his and drew his hands to her lips. Ever so slowly, she kissed his knuckles, one by one. Her gaze met his, soft and bright with emotion.

"You are the bravest man I know," she told him. "You may have felt out of your element and uncertain, but you did what you had to do. You had Cade's back. The way I see it, if Cade had gone down for the count, you would have been the last man standing. You're a hero, Rhett Evans."

A *hero?* The woman wore rose-colored glasses. Her praise, however, massaged the tightness from his chest. He could breathe again. Kimmie accepted his weakness and gave him strength. No other woman had ever built him up when he'd felt so low. He was suddenly pleased he'd brought her with him on the rally. Damn pleased, in fact.

"You deserve a reward," she whispered near his ear.

Sex? He suddenly felt like Superman.

"A kiss for your bravery."

A kiss? Their first kiss? Here, in this hellhole?

Rhett tilted his head. "You want to kiss me now?"

Her reply was a soft smile and a softer brush of her lips against his. It was so brief, Rhett wasn't sure their mouths had even touched.

"H-hmm." Kimmie sighed. "Very nice."

Nice? He wanted naughty. "Where do we go from here, Kimmie?"

"To the hotel and a fabulous Sports Night."

"You're avoiding the issue."

"The issue of my virginity?" She sighed. "Old subject."

The subject wasn't old to him. It was new and hot and inviting. "What shall we play tonight?" he ventured. Sex was a contact sport.

"I love tennis."

He'd love to see her in a tennis outfit. "I'll reserve a court as soon as we reach the hotel."

"Doesn't Athletic Paradise have theme suites?"

Rhett nodded. "Each room is decorated for a certain sport, all the way down to the beds."

Kimmie giggled, her eyes bright. "King-size beds designed as footballs, catcher's mitts, tennis shoes . . . jock straps."

Jock straps, real romantic. "Will you stay with me tonight?" He held up his hand, silenced her, before she turned him down. "No sex, just talking and cuddling. A reward for my bravery."

"I thought to reward you with a naughty story."

Naughty stories were good, but not as satisfying as her body next to his through the long night ahead. "A story? Now? At Roadkill?"

She leaned toward him. "No one's watching us. No one will overhear."

Rhett glanced about the room. The majority of the ral-

213

lyers crowded the pool table and bar. He and Kimmie sat on the edge of darkness. If she wanted to talk dirty, he'd listen. "How about a sports story?" he suggested.

She lowered her voice, her lips near his ear. He heard her breathing, felt the warmth of her breath. "I can do sports," she said, then proceeded to tell him a story about how Wanda the Wood Nymph taught Peter the Golfer to sink a hole-in-one. When Peter became as stiff as his putter, Rhett's own hard-on threatened the seam of his pants. His eyes had glazed, the bar no more than a blur of movement.

"Hey, Evans." Mick Wilcox snapped his fingers before Rhett's eyes. "Mind if we borrow a chair?"

Rhett looked at Wilcox, staring overly long. He had been immersed in Kimmie's story, so much so, the reality of Roadkill had faded. Absently, he nodded. "Sure, help yourself."

Beside him, Kimmie giggled. "Caught in the story?"

Better than being caught with his pants down. He looked at Kimmie, at her lush mouth. Sexy lips, sexy body, naughty storyteller. She was an erotic blend of sin and innocence. Rhett wanted her with a sexual ache that would surely kill him.

He released his breath. "It's almost time to resume the rally. Let's locate Sam Mason and head for the Jag."

"Athletic Paradise is a thirty-minute drive south," Kimmie informed him. "I can't wait to hit the courts."

Tennis. Even if he won a set, victory would not be his. He couldn't claim Kimmie with a raquet.

Two tables over, Mick Wilcox sat on the edge of his chair, ready to split should Marisa Ashton-Lord piss him off. The woman had approached him near the bar, cleared her throat like a queen and requested a private moment of his time. His curiosity had nudged him to the one empty table by the far wall.

He'd borrowed a chair from Rhett Evans's table. If he hadn't known better, he would have thought Evans was stoned. Rhett had the dilated, glassy-eyed expression of someone on drugs or a man ready to climax. Who knew what Kimmie Thorn had whispered in Rhett's ear? Hell, Mick would listen to her recite the alphabet.

"What do you want?" Mick asked Risa the moment she joined him.

Ignoring him, Risa bent slightly and brushed her hand across the seat of the second chair. Dust collected on her palm. She looked down her nose at him. "It's filthy in here."

"Maid's day off," Mick said, grunting. "There's plenty of fresh air outside. Feel free to hit the door at any time."

"I'll be on my way in a minute."

"One, two, three, four—"

"Stop counting," she said.

"Then start talking. Get to the point."

Her lips moved, but no words were voiced. She appeared to have trouble breathing. "Th-thank you for—for—"

For what? Mick couldn't imagine what he'd done to deserve her gratitude. Gratitude she had trouble expressing.

"For pushing me out of harm's way when those disgusting bikers were itching for a fight."

Mick understood. In a moment of weakness, he'd told Risa to run for the door so the bikers wouldn't snap her like a twig. In that moment, he'd wanted to protect her if a fight had broken out. He still didn't understand the reasoning behind his idiocy. The woman hated his guts. In a saner moment, his hatred matched her own.

He puffed out his chest, bragged, "The bikers had nothing on me. I'm in great shape."

"You're built in circles, Marshmallow Man."

"Fortunately, nothing happened," he said, grunting. "No one's nose got broken. We walked away with all our teeth."

"Your nose is crooked."

"Your nose is scrunched like I've got b.o."

"You do."

"At least I smell natural," Mick pointed out. "You, on the other hand, cover up with perfume."

"Distasteful man!"

"Disagreeable bitch."

Risa was so angry her toothpick body shook. "No one calls me a bitch."

"Perhaps not to your face, but definitely behind your back."

She turned on her heel. "Good-bye, Mr. Wilcox."

"Never farewell, Ris." A devious thought formed. "I saved your life—you owe me big time."

Her back to him, she snapped over her shoulder, "How big time?"

He wanted to make her life miserable. "A twosome in my Jacuzzi following Sports Night. I also want you to play Eve to my Adam at the costume party tomorrow night."

He'd never seen a woman swoon in absolute panic. "I can't be seen with you," she said tightly.

"Think about it, Ris," he baited. "If another dangerous situation arises, you can fend for yourself."

"I hate you."

"I'll see you at ten. My room. My Jacuzzi."

"I'm thinking about killing myself first."

"Hell's more appealing than me?"

"Walking on hot coals would be a day in the park."

Cade and TZ were the last to leave Roadkill. Even after their time card had been punched, TZ held back, lingering with Legend and the other bikers. Cade waited for her in the Mustang, giving her privacy to accept the money Legend so generously offered. He was glad the biker had taken an interest in TZ's future.

Before the rally ended, Cade planned to discover who had left the anonymous tip with Legend, along with the cash to "welcome" the rallyers. It was pretty obvious the SunCoast Run was being sabotaged.

To the east, the sun had begun to set, red bled into orange, then into gold. The heat of the day shimmered into shadows, casting the lewd graffiti on the building into the darkness it deserved.

It was Elise who nudged TZ to continue the rally. A honk of the horn, a flash of emergency lights, and TZ tucked the bank bag under her arm. She then gave Legend a final hug that lasted longer than Cade liked.

She settled in the 'Stang with a smile and a sigh. Then, leaning over the seat, she stuffed the bank bag in her leather tote. "Sorry I took so long. Legend and I had—" she hesitated—"a transaction."

Cade didn't push her for an explanation. TZ would tell him about her garage debt when she was good and ready.

"No need to apologize. Walter Brown deducted one hour from our rally time for being the first to enter Roadkill. We're sitting pretty."

TZ picked up the map and instruction packet. "Backtrack to State Road Seventy-six, then head south. Athletic Paradise sits on a peninsula, a combination hotel, sports complex and golden door spa."

"Plans for the evening?" Cade asked.

TZ studied the hotel brochure. "In-line skating, perhaps a swim. The pool is shaped like a sailboat. The hull is the main pool. The narrow mast leads to the sails, which form the kiddie pool."

"I need to hit the weight room," Cade told her. "Then we can meet up at the pool. How's that sound?"

She folded the brochure. "Good to me."

The hotel sported more athletic memorabilia than a museum. All along the hallway leading to their room, autographed photographs from the legends of baseball to present-day heroes lined the walls, along with framed sets of their original uniforms.

She was pleased to see the baseball theme extended to her and Cade's suite. The moment TZ entered the door, she felt as if she'd walked into a stadium. People in tiered stands had been painted on every wall, waving pennants, their expressions ones of excitement as they cheered on their favorite team. TZ could almost smell the popcorn, nachos and hot dogs. Hear the vendors hawk soda and beer.

Across the floor, dark green carpeting displayed a baseball diamond. Home plate sat at the foot of the bed, shaped like a giant baseball: round, with white satin sheets and matching comforter.

Score, home run, ran through TZ's mind. She shivered, uncertain if the terms referred to baseball or the night ahead with Cade.

Behind her, Cade dropped their luggage on a players' bench taken from a dugout. "I'm going to change, then hit the gym."

He was in and out of the bathroom before TZ had decided what to wear in-line skating. Cade looked damned fine in a navy T-shirt and gray athletic shorts. His hair was pulled back in a leather tie. His features were chiseled and strong.

TZ had been around a lot of men in her life. None compared to Cade. He was built, powerful and solid, with an inner strength that gave him presence. No one could ignore the rally man. Especially women.

For a split second, she thought watching him lift weights might raise her heartbeat to the point that she could forgo skating. Her pulse rate was already high.

Bending slightly, Cade snagged his black swim trunks from his gym bag. TZ admired the way his muscles flexed, the easy grace of his movements. He was one well-oiled machine.

He turned suddenly, catching her checking him out. He cocked one brow. "You into me, sweet cheeks?"

Way into him. "I was looking at your nose." Along with your chest, abs and butt. "Wondering if it was still sore."

"My nose is on my face," he said with a knowing grin. "You were checking out my butt."

And the faint bulge beneath his athletic shorts. "Was not."

"My mistake." His grin widened. "Pool in an hour?"

"Make it ninety minutes," she returned.

He nodded and left through the doorway designed as a tunnel leading to a locker room. TZ stared at the door for several long minutes. Sensation sifted through her, sharp and intense, leaving a yearning that started in her heart and settled low in her belly. She wanted Cade Nyland. Admitting such a fact made her vulnerable. Vulnerability was a life hazard when one fell in love. Especially with a heartbreaker.

Fell in love . . . Her jaw dropped, and she couldn't catch her breath. If just the thought of making love with Cade had her hyperventilating, she'd surely pass out from lack of oxygen once engaged in the act.

Exercise, she needed to work Cade out of her system. She changed clothes, slipping into a pair of baggy red shorts and a large white T-shirt designed with a sequined American flag.

She grabbed a thick pair of athletic socks to wear with her Rollerblades, and her navy tank suit for the pool. Slipping on a pair of red Keds, she headed for Shoe Stop, a shop near the hotel lobby that rented everything from football cleats and bowling shoes to Rollerblades.

Color bloomed throughout the hotel grounds. Birds of paradise mixed with white orchids and pink hibiscus. She had just spotted Shoe Stop when she heard a child's sob over the hedge on a parallel sidewalk.

"Just one round of miniature golf, Mommy. Just one, please."

TZ stopped, listening for the mother's reply. "I can't play with a broken arm, sweetie. How about a movie instead?"

A child's long-suffering sigh rose on the air, followed by a dramatic sniffle. "But I really wanted to play golf."

TZ parted the bushes and peered around the bougainvillea vines. A small blond girl of six or seven stood with her arms wrapped around her mother's waist. Her mother, looking tired, patted her daughter on the head with her left hand, her left arm set in a plaster cast. "As soon as my arm's healed, I promise we'll play miniature golf every afternoon after school for a month."

"Calbourne Creek's Putt-Putt Golf isn't as nice as Champion Putter," the little girl said softly into her mother's skirt.

"How about if I watch you play, Lily?" the mother suggested.

"It's no fun to play alone," the daughter replied.

The mother looked heavenward, blew out a breath.

On impulse, TZ stepped through the hedge. She looked past the mother and daughter and out over the miniature golf course, which was well-lit with spotlights. Each of the eighteen holes promoted a specific sport. How long could it take to play a round of mini-golf? TZ wondered. An hour?

Standing with her hands on her hips, her back to the mother and her daughter, TZ spoke out loud. "Champion Putter looks like a lot of fun . . . wish I had a partner to go a round."

The blond girl spun around so fast, she made TZ dizzy. A bright smile broke across her face, and deep dimples flashed. "I'll play! Can I, Mom, please, please?"

The mother looked at TZ as if she'd been heaven-sent. "Do you mind?" she asked cautiously.

TZ shook her head, held out her hand. "TZ Blake."

The little girl grabbed TZ's hand and held on to it as if it were a lifeline. "Lily Baxter."

"I'm Mary Beth," the mother said. "While the two of you golf, I'm going to sit in the gazebo near the sixth hole. From there I've got a great view of the course."

Lily tugged TZ toward a booth near the entrance to Champion Putter. At the booth they each selected a colored putter and matching ball. TZ played with red, and Lily powder blue to match her sundress and jellies.

"How about a side bet?" Lily asked at the first hole.

The kid had a gambler's heart. "How much?"

"Not money, silly, for Popsicles. Cherry's my favorite."

"Mine, too," TZ agreed. "You want to go first?"

Lily giggled. "Age before beauty."

TZ grimaced. The next day, she turned thirty.

It didn't take long for TZ to discover the eighteen-hole course was created with lots of mounding and varying elevations. Rippling streams and waterfalls accented the landscape. Various robotic athletes, lifelike and mobile, were activated at each hole.

Putting like a pro, TZ knocked the golf ball between the front hooves of a galloping polo pony, around the front tennis shoe of a basketball player dribbling a basketball and finally directly into the net of a hockey goalie, who was skating side to side. Lily also played exceedingly well.

Not until she hit the fifteenth hole did TZ falter. Eleven tries, and she still hadn't hit the cup. The timer on the automated figure running track was set so fast, the man ran the three-yard dash in under two seconds. TZ was unable to sink the putt before the runner hit the finish line.

Lily's laughter echoed over the course. "Want me to take the shot for you, TZ?"

TZ glanced at Lily and chanted, "I think I can, I think I can." And with a push from the Little Engine That Could, she finally sank the putt.

Lily jumped up and down, jabbing her putter in the air. "You did it!"

TZ grinned. "I'm still in the hunt."

Lily held up their scorecard. "You're eight shots down."

"Ever heard of a comeback?"

"Difficult with three holes to go."

TZ came up beside Lily and tickled her in the ribs.

"No tickling, that's cheating." Lily was laughing so hard she could hardly speak.

TZ released her. "I'll do anything for a win."

In the end, TZ bought Popsicles for both Lily and her mother, and a lemon ice for herself. They sat in the gazebo, enjoying the coolness of their treats amid the heat of early evening.

When Lily had finished her Popsicle, she collected the putters and balls and took off to return them.

Seated beside TZ, Mary Beth rubbed the fingers of her left hand, which had begun to swell. "You need to return to your room and get your arm elevated," TZ said, concerned.

Mary Beth nodded. "I will shortly, as soon as Lily returns."

"She's a sweet little girl."

"Sweeter still, now that she's challenged Champion Putter and won. Thank you for playing the course with her. Being a single parent, and"—Mary Beth held up her cast—"athletically challenged, it's tough keeping up with her. We appreciate your kindness."

"It was fun," TZ admitted as she finished off her lemon ice. "Wish I could stay longer, but I've made plans to meet a friend at the pool."

Mary Beth smiled. "Enjoy him."

TZ blinked. "How did you know I was meeting a man?"

"Your tone of voice, the softness in your gaze."

TZ cringed. "I was that obvious?"

"I'm a psychiatrist," Mary Beth confessed. "I observe body language, emotion. My advice to you: have a good swim and an even better night in bed."

"How much do I owe you for this office visit?" TZ asked.

"My payment comes in people living life to the fullest."

TZ was about to enjoy Cade Nyland to the max. "Enjoy your stay at the hotel."

"We're here for two weeks. Lily believes in long vacations."

"I'm with Lily," TZ said. "Bye for now."

"Good-bye, TZ Blake."

TZ wandered back down the path from which she'd originally come. Shrieks and laughter guided her toward the Sail Pool. It was a beautiful pool designed with green ceramic tiles, water slides and low and high diving boards. TZ headed to a small cabana and changed into her tank suit. She then walked the perimeter of the adult pool, looking for Cade. There was no sign of the man.

"Marco?" She would recognize Cade's deep baritone anywhere.

"Polo!" came a chorus of excited squeals, followed by wild splashing.

The rally man was in the kiddie pool.

TZ quickened her steps to the shallow end. That was where she found Cade, surrounded by children. Eyes closed, he stood waist-deep in the water, tall and tanned, with hot-pink water wings wrapped about his wrists.

"Marco?" Cade called out a second time. He could feel the water ripple beside him, and knew those children closest to him were not responding. They didn't want to get caught. Chickens!

He took a step forward, made a wide sweep of his arms, heard someone dive beneath the water, just beyond his reach. Slippery little eels. So close . . .

"Polo." The voice was soft, a little breathy, the pitch, female. TZ Blake. If he guessed correctly, she was five or six feet to his left.

Faking a dive to the right, he flipped underwater, opened his eyes and headed for a long, slender pair of legs. He watched her hop up and down, trying to escape when she realized his direction and intention. She wasn't getting away from him.

He caught her near the kiddie slide. She was laughing so hard she couldn't pull herself out of the pool. Rising before her, Cade trapped her between the ceramic tiles and his body. Her hair was damp and curly, her smile wide. The silky, clinging wetness of her suit accentuated her full breasts and sweet, sweet ass.

He looked into her eyes. "You're it."

"Who's playing?" she asked.

Cade stepped back. "Everyone in the pool."

She tugged on his wrist. "Do I get to wear water wings?"

"The wings belong to Carley, the little red-haired girl sitting on the side of the pool with her father," he explained. "She made me promise to wear them when rough-housing with her brothers."

TZ looked toward Carley's brothers. "Those two adorable redheads with freckles?"

"Adorable?" he asked, skeptical. "They're stranglers. Don't let them grab you around the neck."

"I'm tougher than I look."

Cade slipped the water wings from his wrists and handed them to TZ. "I need a break. Go play, sweet cheeks."

He watched TZ play for more than an hour. Watched her laugh and shriek and be a kid. The children loved her. Especially the boys. They tagged in her wake, scoping her out as if they were sixteen instead of six.

Eventually, she came to sit beside him on the kiddie pool steps. She squeezed the water from her hair. "I'm out of breath," she said, panting.

Cade liked the sound of her breathing. Deep and winded and sexy as hell. It was the way a woman sounded when ready to climax. Cade wanted to hear her pant in his bed.

"Have you eaten?" he asked.

She shook her head. "I got involved in miniature golf—"

"I thought you were skating."

"Minor change in plans," she said. "I'm starving."

"Formal dining or fast food?"

"Whichever has the best desserts."

"Eat, then sleep. It's getting late. We've a big day ahead of us tomorrow."

Dinner consisted of a medium-rare cheeseburger and chocolate shake for Cade, and a slice of raspberry cheesecake followed by a veggie burger for TZ. They sat on beach loungers near the pool, listening to the night close in around them. TZ had grown quiet and a little nervous, gnawing her bottom lip when she thought he wasn't looking.

Cade hadn't taken his eyes off her. He liked her wrapped in a big fluffy beach towel, her hair drying in the night air, the faint scent of chlorine clinging to her skin.

He caught her yawn. "Tired, sweet cheeks?"

"The kids wore me out."

"They had fun with you." He looked at her thoughtfully. "You'll make a good mother." He'd never once thought that of another woman.

She dipped her head. "My children will be born with oil in their veins. They'll play with inner tubes and hub caps. The first words out of their mouths will be *oil change?*"

"How many kids, TZ?" A part of him hoped she wanted a big family.

She looked up. "Four boys and two girls."

"A little male domination?"

"I've been surrounded by men all my life," she confessed. "Little boys are a must."

"Little girls to balance the rough and tumble?"

"I'm sure they'll be tomboys. They'll be able to handle their brothers." She licked her lips, her voice low, yet curious. "How about you? Family man or dedicated bachelor?"

He took a moment to answer. "The right woman could have me changing diapers."

Silence settled between them as peaceful as the night

until TZ stretched, then stood. "I need to check on the Mustang before it gets much later."

"Want some help?" Cade asked.

She shook her head. "I'm the mechanic, rally man. That's why you're paying me the big bucks."

He glanced at the pool clock, hanging near the water slide. "If you're not in our suite in an hour, I'll come looking for you."

"You could just go to sleep."

"I'll be waiting up for you, sweet cheeks."

She flipped back her damp curls, her expression one of exasperation. "I don't need you to watch over me."

"Oh, yes, you do. I'm your temporary keeper."

Cade her keeper? The concept was unnerving. Turning on her heels, TZ headed toward the cabana where she'd left her shorts and top. Changing quickly, she took the path toward the underground garage where the classic cars had been parked for the night.

Although the garage was well-lit, there wasn't a soul around. TZ found the 'Stang three parking places over from where Cade had originally left it. Apparently Elise found the '69 bull-nose Trans Am better company than the '58 British-born Morgan. The windshield wipers swished, and the emergency lights flickered. Elise was flirting with the Trans Am.

TZ popped the hood and thoroughly checked the engine. The Pony car was ready to run at first light. Lowering the hood, she caught sight of Sam Mason weaving his way around the antique cars. Sam looked pale and weak. TZ prayed he hadn't been drinking.

As he closed in on her, TZ realized Sam was pulling a wobbly cart bearing a car battery. "I need to replace the battery in the Jag," he told her. "The XKE's running low on juice."

She followed Sam to Rhett Evans's Jaguar. Raising the hood, Sam attempted to pull the dead battery. His body shook as he struggled; sweat beaded his brow. He couldn't lift it.

"Don't have a hernia, Sam," TZ scolded as she bent in to help him.

Sam grunted. "Cade will have your hide if he knows you're helping me."

"He need never know," she whispered conspiratorially.

"*He* already does," Cade said in low, drawn-out tones.

TZ nearly dropped the battery. Grease smeared across her T-shirt and several sequins tore from the American flag as she set the old battery on the cart. Her heart slammed against her ribs as she turned to face him. "Don't you ever knock?"

His features were tight, his tone grim. "It's what you're doing behind closed doors that concerns me."

Sam stepped forward, a slight man who could hide in Cade's shadow. "It's my fault, Nyland," he said. "I have no strength. TZ was helping me shift batteries."

Cade studied Sam. "You'd planned to do the hook-up yourself?"

Sam smiled weakly. "That I can handle. It was the lifting that left me winded."

"No need to tire yourself further." Cade then retrieved and replaced the new battery without flexing a muscle.

TZ stood with her mouth open.

Cade wiped his hands on his jeans. "You have all the tools you need, Sam?"

"I'm all set. Thanks."

"Then our work here is done," Cade said. "Upstairs, sweet cheeks."

Upstairs, to a suite where Cade would certainly score a home run tonight. After what he'd just done for Sam Mason, she was his.

"Night, Sam." TZ waved to him just before he ducked under the hood of the Jag.

The Mustang honked softly. TZ smiled. "Night, Elise."

Cade took her hand, and led her across the parking garage. She hung back, as apprehensive as she was excited about the night ahead. Cade noticed her dragging her feet. "Tired?" he asked.

She was running on adrenaline. "A little."

He hunkered down. "Hop on."

"A piggyback ride?" She hesitated. "I'll get grease on the back of your shirt."

"It's an old shirt."

She climbed on, wrapping her arms about his neck, her legs about his waist. She snuggled in close, feeling the warmth of his back, the broad width of his shoulders.

Reaching back, Cade cupped her bottom with his hands. "Hang on," he said as he headed toward the emergency stairwell.

TZ's eyes widened. "You're taking the stairs?"

"Between SunCoast Run, a psychic connection and a Shriners convention, the elevators are packed and moving too damn slow."

"It's five flights to our suite! Put me down."

Cade shifted his shoulders, adjusted her on his back. "The climb would be a whole lot easier if you'd stop wiggling."

TZ stilled. Resting her head on his shoulder, she held

on tight. She liked the feel of his body as he moved up the stairs. Step by step, she rode the movement of his body. Her breasts rubbed against his back, and her pelvis pressed intimately against the lower curve of his spine. The power of the man beneath her soon became more of a turn-on than the vibration of the 'Stang. TZ was breathing hard by the third-floor landing.

The sound of footsteps coming toward them had her looking up. It was Mick Wilcox lumbering down the stairs. "Interesting means of transportation," he commented as he leaned against the wall to let them pass.

"Headed down to the garage?" Cade asked.

"Forgot my shaving kit," Wilcox replied.

Cade kept moving. At the top of the next landing, they met up with rally master Walter Brown, wrapped in a long terry-cloth robe. The legs of his blue-and-white-striped pajama bottoms were visible beneath its hem, along with a pair of navy socks.

"The stairs are well-traveled tonight," TZ whispered near Cade's ear.

Cade lifted a brow. "Out for an evening stroll, Walter?"

"I'm headed to the garage," Brown explained. "I wanted to make sure the cars were safe before I turned in for the night."

"We just passed Mick Wilcox," TZ told Brown.

Walter shook his head. "That man makes me uneasy. His partner, Skinner, even more so."

"Wilcox stood up to the bikers today," Cade reminded Brown. "We know where his loyalties lie."

"With himself," Brown returned. "He took your side so he wouldn't get beat up."

"Whose side did you take, Walter?" Cade asked. "The jukebox's?"

"I stayed safe," Brown said. "If all hell had broken loose, someone had to remain in one piece to run the rally."

"There wasn't even a fight," TZ said over Cade's shoulder. "Legend was just putting you on."

Brown jammed his hands in the pockets of his robe. "So you say now. Let's hope tomorrow isn't a repeat of today." Without another word, Walter pushed by TZ and Cade and headed down the stairs.

They watched him go, catching only the bob of his head. When Brown was completely out of sight, Cade continued his climb.

Once they reached their floor, he strolled down the hall, his breathing as even as when he'd started up the stairs. The man was fit. Once they reached their suite, she caught the flex of his tattoo as he released her, and she slid slowly down his back. He turned toward her then and smiled, a carnal smile with the hint of seduction. "Care to play a little fast ball, TZ Blake?"

Chapter Thirteen

Fast ball? She swallowed hard. "I've been known to hit a home run or two," she finally managed. "How many zeros do we add to your scoreboard?"

Cade inserted the plastic key into the lock, then pushed the door wide. "Not as many as you might think. I'm selective. When I take a woman to bed, I take time to know her mind, her body."

TZ stepped into their suite, with Cade close on her heels. They stood behind closed doors. The curtains had been drawn back, and the room was steeped in moonlight. The bed had been turned down, the white satin sheets stark against the darkness. She felt suddenly vulnerable.

Standing on the carpet at third base, she stared at Cade. Neither one moved, until the room pulsed with intimacy and the world outside ceased to exist.

"Who am I to you?" she finally managed.

His gaze narrowed, dark and intense. "I like you, sweet cheeks," he admitted. "You're pretty and funny and kind.

You're good with people. I admire your zest for life. In the short time I've known you, I've experienced more excitement, more curiosity, more desire than with any other woman I've ever met. You're unique and impulsive. You match the beat of my heart."

He paused, ran a hand through his black hair. "I think I've wanted you from the moment you slammed your car door into mine. You've stirred my soul, my senses, and"—he looked down his body, at the ridge beneath his zipper—"all visible signs of life in my body. I want to make love with you."

He wanted her . . . The man had said all the right things. "I'm attracted to your strength and confidence," she returned. "You do, however, make me nervous. I'm as edgy now as when I'm riding and vibrating in the Mustang."

He stepped closer, cupping her chin in his palm. "I can take the edge off," he said with a slow smile. "We have a long night ahead."

TZ's forehead brushed his chest as she looked down at her T-shirt. "I'm smudged with grease, dirty."

"We can shower together, get you squeaky clean."

"I want a bath, with water so hot it steams."

"Far better than a cold shower alone."

Taking her by the hand, he led her toward the bathroom. Inside the door, full-length mirrors caught them from every angle. He dimmed the lighting. The basin of the sink was constructed like a catcher's mitt; the sunken tub for two formed a baseball bat. A tub built for lovers.

Her body tingled, and shivers ran down her spine. Standing directly behind her, Cade eased her back against him. "Feel me," he whispered as her back molded to his front. Her shoulder blades pressed into his chest as tightly as her bottom snugged his groin. His strength surrounded her, bold and seductive. His erection strained against the small of her back.

Ever so gently, he brushed her auburn curls off her neck. She felt his breath near her ear, warm, almost hot. Her heartbeat quickened when he placed one openmouthed kiss behind her right ear, then lightly blew on the spot. A hot shudder flashed from her breast to her belly.

Moving down her neck to her collarbone, he kissed and nuzzled, kissed and nipped, his ten o'clock shadow abrading her ultra-sensitive skin. Her chest rose and fell beneath the soft cotton of her T-shirt.

Pushing the neck of her shirt off one shoulder, Cade explored the curve with his lips and tongue. "More skin." His voice was deep and dark with sexual intent.

With a maddening slowness that felt more like minutes instead of seconds, he slid his hands down her sides to the hem of her shirt, then eased it up and over her head. All along the way, he teased her belly, her ribs, her breasts through the white satin cups of her bra, leaving her breathless.

He tossed her shirt aside. Unhooked her bra. He ran his fingers beneath the straps, inching the satin off her shoulders and down her arms. Her freed breasts now rose full and firm, catching the dim light on their upper curves.

She dropped her head back against his chest and closed her eyes, feeling his hands return to cup her breasts. He fanned their fullness. Her breasts ached and swelled. Her pink nipples puckered. He traced down her ribs to the smooth, taut hollow of her stomach. Slow hands. Slower burn. Everywhere he touched, he drew fire to the surface of her skin. His foreplay had no end.

She caught her breath, inhaled long and deeply, when he fingered the silver snap on her red shorts. His hair grazed her forehead, her cheek, as he tongued her ear, then bit its lobe, prolonging the pleasure, drawing out her desire. He taught her a lesson in timelessness.

The sound of her breathing sharpened as he unsnapped her shorts, scraped down the zipper. When he slid his hand beneath the elastic of her panties, stretching his fingers toward her sex, TZ went weak in the knees.

Through half-closed eyelids she caught her reflection in the mirrors. She barely recognized herself, naked to the waist. Her skin was flushed, her lips moist and parted. Her red shorts had shifted low on her hips. The zipper was pulled all the way down, the material on either side spread wide.

Cade's hand was visible beneath the lacy sheerness of her thong. She caught the stretch and stroke of his fingers, felt the deep penetration of his forefinger.

Lifting her gaze, she found him watching her in the glass. Watching her reaction to each teasing stroke, to each erotic insertion of his finger. His features bore signs of strain and restraint, and naked longing.

Her body responded to his stare, growing damp and slick, and radiating heat. Filling her with two fingers, he kept her on edge. The pleasure was almost unbearable in its intensity. He drove her wild.

As her climax built, her back arched, and her heartbeat melded with her breathing. She tossed her head, rocked against his hand. The pressure of his fingers increased, sharp and enveloping. The air around her shivered as spasms overtook her. She clutched Cade's arm, moaning, as the hot waves of pleasure shot throughout her body. Fire bursts broke behind her eyelids; there was a charge of white-hot sound in her ears.

When her breathing slowed, he withdrew his hand from her panties, flattened his palm on her belly. "Less edgy?" he asked, his voice so low and sexual she almost came a second time.

"My tension has eased, but what about yours?"

He turned her within the circle of his arms, stroked her hair out of her face, kissed her lightly on the forehead. "There's no rush, sweet cheeks."

TZ ran a fingertip over his lips. "You have a hungry-looking mouth."

"The better to taste you with, my dear," he warned as he leaned in to kiss her.

His kiss was as soft as his breath. Warm. Moist. Teasing. He flicked the tip of his tongue at each corner of her mouth, along the soft crease, then nipped her full bottom lip with his teeth. She parted her lips . . . only to have him pull back.

She frowned her frustration.

He smiled against her mouth. "Let's take that bath."

TZ ran her hands up the back of his shirt, then scraped her nails down his sides. "A bubble bath?" she asked, turning toward the assortment of bath crystals on a glass shelf above the bathtub. "Gardenia, rose, lavender?"

He frowned. "All garden scents?"

She looked at him, grinning. "No one would ever take you for a pansy, rally man. You can shower after our bath."

"Let me help you out of your clothes," he said.

Goose bumps scattered as he eased down her shorts and

panties, and the callused pads of his thumbs skimmed the soft flesh of her inner thighs, the sensitive backs of her knees, then trailed down her calves. Once the shorts reached her ankles, TZ kicked them aside, along with her tennies. She then went to work on Cade, tugging his shirt over his head, yanking his athletic shorts down his muscular legs.

"In a hurry, sweet cheeks?" A muscle jerked in the hollow of his cheek.

"I want you naked."

Sexual heat surged through her body, head to toe and all sensitive spots in between. She wanted more of Cade Nyland. As much as he would give. As much as she could take. And then some.

Going up on tiptoe, she leaned into him. Her breasts brushed the hard contours of his chest, her abdomen flush against his sculpted stomach. Her hands found their way up his back, then down, slowly feeling the outline of every muscle, every bone.

She savored that burning-for-it sensation, that touch of fire before it consumes. Desiring him so much it hurt, she kissed the chiseled arch of his cheekbones, his prominent jaw, sandpapered with stubble, then slanted her mouth across his. Slipping her tongue between his teeth, she kissed him deeply. Though his tongue was hot, his body was hotter. She could feel his desire sifting into her, and she drew it out. Flames licked her belly until he ended the kiss.

"Slow burn," he breathed against her mouth. "I want to talk and touch and watch you go up in flames."

She bit his lip. "I want to take you on the floor."

His mouth curved in a slow smile. "Maybe later. Right

now, I want you hot and steamy and submerged in bubbles."

Buried beneath a mound of lavender-scented bubbles, Cade stretched out his legs, facing TZ. She'd wrapped her arms about his neck, her legs about his hips. His sex was hard and heavy, his arousal almost painful. She was positioned where he could slide into her at any moment. Yet that moment had not arrived. He wanted her so hot for him, the flames would leave them sexual ash.

Furls of steam hit his face, and a thin sheen of sweat filmed his skin. Skimming his hands beneath the water, he glossed over the curve of her waist, her hips, then cupped her sweet ass. He settled her even closer. Her body was sleek, smooth, sensational. Her breasts rose above the bubbles, the pink nipples pebbled. He breathed a kiss against each peak.

He heard the catch in her breath, caught the rapid rise and fall of her chest, when he flicked his tongue just so.

Reaching for the sponge, she squeezed water over his shoulder, then rubbed it over his chest. The scrape of her nails followed the scrub of the sponge. Her helping hands dipped lower. There was nothing sexier than being touched underwater. It was slower, silkier, the sensations magnified. When she stroked his thigh, grazed the tip of his sex, his heart jolted. When she caressed his erection, squeezed it slightly, he nearly came out of the tub.

"Talk to me, TZ," he requested while he could still speak.

"*Now*, with your hands on me? *Now*, when I can barely remember my name?"

He kissed her on the forehead. "Short, simple sentences."

She blew bubbles off his chest. "What do you do when you're not rallying?"

He shrugged. "A little of this, a little of that."

"That was enlightening." She went back to sponging his neck and shoulders. His pecs.

Burying his hands in her wild curls, he massaged her scalp. Her lips parted on a soft moan. He wanted to hear that same moan against his mouth when he brought her to climax.

Flushed and feminine, she traced his eyebrows, circled one eye with her fingertip. "Your eyes are expressively sexy, and dark as midnight. Your wink is downright lethal."

"Your ass should be outlawed."

She pressed her palm over his heart. "You're a known heartbreaker."

He dropped his forehead against hers. "Some women fall too hard, too fast. They oftentimes read more into a relationship than what's actually there." He gently kissed her lips, laid out his past. "I've never told a woman I loved her."

She kissed the tip of his nose, smiled. "No man has ever claimed my heart either."

He felt her smile all the way to his heart. "What's TZ stand for?" he asked.

"Besides 'tease'?" She brushed bubbles off his upper lip. "Your mouth is foamy."

"Your mouth is full and sexy. Kissable." He leaned in, dropped a soft kiss on her lips, savored her taste: moist, sweet with a hint of lavender bath crystals. "TZ . . . Tarzana? Tizzy?"

She tilted her head, asked, "A need-to-know, rally man?"

He wanted to know her completely. "Cadence Andrew Nyland," he gave her his full name.

"Sounds . . . silver spoon."

He stroked her cheek, admitted, "My family has money."

"But you're the black sheep?"

He nodded slowly. "I've made my own way."

The faintest hint of color touched her cheeks. "So have I."

He burst the bubbles on her shoulder, then several more on her breastbone with his finger. "I like being spontaneous. I need a woman who can pack a bag and hit the road in thirty minutes with no destination ahead. Someone who never looks back, never has regrets. A woman who takes life by the balls and squeezes."

TZ took his life in her hands. Beneath the water, she skimmed her fingers over his belly, his thighs, before reaching his sex. He was fully erect. Eight inches of hardness against her soft palm. She lightly squeezed his scrotum. "I'm living large, Cadence."

He cupped her buttocks, drew her pelvis toward him. She was slick and slippery, and rocked against him. He clutched her hips, slowed her movements. His control was almost spent. Their slow burn was getting impossibly hot.

"It's time for bed," he said as he unplugged the tub.

As the water sank away, he reached for the shower massager and began washing the crystalline suds off her heated body. The water fanned as he swept her neck and breasts and belly. She stood slowly, and he rinsed her legs and inner thighs. He then switched the spray to pulse and the water began shooting in forceful bursts. Her lips parted and her eyes glazed as the teasing force jolted through her body, heightening her senses.

Moving the spray away from her, he rinsed himself off. Wrapping her in a fluffy bath towel, he drew her from the tub and dried them both off. He took his time—long, sensuous minutes—to linger over her breasts and at the juncture of her thighs.

"You're beautiful, TZ Blake," he told her.

She ran her gaze from his head to his toes; her eyes returned to his erection. "You're not too bad yourself."

Naked, his body pulsing, he swept her off her feet and strode to the bed. Easing her onto the white satin sheets, he sank down beside her. She was on her back; he on his side. The room was cast in moonlight. Slivers of silver played across his chest and hip, a caress of heaven on primal man.

He stared down at her, whispered, "Marco?" He caught the faint twitch of her lips as she turned onto her side and faced him fully. "Polo," she replied equally softly.

He leaned closer, until their bodies touched. They kissed lips, face, ears and hair. He slipped his leg between her own. They stilled for several seconds, the only movement being his upper thigh as it stroked toward her sex.

A rush of wild longing drew him back to her mouth. Harder and longer; harder and deeper, his mouth enveloped hers. She responded with a rising passion of her own.

She clutched him close. "I want you, Cade."

"Slow burn," he responded, his voice low and as tight as his body. "Let me taste your heat."

Dipping lower, he kissed her throat. The point of both shoulders. Raw pleasure pushed him down her body. His dark hair whispered across her naked breast and down her stomach like the touch of a shadow. Excitement pounded through him like a thousand primitive drums. His cheek rested just below her breasts as he placed openmouthed kisses across her belly, her hips, slowly reaching the center of her heat and all sensation.

A flick of his tongue, and he tasted her: fresh, wet, womanly. Her hips came off the bed, and he cupped her sweet ass. He made love to her with an intimacy that threatened his sanity.

Feeling the tightness in her body, the throbbing between her legs, he knew it was time to protect them both. He rose, and within three heartbeats had unzipped his gym bag, removed a condom from a side compartment and returned to their bed.

"Let me put it on you," TZ requested.

Her hands shook slightly as she opened the foil packet and fitted it over his erection. Her touch alone had Cade fighting for control. The moment had arrived when the air between them was saturated with lust and longing and a need for release.

Her kisses demanded his fire.

Tongue to tongue, hip to hip, he climbed into her flame.

She was tight. Incredibly tight. His legs strained as he took her slowly. Once she'd received him, their joining proved as fierce as the first converging of human hunger. Time had no meaning, and reality was lost to flesh sliding over flesh. The motion, all flow and thrust, was driven by sharp breaths, arching backs and undulating hips.

He felt her fingernails sink into his shoulders, then score his back. White-hot sensation singed their flesh. They breathed in rhythm, the pounding of her heart resounded in his soul. The rise of intense pleasure took them to the edge, then over.

She went suddenly rigid, gasped, then exploded.

His whole body heaved, shuddered and sank into her.

Sated, he rolled onto his back and TZ curled into his side. She stroked his chest, kissed him on the cheek. "Taryn Zane Blake," she said barely above a whisper. "Zane was my mother's maiden name."

Taryn Zane *Nyland*. Cade closed his eyes, drifting toward sleep. He'd never joined another woman's name with his own. Their names fit as perfectly as their bodies.

Marisa Ashton-Lord was so uptight her stomach knotted and her legs barely carried her down Pit Road, the Nascar theme hallway, to Mick Wilcox's suite. Beneath the black wet suit, she'd grown hot and sweaty. Her goggles fogged from her ragged breathing and the awkwardness of wearing swim fins tripped up her steps.

She knocked three times on Mick's door. Light little taps in hopes he wouldn't hear her arrival. That way she could leave when he didn't answer. She counted to five, planning on going only as high as ten. "Eight, nine—"

Mick opened the door, a big man in a narrow doorway, wearing nothing but an orange Speedo. He was a hairy man, one whose primate ancestry was in no doubt. He narrowed his gaze. "You came disguised as frog woman?"

"I couldn't afford for anyone to recognize me."

He stepped back. "Get inside before someone sees me with you."

Her jaw dropped. "You're embarrassed to be seen with me?"

He grabbed hold of her arm, pulling her inside. "Damn straight. You walk around with your nose so high it breaks the ozone layer."

He then took a ketchup-stained, black-and-white-striped tie from the knob on the back side of the door and slid it over the front handle.

"Why did you do that?" Risa demanded.

"So Skinner knows I have a woman in the room and won't disturb us."

She snagged the tie off the handle before he could close the door. "That won't be necessary." She handed it back to him. "I'll only be here long enough to stick my flippers in the Jacuzzi. All of five minutes. No longer."

Mick tossed the tie on a tripod table decorated with model cars. Turning back toward the door, he secured the chain.

Her fins flip-flopped as she worked her way down the hall and into the main room. The Nascar theme was evident throughout his suite: the gray carpet resembled an oval track; the dressers had been designed as Craftsman tool chests. The bed was modeled after Ryan Newman's Dodge. She could almost hear the engine rev.

"Jacuzzi's on the balcony," Mick told her as he slid open the glass doors and stepped out into the night. A night of a million stars.

Risa stuck her tongue out at his back. The man didn't have the courtesy to wait for her. On a flagging sigh, she followed him outside. One dip of her fins, a splash of water in his face, and she could make her escape. This was the worst night of her life.

Mick Wilcox was surprised when Risa joined him at the Jacuzzi. Her brown eyes looked big and bugged-out beneath the goggles. Those swim fins would be the death of her. She wasn't headed out to sea. Although given her skinny ass, the bubbling jets in the Jacuzzi could toss her like a wave.

He eased into the water, was just getting comfortable, when the web on Risa's flippers caught the tiled edge of the Jacuzzi. Her arms flailed, and her rubber-covered body swayed wildly.

"You're one clumsy broad," he muttered as he dived to her rescue.

He grabbed her before she landed face first in his lap. Her cheekbones were so sharp they could cut off his balls. He caught her, one arm circling her breasts while the other wrapped her hips. Her gratitude came in three slaps to his left arm and a swim fin to his groin. He dropped her with a splash, growling, "You can drown next time."

Risa surfaced, sputtering and swearing. She bared her teeth, her tone cool and not especially civil. "Drowning would be preferable to sitting with you in the Jacuzzi."

Mick put his hand on her head and dunked her. He held her underwater until bubbles rose in rapid succession. Once released, she shot out of the water, spewing threats to his life.

He ignored her. Resting his head on the rim of the Jacuzzi, he closed his eyes and allowed the swirling, gulping water to relax him. Within a very short time, all tension left his body. Up until the moment Risa jabbed him in the chest with her elbow. Damn, she had sharp elbows. No doubt sharpened by pumice stones.

"Stay on your own side of the Jacuzzi," he said, growling.

"The jets are too strong," she complained. "You take up most of the whirlpool. Scoot over!"

"Any farther over and I'd be out of the Jacuzzi."

"Out is an option."

Mick reached toward the panel that controlled the jet spray. He turned the dial from stream to pummel. The sharp spray from the jets flipped Risa on her back. Seconds later, her swim fin caught him beneath the chin.

"Turn it down!" she shouted in his face.

"Take off that damn frog suit!" he returned equally loud.

Her nostrils pinched along with her lips. "Fine!"

With a flick of his wrist, Mick killed the shooting spray. The waves between them settled to a soft haze of steam.

He watched as she pulled off her goggles, flinging them to the side. Her flippers came next. She fought the zipper on her wet suit, struggled out of it like a spastic stripper. She wore an itsy-bitsy silver bikini beneath the layer of black rubber.

Mick stared at her. The woman was all porcelain white skin, tiny breasts and reed-slim legs. Her ribs were as bony as her spine. She had no ass.

His sex twitched with interest.

Mick sank deeper into the Jacuzzi. He was one sick pup to be aroused by a woman so thin she could fade into her shadow and never be seen again.

"I'd like a drink." Risa spoke as if to a servant.

"Wet bar's by the bed."

"Bacardi Orange, light on the ice."

Mick's erection tented his nylon Speedo. The last thing he needed was for Risa to see his hard-on. Her icy glare could freeze his genitals. "Help yourself to that drink," he directed. "I'll have a beer."

Risa looked ready to kill him. The woman wasn't used to waiting on herself or anyone else. When he didn't budge, she eventually climbed out of the Jacuzzi—her platinum hair plastered to her skull, her body shaking with anger—and crossed to the wet bar.

Slipping and sliding across the wet tiles, she returned with both their drinks and a bag of peanuts.

"Hey, don't spill my beer," Mick said as she skittered toward the edge of the whirlpool, set down a Bud and the nuts. "Why the peanuts? That small bag costs three bucks."

Submerged once again, Risa glared at him from across the Jacuzzi. "I'll pay for my drink, now pass me one peanut."

"One?" Had he heard her correctly?

"Just one. I limit myself on snacks."

He passed her the bag and she selected one nut. While she nibbled like a squirrel, Mick tossed the remaining handful of peanuts into his mouth, chewed, swallowed. Belched. Risa, on the other hand, nibbled and nibbled, taking ten minutes to finish her snack.

"Do you always *nibble?*" he eventually asked. "Don't you ever sink your teeth into a thick, juicy steak?"

She looked down her nose at him. "I eat, but watch my weight."

"You've the body of a preteen, no tits or ass. You're a walking advertisement for third-world hunger."

"While you, Mr. Wilcox, are the *before* picture for Slim-Fast."

"Men like a few curves on a woman."

She looked at his chest. "Women prefer fewer love handles."

"Don't you ever get hungry?"

Hungry? Risa had been starving all her life. She'd

starved for fashion, starved for the position of trophy wife. She couldn't remember when she'd eaten more than a few bites at any given meal. When she did eat, she forced down carrot and celery sticks and romaine lettuce. She never felt full.

Staring beyond Mick's shoulder, she looked out into the night. Countless stars joined a full moon in lighting the heavens. It was a romantic evening meant for lovers. A night to be spent with anyone but Mick Wilcox.

She sipped her Bacardi Orange, sighed, clutched the glass between her breasts. The coldness of the glass made her nipples tighten. Without conscious thought, she rubbed the glass right, then left, teasing her breasts with the sweating glass.

"Feel good?" she heard Mick ask. Heat crept into her cheeks and she immediately set the glass on the tiled rim of the Jacuzzi.

"I was warm," she returned sharply.

"Don't be so defensive," Mick returned. "I like a woman who pleasures herself."

Risa's color heightened. "I wasn't *pleasuring* myself."

"Looked that way to me."

"You weren't gentleman enough to look the other way?"

Mick actually smiled. "I liked what I saw."

"Voyeur."

He shrugged. "Whatever it takes to get you through the night."

Risa rose from the Jacuzzi. Water sluiced down her body, in between her thighs. "My evening obligation has ended. I'm leaving. Good night, Mr. Wilcox."

"Don't forget your wet suit."

"Wet suit, goggles, fins, waterproof wallet," she ticked

off what she needed to return to Ziggy's Surf Shop. Unzipping the wallet, she plucked out two twenties and tossed them by her drink. "That should cover my drink, peanut and any service charge."

"You and your money have a good evening now, you hear?"

The man looked like a redneck, spoke like a hick. "My wealth has outlasted three marriages," she shot back as she collected the swim fins and goggles. "I take great comfort in a fat bank account."

"Money can't love you back," Mick pointed out. "I'm a bigger bang for your buck."

Bigger bang . . . Sex with Mick Wilcox? Surely he was joking!

Meeting his gaze across the Jacuzzi, she saw no laughter in his eyes. The man had turned serious. His gaze was narrowed, bright and fixed on her. When he rose from the whirlpool—large and looming, and momentarily blocking the moon—her fingers spasmed and the goggles slipped from her grasp. As he climbed from the whirlpool, her gaze was drawn to his erection, hard against his belly and stretched out like a ruler.

"Stay right where you are," she ordered, clutching the wet suit to her chest, suddenly nervous. "Don't you dare come any closer."

"And if I dare?" He took one step, then a second.

She didn't know what she would do. Scream? Run? Have sex with the man? The thought of coupling with him made her shiver. She liked her lovers powerful, well-built, monied. Not men who thrived on beer and peanuts and considered burping foreplay.

Yet her mind ran down a naughty little path. It had

been months since she'd been kissed, close to a year since she'd had sex. If she remained discreet, and he kept his mouth shut, who would ever know she'd slept with the man?

"You must never tell a soul we've slept together," she ordered him, waiting to see if he'd keep her secret.

"I wouldn't utter a word," he returned. "Sleeping with money would ruin my reputation with ten-dollar whores."

"You're disgusting!" she snapped.

He moved to stand before her. "So disgusting you want me."

She flinched when he tugged the wet suit from her grasp. Cringed when he ran his thumb over her upthrust breast. Moaned when he squeezed the tip between his thumb and forefinger.

When he tilted up her chin with his finger, she looked everywhere but at his face. Her body jolted when he kissed her hard, plunging his tongue into her mouth like a marauder.

Withdrawing his tongue, he soon gentled his kiss. This time when he teased her tongue with the tip of his own, she sucked him into her mouth, taking him slowly.

She grew warm and pliable to his touch. She touched him in turn, running her hands over his big body, no longer repulsed, but oddly excited.

"How long has it been since you've had sex?" she asked after a second hard kiss, wondering if he packed protection.

"With myself or with a woman?"

"Do you have condoms, hand man?"

"Two," he returned.

"I'm good for one, then I'm out of here."

"You'll wish I had a box."

Risa never knew how Mick got her to his bed. Got her there naked. One minute they were on the porch arguing—he bragging he could rewire the bedsprings with his sexual moves; she betting he'd come before he entered her—then several heartbeats later, she found herself flat on her back, panting, desiring, navy satin sheets crushed in her moist palm.

"You're too damn thin, Ris," he complained, his voice hot and moist against her ear as he entered her. "Your tits are sharp little peaks and your hipbones feel like flint arrowheads."

"You're smothering me, Shamu," she said, panting once he'd filled her. Her body felt swollen and stretched, and sweaty.

Mick's body strained. "You could move a little."

Risa wrapped her legs about his hips. "You could move a lot."

He withdrew, drove deeper. The Nascar checkered flag above the headboard fluttered. *"Gentlemen, start your engines."*

Sheets soon twisted, and bedsprings squeaked. Their breathing came fast, their bodies grew slick as Mick Wilcox gave Marisa Ashton-Lord the best orgasm of her life.

Afterward, Risa lay sated and shaken, and disbelieving of the fact a man like Wilcox could bring her such satisfaction. The thought frightened her. When he rolled off her, reached for the phone and ordered room service for two, she pulled the sheet to her chin, remaining in his bed.

By two o'clock in the morning, a petite filet, twice-baked potato, a sampling of green beans and a slice of pecan pie filled her belly to bursting. Her jaw ached from chewing. It was the first time in her life she hadn't thought about her weight, hadn't cared if she'd gained five pounds.

Stacking pillows behind her head, she dropped back on the bed, still naked, and watched Mick polish off his second piece of pie. A la mode. She realized if he lost fifty pounds, added exercise to his diet, he might firm up to be a halfway decent-looking man. Of course, he'd have to get a haircut, shave. Buy some new clothes. Stop grunting. Learn some manners.

She couldn't, however, fault his lovemaking. They'd used up both condoms, then grown inventive. When he scooped the remainder of the ice cream from his dessert plate onto his palm and covered her breast and belly with French vanilla, she melted as fast as the ice cream beneath his heated mouth.

As dawn pushed darkness from the sky, Risa sneaked from Mick's suite, praying she would make it to her room undetected.

However satisfying, no one could ever know where she'd spent the night.

Two suites down Pit Row, Rhett Evans lay wide awake on his bed with Kimmie Thorn curled beside him. He'd finally gotten her to sleep with him. Sleep she had, deeply and fully clothed, all the way down to her shoes.

He stroked her blond hair off her cheek. Her breathing was slow and deep, her mouth slightly parted as if waiting to be kissed. He debated kissing her, thought better of it. He'd promised he wouldn't kiss or touch her. Keeping his word had strained every nerve in his body. It had been a long, long night.

Earlier in the day, they'd played tennis. He hadn't known Kimmie could be so competitive. They'd entered a round-robin tournament and would have won if Rhett had kept his eyes on the tennis ball and not on Kimmie's curves. By their second game, he'd been hot and horny and unable to cover the full range of the back court. He was walking funny by the final game, which they had lost due to his inability to run.

"Good morning," Kimmie said on a soft sigh as her eyelids fluttered. "Is it time to rally?"

"We have an hour," he replied.

Tucking a pale yellow broomstick skirt beneath her legs, she eased to a sitting position and straightened her white linen blouse. "Did you sleep well?" she asked.

He hadn't slept a wink. "Slept a good six hours."

She licked her lips. "I liked sleeping with you, Rhett."

He'd have preferred spending the night naked and burning together like liquid nitrogen. "I'm glad you stayed."

"I'd like to stay with you again."

He'd be a walking zombie without sleep. "Tonight?"

She nodded. "After the costume party, I might let you kiss me good night."

"I'd let you take full advantage of me."

"I'm not you, Rhett Evans."

He didn't need her reminder. Virgin Kimmie had him caught between his desire and his honor. He didn't have a white horse, and a knight's armor itched in the Florida heat. He was close to broke; his self-esteem was sadly tarnished.

Yet when Kimmie looked at him with those big green

eyes, all trusting and adoring, she made him believe in himself. Maybe he had a little Sir Lancelot in him, after all.

His patience protected her virtue.

Chapter Fourteen

TZ rode down in the elevator beside Cade in a euphoric haze. She was a woman well-loved. From the moment they'd touched, any thoughts of sleep gave way to orgasms and pillow talk. He'd found the sex points that made her shiver, along with her moan zone.

Between climaxes, they had discussed what made them tick: their likes and dislikes in books, music and movies; best memories; darkest moments, all highlighted by Cade's knowledge of car engines. TZ had been impressed. She glanced at him as he adjusted the strap on his gym bag then shifted his stance. His hair remained damp from their morning shower, his strong jaw stubbled and sexy. Dark circles underscored his eyes, which were no longer bruised, but showed lack of sleep. His mouth was relaxed, its hard line visible, but not pronounced.

A khaki pullover covered his chest and was tucked into black jeans. His body emanated strength and health and hot-blooded masculinity.

The elevator settled on the garage floor with a jerky little bounce. The doors opened slowly. TZ blinked, believing the sight before her a nightmare.

"More damage?" Cade stormed from the elevator.

TZ moved more slowly. Her legs felt weak, her body numb.

The underground parking lot looked like a Demolition Derby.

Walter Brown stood beside a battered Barracuda. He ranted and raved and waved his arms wildly. "This is a disaster, an absolute disaster. Sometime during the night, the garage became a junkyard heap. We've yet to determine how or why."

Two policemen rounded a cement barricade and approached Brown. Officer Davis spoke first, "There appear to be tracks from heavy machinery, perhaps a bulldozer or backhoe, leading down the dirt access road behind the garage."

Officer Caperton took out a notepad and began writing. "We need to check with maintenance as to what equipment is missing."

"Do so quickly," Brown insisted. "We need immediate answers."

"Elise . . ." TZ whispered as she scanned the garage. She prayed the Mustang wasn't one of the cars buried at the bottom of the heap.

Cade returned to her side, laced his fingers through hers. "Deep breaths, sweet cheeks. We'll find the 'Stang."

TZ circled the parking garage once with Cade, then they separated to cover more ground. She hit sections two and three, while he took the stairwell to the upper levels.

She had just started up the incline, rounded the first

bend, when she spotted Marisa Ashton-Lord's pink Cadillac pushed against the cement wall. The chrome strip along the side panel had peeled back; the steep, wraparound windshield looked as if it had been smashed by a sledgehammer.

Several feet farther, and a faint honk drew TZ's attention to a set of bright orange barricades, blocking off repairs being done on several parking spaces. Behind the safety barriers, TZ caught sight of the Mustang, Mick Wilcox's Bug-eyed Sprite and Rhett Evans's Jaguar.

"Elise, thank goodness." She breathed a sigh of relief. Only to have all the breath leave her body when she got close enough to see the damage to the three vehicles. The pain in her chest was as powerful as if she'd found someone hurt or discovered an animal hit by the side of the road.

"Cade!" Her call echoed through the garage. "Level Three, Section D. Hurry!"

He arrived in a flash. "How bad is the damage?" he asked.

"Doesn't look good," TZ said softly.

Both windshield wipers jutted out like broken elbows. The radio antennae had been snapped in two; the left headlight was shattered. One end of the front bumper lay on the ground; the wheel well on the driver's side was pushed in and scraped the tire.

"Get me a crowbar," she requested. Cade was one step ahead of her, already removing the needed tools from the trunk.

Together they pulled the bumper, laid it on the ground. TZ ran her hands along the chrome. "The indentations appear deep and round like taillights," she murmured.

Cade looked closer. "Marks like that show up when different makes of cars push each other and the connection is off."

TZ swallowed hard. "Do you think Elise tried to save the Sprite and Jag? Had to give up on the Caddie?"

Cade nodded. "I'd say she made a valiant effort."

She inserted the crowbar behind the wheel well and pulled. The metal gave; it was still somewhat dented but no longer rubbing the tire. She then circled the car. Both the front and side mirrors followed her progress. A part of TZ died with each nick and scrape. The front passenger door was concave.

"I don't know if we can continue the race," she finally managed.

Cade wrapped his arm about her shoulders protectively, snuggling her close. "If we can't, we can't."

The Mustang made its own decision. The engine choked and sputtered and after several attempts turned over. One windshield wiper waved, the emergency lights flashed, and the horn honked. The gears ground as the 'Stang inched forward, demanding they continue the SunCoast Run.

"There's the Sprite!" Mick Wilcox approached them at a jog. TZ had never seen the man move so fast. Sweat beaded his forehead and stained the front of his T-shirt inscripted with DO IT TO ME ONE MORE TIME, ONCE IS NEVER ENOUGH. "Evans, your Jag's here, too."

Rhett Evans and Kimmie Thorn came running up the ramp. Sam Mason was close behind. Rhett skidded to a halt, dropped Kimmie's hand and stared unblinkingly at his XKE. TZ watched his Adam's apple work. The once sleek hood had been pounded to look like a hammerhead shark.

"The Mustang started," TZ told Rhett. "There's a possibility your Jag may also."

Cade climbed into the 'Stang, moved the vehicle ahead so Rhett could get a closer look at his Jag. "How did the cars get all the way up here?" Rhett asked.

TZ jammed her hands in the pockets of her baggy sea-green capris. "We have no idea," she said, hedging.

Rhett opened the car door, and the hinges squeaked as one corner of the door dipped, angled toward the ground like a broken wing. He slid onto the seat, turned the key in the ignition. Nothing.

TZ used the crowbar to pop the hood. Peering at the engine, she noticed the distributor cap missing, along with a rotor. Someone had dismantled the vehicle prior to the demolition.

Wiping her hands on her capris, she straightened, called to Cade. "Sam and I need to run to the hardware store. Go talk to Walter Brown, stall the start of the race for as long as you can."

Rhett blew out a breath. "There aren't many vehicles left to rally."

"What about Mick Wilcox?" TZ asked.

"Sprite starts," Mick shouted. He drove forward, only to have the muffler drop off. The Sprite rumbled like a muscle car.

TZ nodded to Sam. "Let's locate an auto parts store."

Cade drove them to the bottom of the ramp, then leaped out to talk to Brown. Twenty minutes later, TZ pulled up in front of Action Auto Parts. Finding the parts they needed took little time. The checkout line, however, stretched down the front aisle of the store. TZ glanced around, at the sale signs, the promotional banners, the black-and-white framed photograph on the wall beneath the store's logo.

The owners of Action Auto were all good-looking men, she noted. Dark-haired, with wide foreheads and strong jaws. One such jaw was set at such a stubborn angle, TZ actually smiled. Her smile slowly faded as her gaze rose, over the hard set of the man's mouth, across angular cheekbones to his unconventionally long hair. Her stomach dropped as she stared into his midnight dark eyes.

Cade Nyland! The man was heir to the largest auto parts chain in the country. The silver spoon in the black sheep's mouth had just turned platinum. The subject of his inheritance would arise before the sun set.

After paying for the distributor and rotor, TZ and Sam returned to the hotel. Pandemonium still reigned. The crushed cars were being loaded onto flatbed trucks, while those in need of major repairs awaited a tow.

Cade motioned to her. He stood by Walter Brown and within a circle of irate rallyers. "What's going on?" she asked as she squeezed through the crowd to stand between Cade and Kimmie.

"Walter has accused Mick Wilcox of staging the Demolition Derby," Cade informed her.

"Wilcox was the last one to leave the garage," Brown said loudly. "He claims he was retrieving a shaving kit. I say he was casing the garage for cameras and locating a bulldozer."

"You're crazy, man!" Wilcox defended himself. "You saw me head back up the stairs. I never returned."

"Prove it," Brown demanded. "Can anyone vouch for your whereabouts?"

TZ saw Mick close his eyes, breathe deeply through his

mouth. She didn't want to believe the big man was behind the damages.

"Come on, Wilcox," Brown persisted. "Who saw you when? The bartender? Skinner? Another rallyer?"

Wilcox ran one hand through his uncombed hair. "Room service delivered to my suite around two A.M."

"You ate and then what?" Brown ground out. "Came back to the garage and started piling up cars?"

Wilcox shook his head. "I didn't do it."

Brown turned to Officer Davis. "Take him down to the station and grill him further. I'm sure you'll find him guilty."

TZ watched Mick as he scanned the crowd, his gaze resting on Marisa Ashton-Lord for a second too long. The woman blushed, dipped her head, refusing to meet his eyes.

Was Risa his excuse? TZ wondered. If so, why hadn't she stepped forward? How could she let an innocent man go in for questioning?

Officer Davis pulled handcuffs off his belt. "Mick Wilcox, you are under arrest for the destruction—"

"He was with me." Silence descended, thick and heavy, as Marisa Ashton-Lord parted the crowd with her words. She stepped forward, perfectly coiffured and elegantly dressed in a silky pewter slip dress.

Her cheeks were pink, her gaze directed at the policeman who was about to cuff Mick's wrists. "Take those handcuffs off him immediately," she ordered in her most aristocratic voice. "Mr. Wilcox"—a short pause as if she were collecting herself—"was with me last evening."

"What part of the evening, ma'am?" Officer Caperton

tapped his ink pen on the notepad. "Be specific as to the time."

Risa looked at Mick. The big man shook his head ever so slightly as if trying to discourage her confession. Apprehension darkened Risa's brown eyes before she straightened her shoulders and gave her statement. "We-we spent the night together."

"Has hell frozen over?" Skinner's voice held so much surprise, it drew nervous smiles from several of the rallyers. Others stood in utter disbelief. Many in total bafflement.

Officer Caperton lifted a brow. "You'd stand by your statement in a court of law?"

Risa nodded. "Hand on the Bible."

"Wilcox isn't your man," Caperton told Brown.

"Then *who* the hell damaged the cars?" Brown ground out.

"We'll need to take statements from everyone," Caperton said. "Obtain fingerprints."

"What about the rally?" Rhett Evans asked.

"The race may proceed, but only after we've documented the evidence," the policeman replied.

"Damn strange bedfellows," Brown muttered as he pushed his way through the crowd, mumbling all the way back to the hotel entrance.

TZ motioned to Sam Mason. "I'll help you install the distributor cap while we wait."

She noticed Cade didn't flinch a muscle when she and Sam broke from the group and headed for the Jag. Afterward she made the rounds to every car owner and mechanic, offering her services. Many took her up on her offer.

Two hours later, TZ and Cade climbed into the Mustang and fell into line at eleventh place. Twenty-five classic cars remained in the rally, all either dented, scraped or limping along.

TZ slipped on a pair of sunflower sunglasses. The lenses were round and dark brown, the rims made up of bright yellow petals.

As they approached Walter Brown and the time clock, the Mustang bucked and bolted so close to the man, he was nearly sideswiped. "Damn car!" Brown growled when Cade handed him their time card.

The engine roared, a deadly growl. "What was that all about?" Cade asked as he pulled the 'Stang onto the main road.

"Elise sounds mad. Perhaps she blames Brown for not assigning security to the parking garage."

"Perhaps she knows who caused the damage."

TZ tilted the rearview mirror toward her. "Elise?"

Dark gray hazed the glass, but no image formed. TZ straightened the mirror, dropped back on her seat. Opening the instruction packet, she directed, "First checkpoint is a brainteaser: 'Ten Winks.'"

"Coordinates?" Cade asked.

"Left at the stop light. Then straight on Alico Road."

"Watch for signs and storefronts," Cade instructed as they cruised Alico, from one end to the other, then back again. They passed each remaining rallyer at least once. "Ten Winks. Twenty winks is a cat nap, ten, just barely closing the eyes or—"

Cade's words faded as the Mustang accelerated, whipping right, then shooting down a narrow alley toward a fenced-in warehouse. Cade held his hands high. "Car's driving itself."

TZ clutched the dashboard as the 'Stang swung left, taking the next corner on two wheels. Faint laughter rose up, along with the strong scent of lavender.

"I hope Elise knows where she's going," TZ said between clenched teeth.

Without warning, the car slammed to a stop outside an aluminum-sided building with mattresses stacked across the front windows. TZ craned her neck to read the sign above the doorway. "Bubba's Half-Price Bedding. Half price would be ten winks instead of twenty."

There were beds everywhere, TZ noted as she followed Cade into the enormous display room. Her cheeks heated with the memory of their lovemaking.

"Can I help you pick out a mattress?" A young woman wearing pink-flannel footed pajamas approached them. She looked Cade up and down. "You look like the firm mattress type."

"We're looking for Walter Brown," Cade told her. "The rally master for the SunCoast Run. He's short, balding and carrying a time clock."

"Try back by the waterbeds." She pointed toward the far wall. "Either there or at the California kings."

Cade took TZ's hand and led her down an aisle of canopied beds. "So many mattresses, so little time."

TZ wished they had the privacy and the time to initiate a few of the beds. She'd never had sex on a gel bed or a futon.

They eventually found Walter Brown stretched out on a waterbed in the far corner of the store, his eyes closed.

"Walter, are you awake?" TZ shook the older man's shoulder.

Waves rippled, and Brown slowly opened his eyes.

"How did you get here so fast?" he asked, yawning. "I'd planned on a good hour's nap."

"Ten winks is all you're allowed," Cade said, holding out his time card. "Punch our card, and we're headed across the state to Sandy Key."

Brown rolled off the waterbed, stretched. "Traffic will be heavy on the east coast," he said as he punched their time card. "The next checkpoint's well-hidden in the cement jungle."

Cade nodded to Brown. "Later, Walter. We'll see you at the Sandcastle Hotel for the costume party."

Brown's smile was tight. "Come dressed as last-place rallyers."

"Or as the trophy," Cade said arrogantly. "TZ and I will cross the finish line first."

Brown sniffed. "Tell that to Marisa and Rhett, and that fool Wilcox. Each one sees himself in the winner's circle."

"I deserve to win," Marisa Ashton-Lord said as she came up behind TZ and Cade, her entourage fanned out behind her. "The things I've endured on this trip—"

"Sleeping with me doesn't qualify as a hardship." Mick Wilcox strolled up behind Risa with Skinner at his heels. "I did you a damn favor."

"A favor?" Risa said.

Wilcox actually grinned. "You had your first taste of food and sampled a real man."

"I hate you!" Risa's mouth was so tight TZ could barely see the outline of her lips.

Wilcox didn't appear the least bit phased. "Make-up sex after a lover's spat really turns me on."

TZ tugged on Cade's arm. "Let's hit the road, rally man."

Outside, the Mustang was already running. The engine rumbled strong, all pistons firing. To TZ's dismay, the 'Stang vibrated with such force, she could barely fasten her seat belt. She felt on edge and wished Cade could take the edge off.

"Coordinates?" Cade asked.

Avoiding the color codes, TZ matched her directions to the map. "Go south on Fairway Terrace until we hit the interstate. Then head east. We should arrive north of Miami by four o'clock."

Traffic was light. The sky overhead looked as if it had been drawn with a bright blue crayon. Reaching into her straw bag, TZ selected a pair of Bugs Bunny sunglasses for the trip. The rabbit's ears shot inches above her head.

Beside her, Cade shook his head, smiled and reached for his Ray-Bans. Afterward, he offered her a stick of Doublemint, which she declined. She watched his hands—long fingers, wide palms—as he unwrapped a piece and popped it into his mouth. She liked the way he chewed gum. His stubbled jaw worked slowly, his lips slightly parted.

Once he'd shifted into high gear and hit the speed limit, he casually rested his hand on her thigh. Casual soon left TZ uncomfortable as he brushed her knee with his thumb, slowly, suggestively, teasingly soft. A tangible sense of closeness induced by desire settled between them. With each shimmy of the 'Stang, Cade's hand drifted higher, his palm pressed against her pelvis. Two fingers slipped between her legs, stroking upward, near the juncture of her thighs.

"Aunt Elise?" TZ asked, her breathing uneven.

Cade tilted up the rearview mirror. "Not visible."

The Mustang shook and TZ shivered. She shifted on

the seat, hot and unsettled. Her shifting spread her legs, and Cade centered on her heat. He rubbed the heel of his hand against her, then ran his fingers along the inner seam of her capris. She felt the rough pads of his fingers through the thin cotton fabric, the tingling friction, the throbbing sensitivity.

He teased and she rocked her hips.

She panted and he pressed deeper.

He stroked and she suppressed a scream.

She was hot and wet and ready to come off the seat. Two seconds later she climaxed, connecting with the air and sunshine and panting for breath.

Cade brought her down slowly. He gently stroked her thigh, squeezed her knee, until she could again focus on the road signs, see the white line that ran the center of the highway.

"Is the edge off?" Cade asked with a knowing grin.

So off TZ wanted a nap. She stretched on the seat, feeling relaxed and sated. She'd drawn such pleasure, such satisfaction from Cade Nyland and the SunCoast Run. Rallying was now her favorite sport.

As the orange groves thickened to the south, TZ glanced in her side mirror and caught sight of Marisa Ashton-Lord's pink Cadillac, minus the front windshield. Wind blew Risa's hair away from her face, and her features stood out starkly. Less than a car length behind, Mick Wilcox's Sprite rode her bumper. TZ couldn't believe the battered little Sprite could keep up with a Caddie hosting an engine the size of Texas. Mick must have the accelerator floored. Either that, or he'd jammed his feet through the floorboards and was running like Fred Flintstone.

Tied to the Bug-eye's round rump was a twin-size mattress. The ends bounced and flapped and looked ready to lift the Sprite right off the highway. Why Wilcox had bought a mattress was beyond TZ. Unless he was taunting Risa.

Cade snapped his gum. "Mick's chase might eventually catch Risa. But not until the rally ends. The woman's damn competitive."

"She wanted you," TZ said softly.

He shot her a smile, slow and knowing. "She didn't get me though, did she?"

Cade was hers for the moment. To be exact, for the next twenty-eight hours. She refused to think of his departure after the rally. She wanted their time together to be exciting and fun and very sexual.

"Exit Ten," TZ pointed out as they approached the down ramp. "Gladiolus Boulevard. Burger Joe's is two miles west. We have an hour for lunch."

Running twenty minutes behind the Mustang, Rhett Evans pulled his Jaguar into a parking space two classic cars down from Cade Nyland. From the moment Rhett had laid eyes on Nyland and TZ Blake earlier that morning, he'd known they had become lovers.

Their expressions were dead giveaways. They bore the look—did it, loved it, plan to do it again. And again. TZ's cheeks were flushed, her eyes all soft and bright. She walked with a languid tiredness that came from a night of lovemaking. Cade's loose gait came from hips having pumped well into the night.

Jealousy stabbed like a sharp little knife. He wanted to strut from having sex. He was damn tired of walking funny. If Kimmie asked him one more time if his briefs were too tight, he was going to show her the reason behind the tightness.

"Do we have to eat here?" Kimmie asked, gnawing on her bottom lip.

"Burger Joe's is our checkpoint," Rhett replied. "We can eat in the car or inside the diner, your choice."

"Inside is good." Exiting the vehicle, Sam Mason dodged a waitress on roller skates. "I need to move around, stretch my legs."

Kimmie was slow to stretch, Rhett noticed as he helped her from the Jag. Dressed in pale pink jeans and a pink, peach and yellow paisley-print blouse, she looked soft and young, but not so innocent. Her pants were so tight they made his groin ache.

A leather headband held her blond hair off her face. A face that broke into a smile when she found a penny on the sidewalk.

"Head's showing," she said excitedly. "I get to make a wish." She held the penny to her chest, eyes closed, thoughtful. "I wish for—"

"Me?" he cut across her wish.

Her eyes remained closed. "Maybe . . ."

He jammed his hands in the pockets of his black slacks. "People don't always get what they wish for." Hell, if they did, he and Kimmie would be heating the sheets.

Kimmie peeked at him through her lashes. "I believe in destiny," she said softly. "Horoscopes, fortune cookies, shooting stars. The way my heart beats a little faster whenever I look at you."

He blew out a breath. "Those are not signs from God that you and I are meant to be together."

"Perhaps if you believed a little harder."

Apparently all his beliefs had dropped below his waist. He couldn't get any harder. "Make your wish and let's go inside."

Kimmie did. When she handed him the penny for good luck, he sighed and dropped it in his change pocket.

Burger Joe's swarmed with activity. Straight out of the 1950's, the fast food chain bore a nostalgic warmth that enticed customers to return to an age of ducktails, poodle skirts, tight white T-shirts and smoking in the boys' room.

Rhett and Kimmie joined Sam at a booth near the front where they could watch the waitresses on roller skates and not go deaf from the rock 'n' roll music on the jukebox. Sliding across the red vinyl-covered seat, Rhett rested his elbows on the Formica tabletop.

When the waitress arrived, the three of them ordered the diner's specialty: half-pounder with the works, fries and thick chocolate shakes. The food was delivered before they got deep into rally talk.

Rhett had eaten nearly all his burger before he stopped, took a breath and said, "Burger Joe's has the best food. If I had the financing, I'd open a franchise."

Beside him, Kimmie came close to dropping her chocolate shake. He saw her jaw go slack as the glass slipped through her fingers and landed on the table with a *thunk*. She'd turned as white as the whipped cream topping. "Kimmie, what's wrong?"

Nothing was wrong. If anything, her world had just righted itself. Until that moment, she'd never have pictured Rhett Evans working in the fast food industry. The man was pure GQ with his gelled hair, designer shirts and knife-sharp creases in his chinos. Now, however, there was a slip of a chance she could fit him with a spatula and an apron. If her wish on the penny came true, they would be flipping burgers together for the rest of their lives.

She smiled to herself. She had one more day to convince Rhett there was more to her than big breasts and curvy hips. She had a brain beneath her blond hair. If only they could get out of the diner without Rhett catching a glimpse of her picture . . .

Once they'd finished eating, Kimmie rose to pay the bill. She didn't want Rhett near the cash register where her photo hung as Burger Joe's poster girl.

Just as she'd received her change, Rhett's body touched her back, and his warm breath fanned her ear. "Thanks for lunch, Kimmie."

She nodded, praying his concentration would remain on her and not wander behind the counter. Turning to face him, she ran her hands lightly up his forearms. He'd rolled the sleeves of his maroon silk shirt to his elbows. Kimmie loved the feel of his skin, so warm and inviting. "Ready to go?" she asked, attempting to keep her voice steady.

Rhett looked over her head, studied the road maps on the shelf behind the register. "I'd like a map of southern Florida and the Keys," he said. "And perhaps . . ."

Kimmie caught the tilt of his head, the narrowing of his eyes as his gaze connected with the poster girl. He stared at the photograph for such a long time, Kimmie grew uneasy.

"The girl is beautiful," he eventually said, his gaze shifting from the photo to Kimmie, then back to the girl. "She looks like your younger sister. Any relation?"

"I don't have a younger sister."

"The resemblance is uncanny."

She shrugged. "Everyone has a twin somewhere in the world."

He edged around her, leaned on the counter, squinted. "Would your twin have your same initials?" he asked. "The letters *KT* are scripted over the girl's left breast."

The man had excellent vision. Not many people caught the tiny gray initials on the pink angora sweater.

Caught between Rhett and the photograph, Kimmie sighed deeply. "It's me. The picture was taken thirteen years ago."

His gaze dropped to her breasts. "You're a national sex symbol."

"For fast food, not *Playboy*."

"Why didn't you tell me?" he asked.

She lifted her chin. "If you'd look beyond sex, Rhett Evans, you'd see there's more to me than you think."

Turning on her heel, Kimmie walked out the door. She didn't look back to see if Rhett followed her. She'd left him wide-eyed, his mouth gaping, so surprised he couldn't move.

Once outside, she spotted Cade Nyland and TZ Blake. The restless and the impulsive, so into each other the air sizzled with sex. They looked so comfortable together: Cade sitting on the hood of the 'Stang, his legs splayed, and TZ standing between his thighs. Their expressions were open and unguarded, Kimmie noted, a little enviously.

The sun highlighted TZ's auburn curls as she tilted her head, smiling up at Cade, her gaze warm and teasing, while Cade looked down on her with hungry eyes and a sensual grin.

273

"Kimmie!" Sam Mason called to her. "We're ready to rally."

She caught Rhett's eye as she wandered back toward the Jag. Their glances locked, meeting for one highly charged instant before she looked away. He was as aware of her as she was of him. Too bad he couldn't get beyond her body and climb into her mind.

She was damn tired of him talking to her cleavage.

Chapter Fifteen

Cade glanced questioningly at TZ. "Are we on the right road?"

He caught her squirm. "What's wrong with the one we're traveling?"

"The brainteaser is 'Rock around the clock.' " He enunciated each word slowly. "Which we agreed could be a local rock 'n' roll hall of fame, an oldies radio station or a movie theater hosting a fifties film festival. Yet we've skirted Sandy Key and are driving down a gravel road used for afternoon delight." He shook his head. "The yellow Volkswagen was rocking so hard it could have flipped into the ditch."

"We've hit lover's lane."

"Lover's lane is *not* our checkpoint."

TZ slumped in her seat, slow to confess. "I might have missed a coordinate or two."

"Or three?" Five miles farther, Cade geared down and pulled onto the shoulder of the road. The car idled like a dildo. Why had Elise let them get so offtrack? Their paranormal guide had yet to make an appearance. Cade was sure they were lost.

Beside him TZ unfastened her seat belt, wiggled her thumb, reached for the door handle. "Guess this is where we part company," she said on a sigh.

Hitchhike back to Gulf Cove? The woman had lost her mind. Grabbing her by the arm, Cade pulled her toward him. Tightly wedged between his body and the steering wheel, she had no wiggle room. "An explanation, sweet cheeks."

She dipped her head, her chin glancing his stubbled jaw. "I'm, uh, not very good at reading a road map," she admitted, finally coming clean.

He stiffened slightly. "You're kidding, right?"

"No joke." She swallowed hard, then spoke fast. "The directions all blend together and rally code is like Greek to me. I came on the SunCoast Run out of sheer desperation. All Tune and Lube is in debt, and I needed the prize money to pay off the bank."

Bargained her down. Rhett Evans's words from Lolli's Pops hung over her confession. "You played me, TZ."

She scrunched up her nose. "Not completely. I am a good mechanic."

"You defintely give good service," he said, breathing against her hair.

"Mad at me, rally man?"

"Not mad enough to leave you by the side of the road." He brushed back her hair, kissed her forehead, then the tip of her nose. "I only wish you'd told me sooner. Rally code is cake once you understand the pretty pastels."

She returned his kiss, stretching the fleeting contact

into an utterly erotic exchange charged with sensation. She tasted sweet, a woman of intimacy and desire.

As stroking tongues deepened their kiss, Cade took pleasure in the stolen moments taken from the rally. As TZ buried her fingers in his hair, he rubbed the small of her back, her buttocks and thighs. He couldn't get enough of her. Might never get enough of her.

The rumbling on the road heightened the vibration of the Mustang. A vibration that couldn't be ignored.

He kissed her one final time. "TZ, someone's coming."

Her arms tightened around his neck. "That someone is me in about seven seconds."

He smiled as he eased her off his lap and back onto the passenger seat. "Listen," he said.

"To my heart, to my rapid breathing, to—"

"The dump trucks." Cade pointed to the convoy of trucks headed their way. Big, heavily loaded trucks with a sign on the cab that read KTL STONE QUARRY.

"Stones . . . rocks. Quarry," TZ chanted the words over and over again. She then bounced on the seat, as excited as when they'd kissed. She threw back her head, laughed out loud. "Drive to the main gate." She pointed straight ahead, crossing her fingers. "If the trucks are coming from a twenty-four-hour stone quarry, we've just hit rock around the clock."

Until the day he died, Cade would never forget Walter Brown's expression when he and TZ pulled up at the gate to the quarry. The rally master's face held both disbelief and disdain. He grilled them for fifteen minutes as to how they'd found the quarry. Cade refused to admit it was a mistake on TZ's part. He'd rather believe the Pony with soul had helped them reach their goal. He glanced in the rearview mirror. No Elise, yet he felt her presence.

Cade was riding high as he pulled into the parking lot of the Sandcastle Hotel. The sandblasted structure resembled an enormous castle on the beach. Decorated in Mediterranean blues and greens, and outfitted with enormous aquariums, the lobby looked like somewhere under the sea. The night's entertainment would be held in the Sand Bar, a private ballroom with an ocean view.

He took the elevator to the eighth floor. His heart felt as light as the swift upward climb. The SunCoast win was within his grasp. The Mustang sat in first place. Exactly where he'd wanted to start the final leg of the race.

Earlier, he'd dropped TZ at the hotel so she could get some exercise. She'd complained of bucket-seat butt and had wanted to jog before the costume party. Their time apart had allowed him to connect with Kimmie Thorn and discuss TZ's birthday, then shop for her gift. He wanted her night to be special.

When he entered their suite, the sensation of being underwater engulfed him. Photographs of exotic fish, pink coral and wavy plankton decorated every pale blue wall. A display of conch shells and sea urchins drew him to the coffee table. He picked up a conch, listening to the ocean.

"Can you hear Ariel? Flounder?" TZ asked as she emerged from the bathroom, wearing a terry-cloth ensemble—one towel held to her breast, another turbaned on her head. "When I heard you come in, I grabbed the closest towel on the rack."

"Closest and smallest." He admired the pure beauty of her body. "Need help drying off?"

She unwrapped the towel on her head, shaking out her hair. She then let the hand towel slip, just enough to reveal the fullness of her breasts, the moistness that collected at her cleavage. Lower still, and he caught drips of water as they ran the narrowness of her rib cage, the flatness of her belly, pooling at her navel. He tracked the towel as it fell over the sweet curve of her hip, her triangle of curls and down her slender legs until it lay at her feet.

Cade knew at that moment he didn't want her dry. He wanted her wet and slick, her skin slippery on the satin sheets. Going to his gym bag, he withdrew a condom, then tossed it on the nightstand.

He wanted her. Now. TZ could read it in his eyes. Eyes so hot and midnight dark they made her body tingle. While he openly admired her body, she appreciated how rapidly he shucked his clothes. As he approached, a hot quiver of anticipation ran through her. She felt a shock of desire so strong it was like pain.

This time there was no slow burn in his kiss or touch as he drew her toward the bed. Only a physical sizzle as his body heat absorbed her dampness, her skin quickly drying. Naked, they twisted the sheets with their arched backs and exploring hands.

TZ loved touching him. Her own pleasure heightened as she stroked his shoulders, the tight musculature of his back, the firmness of his buttocks. The hard length of his sex.

The beat of his heart penetrated her chest and surged into her soul with a mating rhythm. She breathed him in. That faint hint of Polo, his building need, his need for her.

His kisses were wild. Deep and hungry. All consciousness blurred as he slipped on the condom and their bodies came together. He was all fire, flesh and motion. Her body responded, reaching that familiar rise toward orgasm. Building up. Sharp breaths. In. Out. In. Out.

Blinding passion. Eternal intimacy. Unforgettable flesh.

She would hold him in her memory until the day she died.

Her muscles contracted, and she climaxed. A farther thrust, and Cade followed her over the edge. Melting together, they lay entangled, shaken, the pounding of his heart resounding through her soul.

When he opened his eyes and smiled, TZ knew she was falling in love with him. A mistake? Perhaps. But one worth making, just to know this special feeling that drove her crazy.

A sudden knock on their door had them both scrambling for hotel robes. "No time for seconds," Cade muttered.

He answered the door in a navy terry-cloth robe. His hair was mussed, his jaw in need of a shave. The robe gapped over his chest, a sexual sheen glistened on his pecs. He looked both agitated and carnal and downright intimidating. His smile when he opened the door and greeted a member of the rally committee did not reach his eyes.

Cade stepped back as Paul Royer pushed a rack of costumes into the room. Royer glanced from Cade to TZ, then spoke quickly. "Select your favorite, then return the rack to the hallway. Someone will be by to pick it up at six. Enjoy your evening." Nodding to them both, he made for the door.

TZ caught the time on the starfish-shaped clock mounted on the far wall. They had thirty minutes to decide on their costumes. Comfortable in her powder-blue robe, she went over the designs, from Wonder Woman to Batman; Darth Vader to the X-Men.

Cade came to stand behind her. He wrapped his arms about her shoulders, tucked her into his body. "I'm not one for disguises."

TZ continued to check out the costumes. "It could be fun. You could go as Spider-Man, Robin Hood or the Incredible Hulk. Perhaps something more adult, a cowboy in buttless chaps."

"I'm not feeling home on the range."

She paused, drawing in a deep breath. "Heir to Action Auto Parts might fit you perfectly."

Cade stiffened behind her. "How long have you known?"

"Since this morning, when Sam Mason and I took off to purchase a distributor cap for the Jag. Action Auto was the nearest parts store. That's where I saw the photograph of your family. You were the only one not smiling."

"I wasn't happy about having my picture taken."

"You look a lot like the older man on the far left of the photo."

"That's Rayburn, my grandfather," he explained. "The man behind my drive to win the SunCoast Run."

"You have a good chance of winning." TZ tried to pull away, but Cade held her fast. She sank into his chest, sighing. "You're rich, Cadence Andrew Nyland." And she was indebted.

"I'm richer from knowing you, Taryn Zane Blake." He breathed against her hair. "I'm crazy for you."

Crazy, but not in love. She swallowed her disappointment. "Do you work the family business?" she finally asked.

"Not often . . ." he hedged. "I mostly close deals."

"A-ah, so you're the muscle."

"I've never broken an arm or a leg."

"You're a hard-nosed negotiator?"

"I like to get my way."

He'd had his way with her. Several times over. The man was definitely hot and persuasive. In business, he'd be both formidable and forceful. And highly successful. While she struggled at All Tune and Lube, robbing Peter to pay Paul. She'd robbed Peter so often he now carried a gun.

He nuzzled her neck. "Money doesn't matter, TZ."

Tell that to her creditors.

No matter his restlessness, his sense of adventure, when Cade eventually settled down, he'd marry money. Her bank account would never match his. Not in a million years.

Tears pressed the back of her eyelids. She blinked rapidly. Emotion wasn't her style. She'd always been a little bit wild and a whole lot crazy. A free-spirit with an escapist heart. An unbidden sadness settled in her chest, squeezing the breath right out of her. She gasped for air.

"TZ?" Cade turned her in his arms, staring down into her face. "What's wrong?"

She ran her fingers down her neck. "Dry throat. Nothing serious."

He released her. "I'll get you a glass of water."

He went to the wet bar, selecting Perrier. She would have settled for tap water. When he returned, she took a slow sip and collected herself. "You should show up at the party as a boxer," she suggested, setting the glass on a small end table. "Black silk trunks, a towel over your shoulders, a spectacular chest."

"How about you?" he asked.

TZ fingered a costume of soft leather. "I'm thinking biker babe. Leather pants and jacket." She scrunched up her nose. "Wish I had some Harley shades."

Cade squeezed her shoulders. "I grant wishes."

He crossed to where he'd dropped his clothes, fished into the pocket of his black jeans, then returned to her side. Holding out a Harley-Davidson glasses case, he smiled, said, "Happy birthday, sweet cheeks."

TZ was too dumbfounded to speak. Her hands shook as she opened the case and discovered gloss-black biker's shades with flame lenses. Her heartbeat quickened as she slipped them on, dashing to the mirror and catching her reflection. "These are so hot!" Cade felt her excitement from across the room. Her pleasure was vibrant, her happiness a tangible force. When she turned, flying toward him, jumping his bones, he threw back his head and laughed out loud.

"I'm glad you liked your gift," he said as he broadened his stance, his hands cupping her sweet ass.

She hugged him close. "I love you . . . them."

Loved him . . . them . . . His heart clutched. Where did her excitement end and her true feelings begin? When she kissed his cheek, the tip of his nose, then captured his mouth, his own feelings surfaced. He loved her. His vision of settling down with TZ Blake had become too strong to ignore. They would discuss their future at the end of the race.

For now, the urge to enjoy this woman a second time was foremost on his mind. Seconds led to thirds. They were the last guests to arrive at the party.

* * *

"We look ridiculous," Marisa Ashton-Lord hissed at Mick Wilcox. "Adam and Eve"—she glanced over her shoulder at Skinner—"and the snake. I'm going to die of embarrassment."

Wilcox adjusted his fig leaf. "Don't drop dead at my feet. I'd just step over you."

"I hate you!"

He shrugged. "Hate me now, make love with me later."

She bared her teeth. "Not a chance."

He waggled his brows. "A *big* chance, if you're lucky."

Marisa straightened her leafy bikini top. "This is my last public appearance with you. The rally ends tomorrow." She jabbed him in his bare chest. "We're over. It's *adios*, Ox."

Mick actually smiled. He liked the way she'd called him Ox. A nickname only used by family and friends. Coming from Risa, it was as close to an endearment as he'd ever hear.

Music swelled around them. "Care to dance?" he asked.

"Only if I stand here and you move across the room."

"You're not real good at following a man's lead, are you, Ris?"

"I'm a better leader than most men." She turned away from him.

He snagged her by the arm, spinning her back around. The spin caused two leaves to fall from her skimpy top. One pointy nipple pressed the green gauze. Moneybags was turned on.

A slow, lazy ballad played. Couples drifted together. "We're going to dance," he said between clenched teeth.

She looked him up and down, snarled. "Me against you? You're all hairy and round and—and"—her gaze centered on his barely covered groin—"nearly naked."

He pulled her into his arms and pressed her close. "I'm also hard, Ris. Ride it out."

She struggled for several seconds, then fit her body to his. She was so much shorter than he, his erection rode the hollow of her rib cage. The tip of his sex inched toward her breastbone.

When the song ended, he expected Risa to split. To his surprise she snuggled closer, dancing as he so often did, slow, even to the fast songs.

"Care for a drink, *Father?*" Kimmie Thorn, dressed as a nun, looked up at Rhett Evans disguised as a priest. "Red wine? Holy water?"

Rhett ran his hand inside the brown robe, scratching his side, then his stomach. "This material feels like burlap. I'll be itching all night long."

"You didn't have to come as a priest," Kimmie reminded him. "You could have been Bozo the Clown, one of the Disney Dalmatians, a court jester."

"The jester would have worked, since I'm a fool for you," he muttered.

Kimmie adjusted the silver cross around her neck. "I'd never marry a fool," she said solemnly. "My man would be strong, sane and financially secure."

She saw him wince. The corners of his eyes and mouth pinched as he took her by the hand and led her to a small cluster of decorative plants along the back wall. The plants granted them a little privacy in a room packed with rallyers.

He dipped his head, looking uncomfortable and somewhat embarrassed. "Confession time," he slowly began as he fingered the rope belt tied at his waist.

"This isn't church, Rhett." Kimmie had grown as uneasy as he appeared. "You don't need to confess your sins."

"Not sins, Kimmie. I merely want to dispel your illusion of me."

"Illusion?" Her heart told her he was a good man.

"I'm not the man you think I am." He swallowed hard, continued. "I'm a stockbroker by day and a gambler by night. I lose money as fast as I make it. The main reason I brought you on the rally was to pay for my expenses. You offered, and I accepted."

A lump had formed and was expanding in Kimmie's throat. She could barely speak. "You're using me to get to Key West?"

He blew out a breath. "If I win, I'll pay you back every dime."

"If you don't win?" Her voice sounded scratchy, out-of-body, even to her own ears.

"It's been . . . fun."

Fun? For her it had been the most incredible time of her life. She'd met the man she wanted to marry, only to have him confess he found her fun.

"We can still be friends, can't we, Kimmie?" he asked.

A fun friend? Not in this lifetime.

She stared down, silent for several seconds. Finally, she looked half at him and half into space, so that their eyes met only for an instant. "It's very uncomfortable to realize what I'd believed would be perfect somehow isn't. It's shaken me up—I'm not really sure where to go from here."

He cleared his throat. "We're together until the rally ends."

"Fortunately for both of us it ends tomorrow."

"Kimmie . . . I didn't want it to end this way."

"How did you want it to end, Rhett?" She had to know.

"With us in bed."

"Would sex have made you love me?"

"Love? Doubtful. I've known want and need and grati-fication. I've never allowed myself to fall for a woman."

"Love is a free-fall," Kimmie said softly. "Your partner's always there to catch you."

"I'm not ready to make a commitment."

"Because you're broke or because you truly have no in-terest in me?" No matter the pain, she awaited his answer.

Rhett Evans saw the hurt in her eyes, felt the tightness in her chest. Over the past three days he'd become so in tune with this woman, he'd read her mind, sensed her moods, knew how much she loved him. He cared for her, so much so, he wanted to protect her from the rise and fall of his lifestyle. No woman deserved diamonds one day and faux pearls the next.

Kimmie needed a man of substance. Rhett didn't qual-ify. A little hurt now would bring her happiness with an-other man. "I've always enjoyed green-eyed blondes," he finally said. "You're more curvy than most. And there was the thrill of the chase; you're a virgin—"

Her eyes bright, her lips trembling, Kimmie turned with a swoosh of her black-and-white habit and walked away from him. All the color in his life faded to gray. His future lacked prospect and purpose. With Kimmie gone, he'd lost the true prize of the rally.

"I'm staying with you tonight, even if I have to sleep on the floor," Kimmie informed TZ at the buffet table.

TZ pushed her biker shades down her nose and studied her best friend over the rim. "I thought you and Rhett had separate rooms?"

Kimmie blushed. "Not tonight. We decided to share a suite, with the promise he'd keep his hands to himself."

"He's already touched you?"

"No, and he never will." Kimmie's voice shook with her disappointment. "The rally is over for Rhett and me."

TZ wasn't convinced. "Rhett's no longer the one?"

"I'm moving on," Kimmie said with as much conviction as she could muster.

"You can stay with Cade," TZ returned, trying not to smile. "After all the damage to the classic cars, I'd planned to sleep in the 'Stang. My rally man is all yours."

"Giving me away, already?" Cade asked, coming up behind her.

TZ turned slightly. The predatory look in Cade's eyes no longer caused her to jump out of her skin; it made her whole body tingle. Tonight, he made one hard-bodied boxer.

"Kimmie and Rhett are parting ways," TZ informed him.

Cade narrowed his gaze. "I thought he'd come around."

"So did I." Kimmie sighed so deeply all the oxygen left her lungs.

"Our suite is your suite," he said casually. "If TZ plans to camp out in the 'Stang, I'll pitch a tent alongside her."

"It's going to get crowded," TZ said.

"We don't need much room," he returned, a lazy smile curving his lips. "I can fit into tight places."

His comment wasn't lost on TZ. Color rose in her cheeks.

The tapping on the microphone drew everyone's gaze to the stage, where Walter Brown stood front and center. "I hope you're having a good time." He paused, and applause erupted. "Tonight we're celebrating more than the costume party. Happy birthday, TZ Blake!"

TZ gasped as red, orange and yellow balloons dropped from the ceiling and the rallyers sang "Happy Birthday" to her. Confetti was tossed, and noisemakers rent the air. One by one, people approached her, giving her gifts, from a Ford key chain to a bottle of champagne.

"Here, TZ." Mick Wilcox was one of the last in line. He handed her a small box, torn at one end. Inside, she found a picture of a gold charm bracelet. "I couldn't afford the real thing," he said. "But if I could have, that's what I would have given you."

TZ reached out and took his hand. "I love the thought."

"I've always liked you," he confessed in a low voice.

She wasn't sure how to respond. Glancing behind him, she found Marisa Ashton-Lord glaring daggers her way. On impulse, she rose on tiptoe and lightly kissed his cheek. "Turn around," she said, playing matchmaker. "You'll find the person who will like you back. Hurry, she's about to leave."

She watched as Mick stepped back, his big foot landing square on Risa's smaller one. "Get off my foot!" Risa shrieked.

"You're not leaving," he said flatly.

"Who's going to stop me?"

He looked down at her, stern and in control. "I am. Get over yourself, Ris, and get used to me in your life."

"You . . . and me?" Her look was incredulous.

"If you start now, you'll get used to the idea."

"Not in a hundred years!"

"Make it two hundred then. As long as it takes."

TZ wasn't the least surprised when Mick pointed toward the main door, and Risa walked out, ten feet ahead of him.

"We're stopping at the gift shop on our way upstairs—" Risa's voice drifted back to TZ. "I'm buying magazines and you're going to point out everything you would buy me, if you had the money."

After two slices of yellow birthday cake with buttercream frosting, TZ went looking for Cade. She found him talking to Rhett Evans at the corner of the bar. "Am I interrupting?" she asked.

"Conversation's over." Cade finished off his beer, shooting Rhett a long, hard look. "Think with your brain for a change."

Rhett hung his head, looking grim and forlorn.

"I came for the room key." TZ held out her hand. "I wanted to change clothes before I camped out in the 'Stang."

Cade took her hand. "Let's gather your gifts, and I'll come with you."

Once they'd slipped out of their costumes and into casual clothes, and gotten Kimmie settled in their suite, Cade and TZ headed for the parking garage. Several overhead lights had burned out or been broken. Eerie shadows danced along the cement walls.

Cade moved the 'Stang from the first to the fifth level. Once there, they rolled down the windows and sat in silence. The night was still and a full moon was rising. They were alone, not another car was in sight.

"I saved the best gift for last," Cade said into the darkness. "You'll find it in the backseat."

She craned her neck, looking over the headrest. "I don't see—"

Two heartbeats, and he'd lifted, then flipped her in the back. She rubbed her tailbone. "You've done that before," she accused.

"But never in a Mustang." He chuckled. "No watching, Elise." After tilting up the rearview mirror, he climbed over the seat.

"My gift?" she asked when he'd joined her.

He spread his arms wide, winked, and her heart fluttered. "I'm all yours, sweet cheeks. Firm and flexible, and fun to play with. I may not be gift wrapped, but I guarantee there's a bow."

Bow? Ever so slowly, TZ unwrapped her present. Off came Cade's navy T-shirt, and down came his gray running shorts. Beneath his blue briefs she found a matching bow. Dipping her head, her auburn curls glanced over his groin as she untied the bow with her teeth. Then with her lips and tongue, she thanked him for his gift.

Chapter Sixteen

Making love in the Mustang proved both inventive and exciting. Minor cramps with major climaxes. When the sun stretched over the horizon, casting morning light through its windows, Cade Nyland woke TZ Blake with a long, deep kiss.

"We need to head back to our suite, shower, then hit the road," Cade said on a yawn.

He climbed back over the seat, and TZ followed. She sat beside him and finger-combed her hair. Her auburn curls bounced back, as wild as the night they'd spent in the backseat of the 'Stang.

He drove the Mustang down to the lower level. The parking garage appeared undisturbed and quiet. He left the Mustang between a GTO Judge and a Ford Edsel, history's ultimate clunker. Elise revved her engine at the muscle car. The Judge remained aloof, as arrogant as the day it was manufactured.

When they arrived at their suite, they found Kimmie

perched on the edge of the bed, her suitcase packed. "I want to ride with you today," she said, her eyes red from late-night tears.

TZ dropped down on the bed beside her. "Ready to vibrate?"

Kimmie managed a grin. "That's more action than I'll ever get from Rhett."

TZ nudged her with an elbow. "Rhett cares for you."

"I rate second to money," Kimmie softly confessed, plucking at a pocket on her blue-jean jumper. "Rhett used me, and"— her voice caught—"I let him."

TZ sighed. "Love complicates everything."

Cade had to agree. He couldn't verbalize his feelings. Yet what he felt for TZ Blake ran deep and permanent. Toward a house, and children, and family rallies.

Hunkering down, he rummaged through his gym bag for a change of clothes. After collecting a white polo and jeans, he caught TZ's eye, nodding toward the bathroom. "I'm off to shower."

"Alone," TZ mouthed over Kimmie's bent head.

He made a face that drew her smile, then proceeded to take a quick cold shower. Ten minutes later, TZ took her turn in the bathroom. In under an hour the three of them were headed for the garage.

They were the last to arrive, and the first to hit the road. Cade patted the eyebrow on the dashboard. "First place and sitting pretty."

TZ shifted the directions and map on her lap. "It's three hours to Key West. Stay on U.S. One South. It's us against the clock."

The Pony car shot down the highway at a dead run, edging slightly over the speed limit, then automatically slowing within range of a speed trap. Cade swore Elise could smell a cop a mile away.

He held TZ's hand the entire trip, stroking her fingers with his thumb, then gently squeezing her palm. He liked touching her, their connection a continuous slow burn.

One hour into the rally, the engine growled like a hungry stomach. They stopped for gas. While Cade pumped, TZ and Kimmie went into the convenience store for snacks. On the road again, TZ fed him bites of cranberry-orange muffin. Each time she touched his lips, she traced light circles at the corner with her thumb. Cade, in turn, flicked his tongue against her fingers, sucking one into his mouth, tasting her along with his breakfast.

In the rearview mirror, Cade caught Kimmie crunch up an empty paper bag and throw it at TZ. "Between the vibration and the two of you teasing each other, I can't take much more."

Cade shot TZ a knowing look. The backseat had known its share of orgasms. Five to be exact.

At noon, they approached Seven Mile Bridge, which led into Big Pine Key. Beneath the bridge, the Gulf of Mexico merged with the Atlantic Ocean. The sun broke from behind a cloud, casting gold across the blue-green water. Key West was a short distance ahead.

Cade caught a glimpse of Rhett Evans's Jaguar in his side mirror. Coming from two cars behind, Rhett passed on a dangerous curve, riding the Mustang's bumper. When the two-way traffic cleared, Rhett jerked the wheel and pulled the Jag alongside the 'Stang.

Rhett's hair was ruffled, his gaze wild. Sam Mason was as white as the divider lines on the road.

"Kimmie!" Rhett yelled out the window. "We need to talk."

"Talk, now?" Cade asked, growling when the Jag swerved, nearly sideswiping the 'Stang. He downshifted, allowing the Jag full run of the road.

Rhett slowed right along with him. "Kimmie!" he shouted a second time. "Pull over."

"Don't stop, Cade." Kimmie sank deeper on the back-seat. "I have nothing to say to the man."

A car approached, and Rhett fell back. As soon as the car had passed, Rhett drew even with the 'Stang once again. "I'm sorry—" His words were cut off by an oncoming semi. He braked, swerving wildly, barely avoiding an accident.

Cade shook his head. "Damn fool. He's going to get himself killed."

"Killed for love." TZ turned on her seat, speaking to Kimmie. "Rhett's trying to apologize."

Kimmie crossed her arms over her chest. "He's not sorry enough."

Cade lifted a brow. "Planning to make the man suffer?"

"Suffer until he comes to his senses," Kimmie returned.

Ten miles of bumper tag shredded Cade's last nerve. Noon traffic had thickened the roadway. Rhett's weaving in and out between cars caused horns to honk and middle fingers to rise. With only six miles to Key West, Cade was about to sacrifice Kimmie to save Rhett's life.

Four miles and counting. TZ sat on the edge of her seat. "We're going to make it, rally man."

Three miles to their goal and the engine choked on her prediction. There was a wild buck and sputter, followed by decreasing speed. "No-o!" TZ moaned as the 'Stang coasted to a stop on the side of the road.

"TZ?" Cade keyed the engine with no response. He dropped his head, resting his temple on the steering wheel. "What's happened?"

"Elise?" TZ grabbed the rearview mirror and tilted it toward her. "Elise!"

Her aunt appeared in a misty haze. "Help us," TZ pleaded.

The engine turned over with a shimmy and a shake, chugging several yards, then died completely. "More, Elise, please. We're so close."

"Elise?" Kimmie questioned from the backseat.

"My aunt's spirit inhabits the 'Stang," TZ shot over the headrest.

"That explains the car braking on a dime when I refused to wear my seat belt. The door swinging wide and spanking me when I left trash on the floor mat," Kimmie grumbled.

TZ's gaze returned to the rearview mirror. Sadness swirled around Elise, TZ sensed her aunt's sigh of defeat.

TZ jumped from the car and popped the hood. "Turn the key," she called to Cade. She listened for the faintest click or clank. To her dismay, the engine refused to start.

An electrical malfunction, she quickly diagnosed. A malfunction she didn't have time to fix.

"There has to be a way . . ." TZ slammed the hood and began to pace. Suspending her thoughts, she prayed for a way to cross the finish line.

Push. Push the car. TZ heard Elise's voice in her mind.

"Get out of the car." She motioned to Cade. "We're going to push the 'Stang."

Cade swung open the door and stepped out. "Rally rules won't allow a bumper-to-bumper push. Yet there's no rule against rallyers flexing a little muscle." He glanced at his watch. "We have one hour to reach Key West."

"Kimmie's going to sit and steer, and I'm going to help push," TZ informed him, her hands on the trunk. "She's wearing sandals, and I'm in Keds."

Sweaty and sunburned they pushed the Mustang for two miles straight. Rhett Evans whipped by, pulled a U-turn, then crawled back toward them. TZ looked up to see Sam Mason waving his arms and pointing at her. She caught the curling of Rhett's lip before he pulled over and let Sam out of the Jag. Rhett then peeled out, spraying them with gravel.

"Looks like you could use some help," a sober and smiling Sam said as he fell into step beside TZ.

TZ wiped perspiration from her forehead. "Why, Sam?"

"You helped me with the battery and distributor," Sam reminded her, as if his decision was as clear as the nose on her face. "It's time to repay you, girl. Let's win this one for Elise."

"Elise?" TZ nearly fell over her feet.

"Your aunt always wanted to win a rally," Sam said. "It was her fondest wish."

An uncompleted life quest. The realization flashed across TZ's mind like a sunburst. Elise lingered to win a rally. It was her soul's final wish. TZ took a deep breath, pushing a little harder.

Beside her, Cade's shoulders bunched, and his tattoo flexed. He'd pulled his hair back in a leather tie, his jaw locked, his gaze intense.

"How are you holding up?" he asked her.

297

She forced a grin. "Aside from the leg cramps, blisters and dehydration?"

"Take a break," he called to Sam and Kimmie, then pulled TZ against his chest.

His body heat wiped the soreness from her muscles as he lent her his strength. She heard him swallow. "We don't have to keep going, TZ. Rhett's crossed the finish line by now. We can call a tow truck—"

She stepped back, breaking their embrace, then jabbed him in the chest with a finger. "Don't bail on me, Cadence. We have to finish this race."

He leaned in, kissing her full on the mouth.

A car screeched to a halt behind them. TZ and Cade turned simultaneously. Mick Wilcox and Skinner climbed from the Sprite. The twin mattress tipped dangerously to the right.

Wilcox made a muscle. And Cade nodded.

"TZ lent us a jack when we had a flat tire at Lolli's Pops," Mick explained. "We're here to return the favor."

The group pushed forward, breathing hard, ignoring the heat that beat down on their backs. TZ's mouth was so dry she could no longer swallow. The blister on her heel had rubbed raw. Sensing her tiredness, Cade slowed. In one fluid motion he'd lifted her off the ground and onto the trunk. She rested the heels of her Keds on the bumper.

"Catch your breath." His tone brooked no argument.

TZ rode backward, watching the traffic for another classic car. "Here comes the pink Caddie," she noted.

To her surprise, Wilcox pushed off the Mustang and moved to stand in the middle of the highway. The Cadillac fishtailed, braking inches from his kneecaps.

Risa shook her fist at Mick, shouting, "Move or be road-kill."

Mick shook his head. "We need your flying monkeys," he told Marisa.

"To do what?" Risa huffed.

"To push the Mustang another mile."

Risa snorted. "Why should they push, when I can win the SunCoast Run?"

"Because TZ changed the sparkplugs when I couldn't," her mechanic, Winston Henry, answered for Wilcox. Winston jerked his head toward the 'Stang. "Turnabout is fair play."

"Plan to walk back to Gulf Cove!" Risa fired at her entourage as they exited the Caddie.

TZ held her breath as Risa gunned the engine and Mick stood his ground in torn-at-the-knee jeans and a BEAT THE MEAT, I ATE A TWO-POUND PORTERHOUSE AT STARLING'S STEAKHOUSE T-shirt. He'd gotten a haircut and a close shave. He looked almost human.

Risa slammed her fist on the steering wheel. "You can't expect *me* to push," she ground out.

Mick didn't reply.

"I don't have the strength."

· Mick continued to stare at her.

"I hate you!" she flared.

And Mick finally smiled. "Pull over and help push. One of your ass-kissers can cruise behind us."

Once Risa had switched places with her timekeeper, she stomped toward Mick in a red island shirt, matching linen pants and low-heeled straw sandals. Slipping between Wilcox and Skinner, she did her best to keep up with the men.

"Half a mile!" Kimmie called from the front seat.

TZ slid off the trunk, again putting all her effort into pushing. Her arms strained and her legs felt like rubber. Her lungs burned; her breathing was painful. Her blouse stuck to her breasts and back. Her drawstring shorts clung damply to her thighs.

Beside her, Cade pointed toward the finish line, where the rally committee had gathered in full force. "Isn't that Evans's Jag?"

TZ craned her neck. "Has he won?"

Cade squinted against the sun. "The car appears parked on this side of the finish line."

"Why hasn't he crossed?" TZ asked.

Her question was soon answered. A quarter mile from Key West, Rhett approached the 'Stang on foot. His hair was mussed, and his shirttail hung out of his rumpled chinos. Walking along the driver's side of the vehicle, he spoke to Kimmie's profile. "I waited for you," he told her. "Even if I'd crossed the finish line I wouldn't have been a winner. Not without you, Kimmie Thorn."

TZ saw Kimmie's jaw drop. The car swerved as she momentarily forgot she should be steering and not staring at Rhett. Seconds later, she hit the brake. Those pushing slammed into the back of the 'Stang.

"Damn, Kimmie, give a man some warning." Cade rubbed his left hip.

"Bruised my balls." Mick Wilcox ran his hand down his zipper.

"Smashed my sex." Skinner dropped to his knees.

"Take Kimmie's place."—Cade nudged TZ forward—"before we're all walking funny."

TZ held the door as Kimmie hopped out and she climbed in.

As they inched forward, TZ heard Kimmie say, "I'm proud of you, Rhett Evans. Cade and TZ deserve to win."

Rhett's reply rose soft and sincere. "You've opened my eyes and my heart to what's truly important."

Kimmie's breath caught. "Is that a proposal?"

"If you'll marry for poorer in hopes of getting richer."

Kimmie's squeal split the air. "I do, I do, I do!"

Ten minutes later, the Mustang crossed the finish line, with only thirty seconds to spare on the time clock. Skinner, Sam Mason and Risa dropped to the curb, exhausted. Risa's entourage slid onto the trunk, their heads lowered, trying to catch their breath. Cade slapped Wilcox on the back seconds before TZ set the parking brake on the 'Stang and sprang from the car. On a wild whoop she jumped his bones.

"We won!" She threw back her head and shouted to the sky.

The rally committee circled them, popping champagne corks, the air sparkling with the richness of the spray.

As TZ tightened her thighs about his hips, Cade brought her hands to his lips. He kissed each knuckle. Twice. "Your helping hands won this race." He gently eased her down his body. "I have people to thank."

Climbing onto the hood of the Mustang, he whistled through his teeth. When the crowd quieted, he smiled and announced, "Today, TZ Blake and I won the SunCoast Run." The rallyers cheered loudly. "We could never have done it alone. Many people participated in our success. I want all those involved to share in the prize money."

An expectant silence hung heavily on the air as Cade

sought TZ's approval. When she nodded, he continued. "Mick Wilcox, Skinner, Marisa Ashton-Lord and her entourage, Sam Mason, Kimmie Thorn and Rhett Evans will all get a cut of the check."

Wilcox raised a glass of champagne. "That should be a year's salary for me."

"You're not blowing it on pretzels and beer," Risa said flatly. "I'm going to teach you how to invest and live off the interest."

Applause rose, and champagne sprayed as Cade jumped off the hood. While those graced by Cade's generosity gathered close, TZ decided to work on the Mustang. She turned the key to *on*, retrieved a toolbox, then lifted the hood. She was soon elbow-deep in the engine.

With nothing but time, she further evaluated the wiring, fly wheel and starter motor. A faint spark ignited when she touched a screwdriver between the terminals on the starter solenoid. With a sputter and a wheeze, the Mustang came to life. Lowering the hood, TZ left the car running.

"Where's Walter Brown? Has anyone seen him?" Paul Royer's question drew an uneasy silence. "It's time to present the check and the trophy."

The rallyers looked around, shrugged, then were soon shouting and pointing as Brown's classic Rolls cruised passed the group. The rally master's shoulders were hunched, and his head was barely visible over the dash as he tried to sneak out of town.

"Brown's leaving?" Royer looked on in disbelief. "Someone stop him!"

TZ gasped as Cade broke from the crowd, with Mick Wilcox several yards behind him. The two men ran, but not fast enough. Once he saw that he'd been spotted, Brown floored the Rolls and the aristocratic chassis responded with precise dignity.

All anyone could do was stare at its taillights.

Amid the chaos and panic, the Mustang rumbled. Slipping into the car, TZ stared into the rearview mirror. A gray haze swirled with a red mist. Her aunt's face appeared, strong and determined, and ready to give chase.

TZ couldn't allow her aunt to face Walter Brown alone.

Her hands shook as she fastened her seat belt. The horn blared, and the crowd parted like the Red Sea. TZ clutched the steering wheel, knowing all control of the vehicle was in the hands of the paranormal. She faced a wild ride.

Lurching forward, the Pony with soul veered around the entrance square on two wheels. *Yee-ha* rose from the engine. In less than a mile, the 'Stang had caught the bumper on Brown's Rolls-Royce. TZ closed her eyes as the Mustang rode the yellow line, causing cars to skid toward the sandy shoulder. The Atlantic Ocean lapped the side of the highway, the road narrow and potholed, without guardrails.

Running side-by-side with the two-ton classic, the 'Stang cut right, sideswiping the Rolls's steely body before clearing the front bumper. Brown shook his fist. TZ watched as the speedometer climbed from fifty to sixty. A short bridge was just ahead. She instinctively knew that if the Mustang didn't stop Brown by the bridge, the man was gone for good.

She gripped the dashboard, praying out loud.

Within seconds, the 'Stang passed the Rolls, then shot sideways. Crushing metal and broken glass crashed around

TZ as the Rolls plowed into the passenger panel, then shoved the 'Stang down the highway like a bulldozer.

Caught between the upcoming bridge and the classic Rolls, TZ felt all blood drain from her face. She was going to die . . .

But not today. A flash of pink, and Marisa Ashton-Lord's Cadillac came into view. She glimpsed Cade behind the wheel, his expression fierce. Driving like a bat out of hell, he cut the wheel and caught the Rolls by the back bumper. Nearly equal in weight, the Caddie swung the Rolls off the road and down a short embankment. The ocean rose and rippled beneath the undercarriage. The sand sucked at the tires like quicksand.

Spinning from the release, the Mustang came to a screeching halt inches from the bridge. The Cadillac left yards of rubber as the brakes locked and it jerked to a stop.

"TZ!" Cade's voice was deep, frightened; his gaze wild as he leaped from the Cadillac and ran toward the Mustang.

Crushed against the driver's door, TZ felt bruised and disoriented. Lavender wafted, and TZ swore someone kissed her forehead. *I love you, Taryn. Thank you.* One heartbeat, then two, and both scent and sensation faded to police sirens, people screaming and a hiss from the radiator. When Cade pried open her door, she fell into his arms. He cradled her close. As her vision cleared, his look of concern nearly brought her to tears.

Cade Nyland cared about her. Possibly loved her.

Her smile drew his frown. "Are you crazy?" he said, growling against her cheek. "You could have been killed."

TZ kissed the darkness from his scowl. "Elise took off after Brown. I couldn't let her go it alone."

He eyed the 'Stang. "Pony's run its last race."

"A good mechanic could have the 'Stang running again in no time," TZ assured him. She then peeked over Cade's shoulder. A tow truck was in position to pull the Rolls from the Atlantic. "Brown's car has suffered major water damage."

"Water damage is the least of Brown's problems," Paul Royer said as he crossed the highway. "Police are taking his statement now. He's confessed to embezzling the rally fund as well as contacting the bikers and causing all the damage to the vehicles during the SunCoast Run."

Stunned speechless, TZ looked up at Cade.

Cade's jaw worked and his tattoo flexed. "What happens next?"

"Brown will be prosecuted and convicted," Royer stated. "He'll be ordered to repay the rally fund."

"Why did he do it?" TZ asked.

"Brown didn't expect anyone to win," Royer explained. "He figured between the brainteasers and damaged vehicles, teams wouldn't finish within the designated time and all the prize money would revert to the rally fund."

Royer shook Cade's hand. "Hope to see you on the circuit next year."

"We'll see," Cade replied, evasive.

TZ turned slightly and wrapped her arms about his waist. "Thanks for saving my ass."

Cade cupped her right buttock. "I voted for your ass in the tight butt contest," he finally confessed. "I have every intention of taking my choice home with me."

"Home with you?" Had she heard him correctly?

He pressed a kiss to her forehead, then nuzzled near her ear. "I want to build a life with you, sweet cheeks. House, babies, an occasional weekend race."

"Can I travel as your mechanic?"

"As my mechanic and my wife."

Her heart slowed, and her body filled with an inner peace. "I love you, rally man," she whispered against his mouth.

"I love you more."

On a highway jammed with cars and gawking onlookers, Cadence Andrew Nyland kissed Taryn Zane Blake with the promise of long life and everlasting love.

Standing at the gates of Heaven, Elise Blake glanced down on her niece and the man she would soon call husband. Elise's life had been full, and with the SunCoast win, she felt fulfilled. Everything she'd wanted to accomplish had been achieved.

Glancing to her left, she caught sight of Saint Peter walking her way. The man stood tall and regal, the gate-keeper for mankind.

Saint Peter slowed several feet before her and softly said, "We've been waiting for you, Elise Anne Blake. You've taken six months to arrive."

Elise fingered her long white robe. "Now that I'm here?"

"Welcome." His smile was kind. "Enough excitement for one lifetime?"

She sighed. "I've earned a rest."

"A little ambrosia?" he suggested.

Elise nodded. "Beats the heck out of high octane."

CURVEBALL

KATE ANGELL

The bad boys of baseball, they are the top power hitters of the Richmond Rogues, and the team's best hope for a shot at the World Series. But when all three have to be benched for brawling, it's the beginning of a whole new ball game, and the opposing team could win something more than a trophy—these ladies are after their hearts.

At the top of the ninth, with the bases loaded, each man realizes that happiness is just within reach, even when love throws a...*Curveball*.

ISBN 10: 0-505-52707-3
ISBN 13: 978-0-505-52707-3

Kate Angell

Strike Zone

SHE'S BACK IN THE GAME

Faced with the love of her life waiting at the altar, thrill-seeking adventure guide Taylor Hannah lost her nerve and ran. Three years later, the gutsy blonde is back in Richmond to reclaim handsome Rogues pitcher Brek Stryker before he makes another trip down the aisle. Trouble is, her ball player refuses to believe she's finally ready to play by his rules.

Stryke hasn't forgiven the woman who left him on their wedding day, but he can't ignore the chemistry that sizzles every time he and Taylor meet. The fireworks between them could light up the ball park, but Stryke won't lose his heart again unless he knows the score.

ISBN 13: 978-0-505-52708-0
